M
l
HEAVEN

## ALSO BY DEBBIE VIGGIANO

# THE
# MAN YOU
# MEET IN
# HEAVEN

## DEBBIE VIGGIANO

bookouture

Published by Bookouture in 2018

An imprint of StoryFire Ltd.

Carmelite House
50 Victoria Embankment
London EC4Y 0DZ

www.bookouture.com

ISBN: 978-1-78681-586-6
eBook ISBN: 978-1-78681-585-9

*In memory of my beloved grandmother, Joan Edwardson.*
*I still miss you, Nanna, and all your wonderful stories! xx*

# Chapter One

'Mum, *please*,' I implored, 'give me a break, eh?' I unhooked my handbag from the back of the kitchen chair and stood up.

'Where are you going?' my mother asked, stubbing her ciggy out on her coffee saucer.

'Tesco. I need some shopping.'

'You're running away from me,' she accused, narrowing her eyes through an exhaled plume of smoke.

I tutted. 'Mother, if I wanted to run away from you, it wouldn't be to Tesco.' I grabbed my car keys from underneath a wrinkled apple languishing in the fruit bowl on the table. 'I'd choose somewhere far-flung, on the other side of the world, where you wouldn't be able to hound me to attend your dinner parties and cosy up to Margery Jackson's buck-toothed and bespectacled unmarried son.'

'What is it with you, Hattie Green?' my mother frowned. She always called me by my full name when irked, probably because she knew it irked *me*. It was high time I abandoned my old married surname. 'I'll have you know,' she sniffed, 'that Mark is a very nice boy.'

'He's nearly forty-three. Hardly a boy.'

'You're forgetting that you'll be that age on your next birthday.'

'Thanks for reminding me.'

'And Mark doesn't have buck teeth. He just has an unusual dental arrangement. And what's wrong with wearing glasses, Hattie? You wear them sometimes! I've seen you, reading those soppy romances, a pair of specs perched on your nose. You could do a lot worse than Margery's boy.'

I refrained from saying that surely I could also do a lot better? I had nothing against buck-toothed bespectacled men. I just didn't want one for a boyfriend. Nor, for that matter, did I even want a boyfriend.

'You're still a nice-looking woman, Hattie, but you don't make the most of yourself. It's almost like you deliberately want to be unattractive.'

'Cheers,' I said huffily, patting my scruffy hoodie's pockets for my mobile phone.

My ex-husband had once told me that I looked a bit like Cameron Diaz. These days I looked more like another Cameron. David. My mother had a point.

'Looks fade, Hattie. You need to stop being so fussy about a potential suitor.'

Only my mother would use a word like 'suitor'.

My son wandered into the kitchen looking for something to snack on. Like most sixteen-year-olds, Fin was perpetually hungry. He picked up the battered apple from the fruit bowl and eyed it suspiciously.

'This looks a bit past it,' he said.

'Like your mother,' Mum murmured.

I ignored her, took the apple from him and chucked it in the bin.

'I'll buy some more,' I promised.

'Never mind the apples,' said my mother to her grandson. 'It's Saturday, and your mum is prepared to spend tonight in front of the telly. Please tell her, Fin, that it's about time she got herself a boyfriend.'

My son gave me a sympathetic glance. He was quite used to his grandmother's matchmaking attempts.

'If Mum wants a boyfriend, Granny, I'll help her get one on Tinder.'

'Tinder?' my mother queried. 'What's that?'

'A dating app. You download it to your mobile phone. It's more or less how everybody meets these days.'

My mother looked shocked. 'Where's the fun in that?'

Fin shrugged. 'Busy people with busy lives seem to like it. Cuts out the middle person, Granny,' he said drily.

But his words were lost on my mother who, even now, was beginning to look distracted as her thoughts no doubt wandered to the possibilities of suggesting a little soirée with pals Edith and Rose. Both of them had middle-aged sons who were recently divorced, and both women were desperate to see them remarried. Edith and Rose wanted their spare bedrooms back, and they were fed up washing size-nine socks and ironing a mountain of man-size shirts. In my village there was a small army of frustrated seventy-something females who'd had their golden years rudely interrupted by balding sons too broke paying maintenance to get back on the property ladder.

'Right, I'm off,' I said to Fin. 'Anything you want in particular, other than apples? Or any special requests for dinner?'

'Yeah,' he said, rubbing his hands with glee. 'Let's have thinly sliced smoked salmon for starters, fillet steak for main, and something full of sugar and cream for pudding. Oh, and a bottle of Tesco's finest wine, Mother Dearest, with which to wash it all down.' He grinned mischievously, instantly reminding me of his father. Thinking about Fin's dad immediately caused a shadow to pass across my mind. A second later the shutters came down. My son was going to be heartbreakingly handsome one day. I just hoped he didn't break hearts. Like my ex-husband.

'Unfortunately my budget doesn't run to that delightful menu, but I'll buy a tub of Tesco's poshest ice-cream.'

Once, I'd been a commuter to London, earning a tidy sum. Now much older and far less confident, I was no longer up to date with essential techie skills. These days my income came from walking the dogs of those who spent their days in glass-fronted City offices. Occasionally I provided doggy board and lodging when those same folks jetted off to the Maldives or America and didn't want to use kennels. I got by.

'Actually, don't worry about cooking for me, Mum,' said Fin, opening the fridge and extracting a yoghurt. 'I'm going around to Ryan's house later. His parents usually order a takeaway.'

'That sounds nice,' I said, salivating at the thought of a korma on the sofa. I'd give Jo, my fellow singleton mate and good neighbour, a ring a little later on and ask if she was up for some company this evening. 'I might get a supermarket curry for myself and Jo. We can enjoy eating it while watching *Take Me Out*.'

'Pity you don't both write in to ITV and ask to be contestants,' said my mother, standing up. 'I suppose I'd better get back to your father. I left him out in the garden filling the patio pots with flowers. You could do with something to brighten up your little garden, Hattie. Do you want me to ask Dad to put something together for you?'

'That would be lovely,' I said, relieved to be talking about something as mundane as winter pansies, and not blind dates. 'Thanks, Mum.' I moved round the kitchen table and kissed her goodbye. 'Will you be in when I get back?' I said, turning to Fin.

He did a seesaw motion with one hand. 'Not sure.'

'Well if I'm not back before you leave, make sure you let Buddy out before locking up, then put him in his crate with a chew to keep him occupied.'

Buddy was my rather fat, food-obsessed rescue beagle. I could see why so many of the breed ended up unwanted. Virtually untrainable, with a penchant for eating anything foolishly left around, Buddy had a low boredom threshold. He was quite partial to chomping his way through chair legs or banister spindles, was a dab hand at opening kitchen cupboards fitted with child locks and would think nothing of upending the bin in his quest to seek out leftovers. Despite being the naughtiest dog in Vigo Village, he was also the most loving, and soulmates with Jo's black Labrador, Buttons, who we often walked with.

'Yeah, I'll see to Buddy,' Fin assured me.

'Good,' I said, slinging my handbag over my shoulder. 'See you later.'

I followed Mum to the front door. This was accomplished swiftly because my terraced cottage had no hallway. One simply stepped from the garden path straight into the lounge, and from there it was a few paces to the kitchen.

I'd lived in my cosy – okay, miniscule – two-up two-down ever since Nick and I had parted company. My mind briefly flitted back to married life. Two years ago, home had been a contemporary detached property in swish Sevenoaks. These days I rested my head under the beams of Honeysuckle Cottage, which sounded charming enough and, indeed, was. But the old bricks were crumbling from Vigo's frequent winter fogs that always added another layer of moss to the uneven roof tiles. Thankfully, now that February had arrived, the promise of milder weather hung in the air, and the previously dark afternoons were steadily growing lighter. Nick had hated dogs, so the first thing I'd done when we'd split up was visit a beagle re-homing centre. Buddy had no complaints about Honeysuckle Cottage's postage-stamp-sized garden, where we sat companionably together during the temperamental British summers. In the old days, I'd hopped on planes with Nick and flown off to foreign sunshine, Fin holding a hand between us… but those days had been stormy for reasons that were nothing to do with the weather. Our marriage had been volatile. Full of tears and pain. My husband had been a serial adulterer. I'd grimly hung in there, telling myself that it was my fault he'd behaved the way he did, and blindly hoped that one day my husband would cease his extra-marital activity, and we'd all live happily ever after. And for a while, I'd truly thought we'd achieved this. Harmony had reigned for longer than ever previously experienced. Until, on a whim, after dropping Fin to school, I'd driven to a mate's house for an impromptu coffee and catch-up, and been surprised to see my husband's car parked outside her house.

Pippa Brown was everything I wasn't: diminutive, stunningly beautiful, immaculately turned out. Nick had always taken the micky out of Pippa and her stockbroking husband, Brian. 'Watch out,' he'd say, at Parents' Evening, 'here come Mr and Mrs Boring-Brown.' They were the sort of couple who always looked at each other adoringly, finished each other's sentences, and never seemed to have a cross word. Which just goes to show that you never know what goes on inside somebody else's marriage. Pippa and I had gravitated towards each other at the school gates when our kids had started secondary school. Both of us had been trying not to cry as we'd watched our boys disappear into the enormous building wearing their too-big blazers and terrified expressions. We'd laughed at ourselves for being so overprotective and hastened off to the local coffee shop to bond.

Over the next three years I thought I'd got to know Pippa very well, including all her secrets. But obviously she'd held one back. Why else would I be puzzled as to why my husband was in her house while her own spouse was out at work? Knowing that Pippa rarely locked her back door when home, I'd passed through the side gate and stepped into the utility room. Laundry was swishing around in the washing machine while a tumble drier rumbled away. My footsteps had gone unnoticed, such was the racket going on upstairs.

My bowels had lurched as I'd climbed Pippa's staircase, the bile rising to my throat as I'd made my way along the landing to Mr and Mrs 'Boring' Brown's master bedroom. There had been nothing drab about the full technicolor discovery of Nick spread-eagled across Pippa's Laura Ashley bedding as she'd impersonated a pneumatic drill, her waterfall of long red hair rippling down her back. Even now, all this time later, an inner part of me shrivelled at the memory of my handsome husband and beautiful friend bonking the living daylights out of each other. As my mother had said at the time, any man and woman who had surnames that sounded like a dreary paint chart were surely welcome to each other. But all that had been two years ago. I'd sworn off men ever since, and had no plans to change this. Until a mind-bendingly surreal experience in Tesco's aisle three.

# Chapter Two

Tesco was packed. Valentine's Day was less than a fortnight away and the supermarket was awash with heart-shaped red balloons. At this time of the year I usually avoided the greeting card aisle, but as so many shoppers seemed to be having a chinwag and blocking the other aisles, I found myself taking a reluctant detour. I trolleyed past soppy gift teddies, my eyes firmly averted, steadfastly ignoring red velvet hearts held in stitched-together paws, plastic eyes looking soulful with sewn-on red lips puckered in a kiss.

My mind wandered back to the last Valentine's Day I'd shared with Nick. He hadn't really been a hearts-and-flowers man but, despite that, had made a romantic gesture and whisked me off to our local Italian, Serafino's Cucina. This was before the Pippa fiasco, of course. The restaurant had been full of loved-up couples holding hands across candlelit tablecloths. Our marriage had been back on an even keel, and I'd tentatively reached across the cotton gingham, taking Nick's hand in mine. He'd looked up from the menu, an expression of surprise on his face. I'd smiled at him and curled my fingers around his. He'd smiled back and allowed me to hold his hand for... ooh, a good five seconds... before gently reclaiming it as the waitress came over. The food had been delicious. The wine delectable. I'd overheard another couple at the table next to us reminiscing about their wedding day. The man had been telling his silver-haired wife that she'd looked a vision in her white gown and hadn't changed one bit. I'd studied Nick under my eyelashes as we'd worked our way through the meal. Had we changed? On the outside, not really. We were a few pounds heavier and had the odd grey hair. But it was on the inside – the side that couldn't be seen – where all the emotional scar tissue criss-crossed around the heart. Another layer had been added later when I'd discovered the waitress's phone number in his jacket pocket. Oh yes, I often did discreet searches through Nick's clothes when the 'signs' came along.

On this particular Valentine's Day, the signs had appeared when I'd returned from the restaurant's loo, and noticed my husband sweeping a hand through his hair as his eyes sought out the young woman dressed from head to toe in black, a snow-white apron tied around her slim waist. Later, after finding the incriminating piece of paper bearing a telephone number, I'd confronted him. He'd been outraged.

'How dare you go through my pockets!' he'd yelled.

'And how dare you keep doing this to me!' I'd yelled back.

'Don't you act all Miss Virtuous with me,' he'd said, stabbing a finger through the air. I'd been the first to look away.

Now, I looked away again, as I passed the sloping shelves full of cards bearing flowery illustrations and declarations of love. However, my exit from the hateful aisle was blocked by a lone man heading towards me.

'Excuse me,' I said politely, trying to wheel my way around him. For a moment we trolley danced, going in the same direction and therefore unable to pass. We both laughed at the same time. The man took this as his cue to speak.

'Trying to escape the Valentine aisle, eh?' he grinned and tutted, and I saw his eyes quickly check out my ringless left hand.

'Yes,' I smiled, adopting a rueful expression. 'As far as I'm concerned, this section of the supermarket is akin to hell on Earth.'

'Ah, a woman who has been burned.'

'Maybe,' I replied. I was still smiling, but the smile had gone brittle around the edges.

'Er, look,' said the man hesitantly, a sudden shyness entering his tone, 'I know I don't know you or anything… and you might think I'm being outrageously forward, but… do you fancy having a coffee?' He nodded his head at Tesco's Costa corner, which, admittedly, was emitting delicious smells of ground coffee beans.

I stared at him in surprise. He was handsome. Very handsome. If my mother had been with me, she'd have physically dragged the pair of us over to the Costa corner and then whipped out her diary and asked when we both had a mutually convenient date to pop into Sidcup Registry Office on the way home. But the last thing I needed was a gorgeous-looking stranger issuing an invitation for coffee. It might not lead to Sidcup Registry Office, but it could potentially lead to my heart being broken. And that was a no-no. I took a deep breath.

'Thanks, but no thanks. I just—' I shrugged helplessly. Hopelessly. 'I can't.'

And before the man could say another word, I put my head down, tucked my elbows in, and pushed my way out of the hateful aisle full of red roses and romance.

As I headed off to aisle three, I pondered, what exactly *was* true love? Whatever it was, Nick and I hadn't had it, although it had taken me far too long to come to that realisation. Pippa and Boring Brian surely hadn't had it either, despite the dewy-eyed looks they always gave each other. Why else would Pippa cheat on Brian? Not that he'd ever found out. She'd begged me not to tell him. I hadn't deigned to respond, but much as I'd wanted to lash out and blast a few holes in her marriage, I wasn't the sort of person who deliberately hurt an innocent. And Brian was innocent.

I sighed heavily. Why on earth was I thinking about the past? It was Mum's fault. All her manic efforts to constantly pair me up with Mr Lonely of Longfield and Mr Desperate of Dartford. The only men currently in my life were my father, my son and my delinquent dog. And that was enough. It was at that moment my mobile phone rang. I glanced at the caller display and pursed my lips.

'Mum,' I said.

'I was just thinking about you,' she began.

'Funnily enough, I was doing the same,' I said wryly.

'Aw, that's nice,' she said, blissfully unaware of me blaming her for my gloomy reminiscing. 'Now I know I only saw you half an hour ago, but I've just got home and was telling Dad about you being all on your own tonight, and he said why don't you come over and join us for dinner? What do you think, hmm?'

There was something about my mother's tone that instantly had me on red alert. She sounded almost desperate for me to accept her dinner invitation. Now, why would that be?

'Thanks, Mum, but I have the evening all planned out. It's just me, Buddy, possibly Jo, a supermarket curry, and the telly.'

'Ah, yes, the dating programme.'

'That's right.'

'Ooh, I know!' she said, practically squealing at her sudden light bulb moment. 'Forget Jo, and watch it here with us. What do you say? Eh, Hattie? C'*mon*,' she wheedled. 'And anyway, Dad's put together a tub of flowers for your patio, so you could take it home with you afterwards.'

'Tell Dad thank you, but I'll drop by and pick it up tomorrow.'

'No, no, Hattie,' she said, her tone unexpectedly emphatic. 'I absolutely insist you join us for dinner.'

'Mum, I only saw you a little while ago. Why the sudden invitation?'

'Well, Fin said he's having a takeaway tonight, so we thought we'd get one too. And we'd love you to join us. That's all.'

But my mother wasn't fooling me. I smelt a rat.

'Who else will be there?'

'Who else?'

'Is there an echo on this line?'

I heard a gasp of frustration crackling down the handset. 'If you must know,' she hissed, 'Margery's here. She was just passing, but your father invited her to stay for dinner. I know I'm a brilliant cook, but even I can't rustle up something amazing at such short notice. So we're having a takeaway.'

'And let me guess. Mark is there, too.'

'Er, I'm not sure, let me think, erm…'

'Oh, Mum, spare me the charade. I can hear him laughing in the background with Dad.'

Apart from Mark's buck teeth and specs that looked like they'd come out of a Third World recycling bin, the man had been bestowed with a laugh that made Sid James sound refined.

'Ah yes,' said Mum brightly, 'you're quite right, he is here. Fancy that!'

'Yes, and I don't,' I said pointedly. 'Apart from anything else, I can't possibly leave Buddy alone for too long.'

'Bring Buddy with you!' Mum cried.

'Are you mad? The last time he came to your house, he chased poor Wilbur up onto the drinks cabinet and barked incessantly.'

'We'll put Wilbur in one of the bedrooms and shut the door,' said Mum. 'So that's a yes then?'

'No!' I howled, causing another shopper to turn and stare in my direction. I huddled over the mobile phone, speaking low into the handset. 'Listen carefully, I shall say it only once.' For one surreal moment I felt like I'd dropped into a scene from *'Allo 'Allo*. 'I do not want to spend Saturday night with Mark Jackson. Not this week. Not next week. Not ever. Understood?'

'Well really, Hattie, I do think you're being terribly ungrateful,' said Mum, adopting a hurt tone. I rolled my eyes at the shelves of baked beans to my left. Why did my mother do this to me? And why was I made to feel so guilty? But before I could answer her, something extraordinary happened. Something enormous appeared in my peripheral vision. Something large, and white, falling from the ceiling. Too late I realised that the sign for aisle three was zooming through the air. As it caught me with a glancing blow, I automatically threw out my hands to fend it off, and sent a shelf full of Mr Heinz's products cascading everywhere. My feet came down on rolling tins and, like a cartoon character frantically running but getting nowhere, there were a few seconds of panicky activity before I tipped backwards, head slamming painfully against the hard floor. My last coherent thought was that I now had a legitimate reason not to spend the evening with Mark Jackson. And then everything went black.

# Chapter Three

When I came to, there was no sign of my shopping trolley, or the scattered cans of baked beans, nor any shoppers looking shocked with their mouths formed in a perfect O. I appeared to be lying down on a large comfortable sofa in an equally large and comfortable room. On the far side, enormous picture windows opened onto a veranda overlooking a panoramic view of green hills. I blinked. Strange. I'd not seen those hills before. In fact, I wasn't aware of any hills in the town of Sidcup. But then again, the back of Tesco ran adjacent to the A2 and actually, yes, didn't the A2 run through a rather verdant stretch? Perhaps I had simply never noticed these hills before as I'd shot along the dual carriageway in my car.

'Ah, you're awake,' said a male voice.

I sat up, swivelling my neck as I did so. A good-looking guy in white jeans and a matching open-necked shirt was seated in a winged armchair to my right. He looked familiar, but I couldn't figure out why. There was a hazy recollection of seeing him somewhere before but... no... it was eluding me. It was as if a veil had been flung over a distant memory. Probably due to the bump on the head. Or maybe it was because he reminded me of the American actor

Bradley Cooper, so just *seemed* familiar? For one fleeting moment, I wished I'd bothered to put on some make-up this morning. That thought had barely registered in my brain, when I dismissed it. *Why are you thinking about making yourself look attractive, Hattie? That's the last thing you want to do. Especially when the guy is a looker like this one. He has 'heartbreaker' stamped all over him.*

'Don't stand up,' he said quickly, as I made to swing my legs off the sofa. 'Just rest for a moment. Take some deep breaths. That's it, well done. That was quite a bump to the head. How are you feeling?'

'Er, fine, thanks,' I answered, carefully sitting up. I had no recollection of leaving the shop floor. I must have blacked out for a few minutes. How odd. After a wallop like that, I'd have thought a headache would have been an absolute cert. After all, that was an almighty smack I'd taken. A part of me winced as I recalled the sound in my ears before I'd lost consciousness. It had been like eggs cracking. Automatically, I put up one hand and tentatively touched the back of my head. Everything was intact. It didn't even feel bruised. How peculiar. 'Are you the manager?'

'No,' he said, giving me a kind smile. 'The manager here is a big shot, and pretty busy right now with other matters.'

Ah. So this guy must be second in command. The assistant manager. I raised an eyebrow at the casual clothes. Perhaps Tesco liked their upper echelon of staff to dress in a relaxed fashion because it made them feel less stressed out when they were studying the profit and loss columns or planning marketing strategies? For a deputy, he had the most amazingly plush office. And I'd certainly worked in a few in my youth, but nothing quite as grand as this. I had no idea that supermarkets looked after their employees so well. Perhaps I should give up my dog-walking 'career' – where I was out in all weathers – and apply for a spot of cosy shelf-filling. There was probably a staff canteen in another part of the building which, if this room was anything to go by, might be like The Ritz, offering staff tea breaks with cream scones on porcelain plates. I made a mental note to look online when I was back home and check out any vacancies.

'Would you like a cup of tea, Hattie?' the assistant manager asked.

How did he know my name? Ah, of course. No doubt some well-meaning member of staff had gone through my handbag and found my driver's licence tucked away in my purse.

'Yes please, I'd love a cuppa.'

I wondered if I should ask for lots of sugar too. It was meant to be good for shock, wasn't it? And I'd certainly had a big one, hitting my head like that.

'Here,' said the assistant manager, getting up and moving towards me. I was astonished to see him holding a cup of tea. On the saucer rested a teaspoon and several packets of sugar. 'You might want to tip all the sugar in. It's very soothing after a trauma.'

'Th-thank you,' I stuttered in surprise. As I took the tea from him, I couldn't help but discreetly glance around the room for an inconspicuous and ultra-quiet tea-making machine. Not finding one, I deduced that the assistant manager's fancy chair must have some sort of high-tech inbuilt gadget that produced a brew in a nanosecond. Good heavens, this supermarket certainly had all the latest technology. I made another mental note to check out the white goods aisle when I left here and see if they sold such machines to the general public. I was about to balance the cup and saucer on my lap whilst opening a packet of sugar, when I noticed an occasional table in front of me. I paused in my sugar opening and stared at it. That hadn't been there a moment ago… had it? I shook my head in bemusement. That bang on the head must have affected me more than I realised. Setting the tea down, I emptied all the sugar packets into the hot liquid. Picking up the teaspoon, a thought occurred to me. *Ah. Hang on a mo…* I stirred the tea, my mind whirring. Yes, it was coming to me now. I was receiving all this marvellous attention in this beautiful room by this charmingly good-looking man because Tesco were worried I was going to slap a lawsuit on them. After all, if their sign hadn't fallen from the ceiling, I wouldn't have accidentally knocked all those tins of baked beans off the shelf, thus falling down and hurting myself.

Bradley Cooper didn't return to his chair, instead settling himself down at the other end of my sofa. I took a sip of tea and eyed him speculatively. I wasn't the sort to jump on the compensation bandwagon, but if I was offered tonight's supermarket korma on the house by way of an apology, I wouldn't say no.

'Incidentally, Tesco aren't worried about you suing them,' he said, eyes twinkling mischievously.

I paused, mid-slurp. 'Pardon?' What a coincidence. He'd voiced aloud the very thoughts I'd been thinking.

'But if you want a Saturday-night korma in front of the telly, then I'm sure the manager will arrange it.'

My mouth dropped open. 'How did you know—?'

'It's a little gift I have.'

'Gift?' I said stupidly. What was this guy talking about? Did Tesco train their staff to read body language? Was this man a bit like Derren

Brown, sussing me out because of the particular way I held my tea cup, perhaps a certain angle meaning I was responsive to suggestion?

'Although,' he added, furrowing his brow, 'regarding the Saturday-night spice in front of the telly, you can't beat the real deal. Caribbean curry is the best – would you like to go there?'

I narrowed my eyes over the rim of the cup as I sipped. Yes, he was definitely reading my body language. It was also becoming clearer by the second that despite him saying Tesco weren't bothered about being sued, this wasn't the case at all. Why else was I being offered a bigger sweetener than all those little packets of sugar? *Because, Hattie, the last thing a supermarket wants is a national scandal!* Indeed. I could see the headlines now.

WOMAN SPILLS BEANS OVER SUPERMARKET HUSH-UP!

SACKED SUPERMARKET MANAGER IS NOW A HAS-BEAN!

INJURED CUSTOMER BRIBED WITH A TRIP TO THE CARIB-BEAN!

'Listen, Mr Cooper, I'm not up for bribery.'

'My name is Iam.'

I stared at him. What sort of weird name was that?

'Tell you what, call me Josh. It's easier to remember.'

He stood up abruptly and walked over to the large picture window, hands in pockets, expression thoughtful, and momentarily stared at the mountains. Wait… a few moments ago they'd been green hills. I frowned and leant forward, staring ahead at the vista beyond. Definitely snow-capped peaks. There were no mountains in Sidcup. Of that I was one hundred per cent sure. In which case… where the flipping heck was I?

'To answer your question, Hattie, I first need to tell you what happened.'

'Are you reading my mind?' I gasped.

'Yes,' he said, with a shrug. 'But don't worry,' he assured me, seeing my look of alarm, 'I can't read anything that is… how can I put this… *sensitive*. So, if you're thinking something very personal, those thoughts are not accessible to me.'

I didn't respond. I was too confused. Perhaps the accident had knocked me out and I hadn't yet come to? Maybe everything that was happening now was, in fact, some sort of strange dream? Why else would tea be appearing without kettles boiling, or tables materialising out of thin air, or hills turning into mountains or…?

My mind screeched to a halt as I stared at the assistant manager in disbelief. His white jeans and shirt appeared to be glowing.

'What on earth—?'

'Firstly, Hattie,' he interrupted, 'you might have *thought* that aisle three's sign fell from the ceiling, but it didn't. It was an illusion created to interrupt your life, and with very good reason. Secondly, you aren't in Sidcup. This room is not an office, and I'm not an assistant manager. Take another sip of that sugary tea, because what I'm going to tell you will be the biggest shock of all.'

But I didn't need this man to deliver any further mind-boggling revelations, because the pennies were rolling around in my brain, clattering into place as the awful realisation dawned. I'd only flaming well gone and died!

# Chapter Four

I dropped the teacup with a clatter, instantly spilling hot liquid over my thighs. Before I could even cry out with pain, the tannin stains evaporated, my trousers were suddenly dry, and the teacup – magically replenished – safely set down on the occasional table. I couldn't deal with this. Nor was I going to.

'I don't know who you are, Mr Cooper... I am... whatever-your-name-is—'

'Josh,' he said quickly.

'—but I cannot, indeed *will not* be stopping here. Is that clear? I have a son who needs me. And a dog,' I added, 'who is currently in his crate and will be cross-legged if I don't get home to let him out. Fin isn't home until sometime tomorrow.' I tore at my hair in frustration. This simply could not be happening. Apart from anything else, I didn't believe in life after death. No, no, no, I'd *definitely* hit my head. I was probably in a hospital somewhere, full of morphine for the injury, and having some sort of psychedelic drug-induced trip. Yes, that was it. It *had* to be it, there could be no other explanation.

'Hattie, please don't panic,' said Josh, turning his back on the huge window and walking towards me. Despite the bewildering circumstances and my immense confusion, Bradley Cooper was giving off a wonderful vibe, so much so that I somehow knew he was both good-humoured and kind. Instinctively I felt I could trust him. He crouched down in front of me, hesitating a moment before gently taking both my hands in his. They felt very real. Very warm. In fact, his touch was sending some pleasantly nice tingles up and down my spine. *Oh terrific, Hattie. Not only are you tripping on morphine, you're having a sexy reaction to a cosmic Bradley Cooper lookalike.*

'I can tell you're thinking something,' he said, 'but I'm not privy to this particular set of thoughts.'

Thank heavens for small mercies.

'I'm truly sorry your trip to the supermarket was so rudely interrupted,' he continued, 'but rest assured, you haven't died.'

I stared at him, feeling a mix of bewilderment at what was happening, and relief at being told I hadn't died.

'So… so am I dreaming?'

'No. This place is real, but you can only access it when asleep or unconscious.'

I sighed gustily, struggling to take on board what he was saying, such was the relief of being told my life wasn't over, even if it had suddenly gone topsy-turvy. *Thank you, God. Thank-you-thank-you-thank-you.*

'Please can you send me back to Tesco?'

'In a bit,' he said, giving my hands a reassuring squeeze, which sent some fresh zingers up my spine. It was a good thing I was sitting down because this guy's presence had reduced my knees to the substance of Tesco's tiramisu. 'The reason you're here, Hattie, is because the Powers That Be have seen fit to interrupt your life. You wandered off the path you were meant to be following, so I was assigned to bring you here to explain a few things.'

'And where exactly is "here"?' I quavered.

'You're in God's Halfway Lounge.'

I had to resist an urge not to laugh. Wow, this dream was getting funkier by the moment.

'I'm not sure I believe in God,' I said, more to myself than Josh.

Sure, like many people, I occasionally flung a prayer heavenwards. It was usually along the lines of: *Dear God, please get the car through its MOT.* Or: *Dear God, please can I win the lottery?* More recently it had been: *Dear God, please can you get me out of a date with Mark Jackson?* But we all did that, didn't we? It didn't mean we truly believed in a heavenly superpower.

'Take it from me, the Boss is real all right.'

I snorted. 'So what exactly is the *Boss's* Halfway Lounge?'

I looked around the sumptuous room with its incredible view.

'It's somewhere between Earth and Heaven. A resting place, if you like. Some people refer to being here as a near-death experience. Others think of it as a dream. Either way, you're going to be here for a while.'

'Oh no I'm not. I've told you, I need to go home and let Buddy out—'

'Rest assured that the concept of time here is very different to that on Earth. What seem like great chunks of hours here, are only fractions of seconds in your world.'

'Listen, Josh, I'm not stopping here for another minute, never mind hours on end,' I protested.

'Then the sooner you understand and act upon why you're here, the sooner you can return.'

'I'm all ears,' I said sarcastically.

'Good. Let me explain. When your marriage broke up, you made a vow never to get involved with another man again.'

'That's right,' I whispered.

*How the heck did he know that?*

'I know everything about you, Hattie.'

I gulped. Okay, he was mind-reading again. I hoped to goodness he wasn't reading my soul too, because it had some very dark depths.

He smiled reassuringly. 'There are other vows too, Hattie, like learning to forgive others, and to forgive yourself. But the vow about never getting involved with a man again has proven so powerful, it's interfered with you falling in love again.'

'But I don't want to fall in love again.'

'We all need to love, Hattie. Living without love is like trying to live without food and water. Love is the Universe's Law.'

'I have all the love I need,' I retorted indignantly. 'I'm showered with love from my parents and son.'

'You need unconditional love.'

'My dog loves me unconditionally,' I said, my tone stubborn.

'I know Buddy does,' Josh replied. I had a feeling he was laughing at me now. His eyes were twinkling merrily, which was doing rather strange things to my pulse. 'But despite Buddy being a slave to your every mood, unfortunately pets don't count. Love is a tough lesson, but it's something we all must learn as we pass through life. You are here to undo old vows. Destiny decrees you are given a second chance to love.'

I tutted, and decided to humour Josh.

'Righty-ho. And how, pray tell, is this vow going to be eradicated and Mr Right capture my heart?'

'It's quite simple,' Josh said, his tone matter-of-fact. But I wasn't at all prepared for his answer which, when it came, had me instantly recoiling in horror. 'We're going to review your life.'

# Chapter Five

I stared at Josh, eyes wide with fear. I didn't want to review my life. And I certainly didn't want somebody else reviewing it with me. Whether they were real *or* part of a dream. It was simply not on. It was an invasion of privacy, that's what it was!

'Don't distress yourself, Hattie,' Josh cajoled. He was still holding my hands and gave them a reassuring squeeze. Once again my heart did some skippy beats, despite my brain screaming at the very idea of dredging up the past. 'We'll do this together; you'll be guided every step of the way.'

I shook my head. 'I don't want you to be with me.'

'But if I'm not with you, how else would you review your life?' he asked gently.

'I… I'll do it when I'm back home. Promise,' I nodded, as if I was talking to one of my old teachers, and back in Lower Three again. *Yes, Miss Osbourne, I promise I'll do my homework tonight.* This was surely the same sort of thing, but in a reflective way. 'I'll sit down in front of the fire and have a good think about things. And I'll make sure the telly is turned down,' I nodded again.

'Unfortunately the type of life review that has been decreed for you is beyond mulling things over, Hattie, and you know that in your heart.'

I inwardly squirmed. Did this man *really* know everything about me? He couldn't possibly. It was preposterous.

'Are you an angel?'

'No.'

'A guide?'

Josh smiled. 'I'm not meant to tell you too much about myself.'

'Why not?'

'Laws.'

'What laws?'

'Heavenly laws, of course. And karma,' he added mysteriously.

I gulped. Karma? Why would karma be involved? I wasn't a murderer. Or a thief. I'd never stolen anything. Apart from a packet of sweets from the local corner shop when I was five years old. But it would be ridiculous if that counted! Wouldn't it?

'Karma is the law of cause and effect,' Josh explained, 'and it's very real. You need to right a major wrong, Hattie. Something momentous. And I'm not talking about stealing a bag of chocolate buttons.'

I flushed to my roots and wished this man didn't have the ability to read my thoughts.

'You know what I'm talking about, don't you?' he prodded.

'I-I'm not sure,' I stuttered, my frazzled emotions starting to collapse upon themselves, like a blanket being folded tighter and tighter before being crammed into a storage box and shoved out of sight. 'Look, before I agree to anything, J-Josh,' I stuttered, 'I absolutely insist on knowing more about you. If you're not an angel or a guide or some mythical being, then what are you?'

'Okay,' Josh nodded, 'that's a fair question and one that I can give some sort of answer to.'

'Please,' I said, looking at him expectantly.

'As such, I'm a representative. I'm here, with you, on behalf of the person you're meant to be living the rest of your life with.'

I stared at him. 'What person?'

'I can't tell you that.'

*Oh, for…*

'So, so, you mean, you're *that* person's guide?'

'There are no easy answers to what you're asking, Hattie, because invariably one question's answer will simply lead to a whole host of interrogations which will make your brain boggle. I could attempt explaining things, but it would probably take two thousand years, and I thought you wanted to get back to let your dog out for a wee?'

I opened my mouth to speak, but nothing came out.

'At this level of consciousness it would be too complicated to work with your own guide. Instead you have me. A co-ordinator. Let's focus on the three things you need to learn before you return home.'

'Which are?'

He smiled kindly, and his eyes crinkled attractively at the sides. He really was very good-looking. But I wasn't finding myself attracted to him just because of his appearance. Mentally, Josh was stimulating. He was making me think. I loved that he knew things about 'the Boss' and the universe and karma and… well, just fascinating stuff that nobody I'd ever met could offer a sensible opinion about. I listened intently to what he was saying.

'Okay, three things. Firstly, trust. Secondly, allowing yourself to believe the unbelievable. Thirdly, falling in love.'

Those last three words had me rolling my eyes.

'You sound like my mother,' I said, cranking up a smile.

'Then she must be a wise lady,' he retorted. 'We might as well crack on with the first lesson,' he smiled, pulling me to my feet. I stared up at him and, for a moment, suddenly felt a bit shy. My goodness he was tall. I was no shorty myself, but he towered over me. I'd never had to lift my lips to a man's before because I'd always pretty much been the same height as them, Nick included. But if I were to kiss Josh it would mean – for the first time ever – tipping my head back. I felt myself go a bit pink. Why was I thinking about kissing a man who lived in another world which, anyway, thanks to a bump on the head, was nothing more than dreams and make-believe?

'I didn't quite get all that,' said Josh, interrupting my musings, 'because I guess some of it was private.'

'All my thoughts are private!' I said indignantly.

'What a shame,' he said playfully, holding my gaze longer than was strictly necessarily.

Oh my goodness, was he flirting? *Don't be ridiculous, Hattie.* He guided me by the elbow across the room to the enormous window.

'As I said before,' he continued, 'this place is not a world of dreams and make-believe. It is the Halfway Lounge, and it's real.'

When I'd been sitting on the sofa, I had presumed the window to have a glass pane, but now I could see there was none. It was possible to walk straight out onto the veranda, which we did. Even though the backdrop was snow-capped mountains, the temperature was mild. A whisper of wind lifted the hair around my neck, its touch as light as a caress. Despite the bizarreness of my situation, I could feel myself relaxing. This place reminded me of a village I'd once visited in Switzerland… all gigantic fir trees sprinkled with the feeling of Christmas. However, my gut instinct was to remind myself this whole experience was nothing more than fanciful imagination.

Suddenly the piercing blue eyes were boring into mine.

'Are you ready for your first lesson, Hattie?'

I stared at him blankly.

'Trust,' he reminded. 'Do you feel you can trust me?'

Yes, I *did* feel Josh was trustworthy, but I wasn't so readily going to tell him that. After all, I didn't know him. Not properly. His eyes were distracting me. They were like two chips of aquamarine, flecked with amber and grey.

'How can I possibly answer that question when I don't know you?'

'Open your mind, Hattie, and open your heart too. What is your inner voice telling you?'

Inner voice? What was this man on about?

'I'm "on about" getting in touch with your feelings,' he said, sounding like a slightly exasperated school teacher.

I put my hands up in the air. 'Okay, okay. I'm doing my best to understand. My general "feeling" is that you seem like a pleasant person. I'm not getting any bad vibes, if that's what you mean.'

'Excellent, now hold that thought,' he said, looking pleased, 'because vibes are very important. People refer to good vibes and bad vibes all the time, especially in relation to other people. Trust that instinct. But right now, I want you to trust *me*. Do you think you can?'

I looked at him. No alarm bells were ringing. No claxons going off. Nothing was telling me to put as much distance as possible between us.

'Yes, I trust you.'

'You're not convincing me,' Josh laughed, revealing beautifully white straight teeth. 'There's time to develop trust, but you've made a tentative step in the right direction. Let's see how much you trust me right now.' And with that, he jumped up onto the veranda's rail.

'What are you doing?' I shrieked with alarm as he flung his hands out, like a tight-rope walker, balancing himself.

'Get up here with me,' he instructed.

'Not blooming likely,' I replied, backing smartly away. 'You're mad. Absolutely barking.'

'You just said you trusted me.'

'What's that got to do with standing on a veranda rail?' I protested. 'For heaven's sake, Josh, if you fall—'

'I'll what? Get hurt? Plunge to my death? That's not going to happen. This isn't Earth.'

I stared, thoroughly confused. Things were going from the bizarre to the downright ludicrous. One minute I was shopping in Tesco, minding my own business, the next I was goodness only knows where with a gorgeous stranger wanting me to stand on the balcony rail of a tall building and all without a safety net. But he was right about one thing. I couldn't die if I was dreaming – and my brain refused to accept this experience as anything other than some sort of wild imagining. I was suddenly reminded of a nightmare that periodically troubled me. Running away from someone… being chased through the corridors of sleep… being screamed at… someone calling me a wicked liar and demanding that a secret – buried deep in my soul – be revealed… that it spurt out like blood from a deep wound. In the nightmare I would run and run, feet pounding through a maze of anxiety until, sweating and terrified, my body would jerk upright in bed, heart hammering wildly. Similarly, what was happening now must be one of those moments. Perhaps I would stand on the veranda's rail, watch the ground below tilt as dizziness took hold, which would be the trigger to me shooting upright in bed at home, whereupon everything would turn out to have been a nightmare. Perhaps I'd never even gone to Tesco? Maybe the supermarket was part of this wacky dream? Yes, that must be it. How stupid of me. I'd probably even dreamt the bit about Fin coming into the kitchen while I'd been talking to Mum. In which case I was now getting to the bit of the dream where wakefulness was only moments away. Hurrah!

Certain that this was the case, I darted forward and scrambled rather clumsily onto the balcony rail. Thank goodness I was wearing trainers that, if I assumed a ballerina's first position, fitted neatly within the wooden rail's width. Slowly straightening up, I stared triumphantly at Josh.

'There!' I beamed, before daring to look down. Flipping heck, the ground seemed miles away. Vertigo instantly consumed me, but I almost welcomed it as my body began to sway like a tree caught in a hurricane. In my peripheral vision, Josh was regarding me with amusement, but I took no notice. It was time to wake up. I tore my eyes away from the chasm below and glanced quickly back at Josh. 'I'm off,' I said. Quite literally. Because suddenly I was falling.

# Chapter Six

The ear-piercing scream that followed should have catapulted me back to wakefulness, but regrettably no such thing happened. The ground didn't rush up to meet me, and I didn't go *splat*. Instead, I found myself suspended in mid-air, arms windmilling frantically as the dizziness increased, making my entire body feel like it was in a washing machine that was revving up for its final spin. A voice cut through the hysterical shrieking.

'Hattie? Hattie! Stop thrashing about, for goodness' sake.' A pair of strong arms grabbed me, and my body reacted so strongly it was a wonder I didn't erupt out of them, like squeezed toothpaste. 'You're safe, I've got you,' Josh crooned, as if talking to a distraught child. I could feel his warm breath against my ear, sending tingles down my spine. I clung to him like a baby, too terrified to let go in case the law of gravity caught up and claimed me. 'You've just had a taster of the second thing I told you about.'

'Which is?' I squeaked, none the wiser, my hands clamping down hard on his wonderfully broad shoulders. *Concentrate on them, Hattie. Forget about the space between your feet and the grass miles below.* Terrified, I stared at the tendrils of golden-brown hair curling around Josh's neck and suddenly had an overwhelming urge to touch one.

'Believe the unbelievable.'

'Get us back on the veranda!' I yelped, wondering if it was possible to vomit with fear in a dream. 'Pl-please.'

I'd barely finished stuttering that final word when there was a sensation of solid ground beneath my feet. Still clinging to Josh, I looked tentatively around. Yes, we were definitely back on terra firma. Josh prised my fingers off him one by one and steered me over to a twee little table and chair arrangement.

'Sit,' he ordered.

I needed no persuasion, and collapsed heavily downwards, trembling rather like Buddy did when it was time for his annual booster.

'Brandy?' Josh asked, his voice full of concern.

I nodded. For now, speech was out of the question. A balloon glass materialised on the table next to me. I shook my head in bewilderment. Did everything here appear as if by magic?

'Only when you want it to,' said Josh, answering my silent question.

I shook my head again. If I wasn't going to wake up any time soon in my own bed, then I guessed I'd have to get used to expecting the unexpected.

'Excellent, Hattie!' said Josh, nodding his approval. 'That thought is a very wise one, and on a par with believing the unbelievable. You're starting to edge along the path of progress, although there's still a long way to go.'

I picked up the glass balloon and, without bothering to warm it between my shaking hands, swigged greedily. The liquid burnt a trail down to my stomach, and I welcomed its fire. Draining the glass, I set it down on the table before looking up at Josh. He was leaning against the veranda rail, looking devastatingly handsome.

I found my voice. 'How come we didn't fall?'

'Because I wouldn't let you.'

'So I could have fallen?'

'Technically speaking,' he nodded. 'Look, Hattie, there's a couple of things you need to know. In this place, nothing can harm you. So even if you'd plummeted down, you wouldn't have been injured, although you would have experienced everything else associated with falling – the speed of the descent… panic… and so on. Secondly, while you're here, you have the power to make something happen just like that' – he clicked his fingers, as if to demonstrate – 'so, if you want a brandy, you simply *think* about wanting the brandy, and you'll get it.'

'Excellent. Well I'd like to go home, Josh, so I'm going to think about that and whisk myself right out of here.'

'Ah, 'fraid not,' he smiled. 'Theoretically, of course, you should be able to do that. But it's outside the Law, so consequently it won't happen. After all, if everyone could do that, we'd have all sorts of people popping in and out of this place whenever it suited them.'

'Are there other people here?'

'Yes and no.'

'Eh?'

'There are other people here in this half-dimension. However, you can't see them, and they can't see you due to different vibrational frequencies. Like you, they are here for a reason. If you could all see each other, it would be too distracting. Therefore, all of you only see your mentor. You're asking some great questions, Hattie, but to answer them would be going into the realms of quantum physics, and I have it on good authority that the subject was never one of your best when you were at school.'

I sighed. He was right. I loved the fact that he knew about quantum physics. Cleverness and attractiveness were a lethal combination in a man.

'So to continue,' said Josh, 'the Law here does not allow you to "think" yourself back home otherwise it would work in reverse and allow human beings to "think" themselves here the moment life got tough. It's important that human beings figure out how to get through difficult situations and stick around to resolve the lesson. Running away from life and all its complexities is not acceptable. What *is* allowed is making the magic happen in *your* world.'

'You've lost me.'

'If you want something hard enough, invariably you'll get it. You just need to put the intention in place. Once the intent is there, a shift occurs. The universe sets things in motion for you.'

I snorted with ridicule. 'You mean like cosmic ordering?' The brandy had hit its spot and loosened my tongue. 'Sorry, Josh, but I'm struggling to keep up.'

'I'm simply talking about the basics here.'

'Yes, well I'll prove you wrong on that little homily,' I said, surprised at the sudden anger in my tone. 'You see, there were lots of things I wanted in life, Josh, but unfortunately they didn't happen, despite the *intent* being in place. I wanted a husband who was faithful. For my son to have his father. To live the proverbial "happy ever after". So what happened to all that then, eh? Answer me that!' I could feel myself choking up. 'Are you telling me I brought that all upon myself?' I demanded.

If silence could ever be deafening, then this was one of those moments. I wiped away a tear that had leaked out of one eye.

Eventually Josh blew out his cheeks. 'That's a lot of questions, Hattie.'

'I didn't ask for Nick to be a bastard who chased anything in a skirt.'

'No,' he said quietly, 'but you unwittingly set in motion the wheels that drove him to punish you with his extra-marital affairs. Remember?' His eyes suddenly pinned me to the outside wall of the Halfway Lounge. Two bright blue headlamps were lighting up dark corners of my soul, like twin spotlights searching out escaped convicts. I stared back defiantly, but my eyes were the first to look away.

# Chapter Seven

'Look,' I said quietly, my gaze sliding away to stare at my tatty trainers. The laces were badly chewed, courtesy of Buddy. 'I hear what you're saying, Josh, and despite the bizarreness of this situation, I do kind of believe you. After all, dreams are usually fragmented. A nonsensical muddle. And yet this place' – I looked up at him, feeling my heart momentarily skip a few beats as I encountered those gorgeous blue eyes that were still trained upon me – 'well, all this seems very sane – in an insane way.'

Josh threw back his head and laughed. 'That's a great way of putting things into some sort of context.' He nodded. 'I'm not judging you, Hattie. That's not my job. You're the one who does that.'

My brow furrowed. 'Judge myself?'

'Yes. But that's rather a harsh word. I prefer the word "review".'

'Ah, yes. You said earlier. I have to review my life.'

'Only when you're ready.'

I chewed my lip. I didn't think I'd ever be ready. Josh must have read that last thought, because he moved away from the veranda rail and came over, hunkering down to my level as I sat on the chair. His face was full of kindness. Ooh no, I didn't want his sympathy.

That would have an adverse effect and, yes, dammit, it was already happening. I could feel a chin wobble coming on.

'I appreciate this whole experience is surreal, and downright confusing. Can I suggest something?'

'Yes,' I said, my chin now quivering rather dramatically. *Please don't be kind to me. It might open the floodgates.*

'Currently you're feeling overwhelmed. Why don't you sleep on things?'

'I don't want to go to sleep here,' I replied in a small voice. 'I miss my son. And my dog.' God, I'd even suffer one of my mum's wretched dinner parties with the buck-toothed Mark Jackson if it meant I could just click my heels, like Dorothy in *The Wizard of Oz*, and find myself back in Vigo Village. Whoever had written that movie script was right. There was no place like home.

'I promise you will go home.'

I looked up at him hopefully. 'Now?'

He shook his head imperceptibly. 'Eventually.'

My heart sank. Never had I felt so despairing.

'Come on,' said Josh, taking me by the hand and pulling me up on my feet. One way or another, we seemed to be doing an awful lot of hand-holding. His warm touch once again sent some high-voltage zings whizzing through my body. He led me across the lounge to a door I'd not noticed before. Pushing down the handle, I was astonished to see a pretty bedroom, just like the sort of room I'd have loved to have at home, cash flow permitting. I'd always been a bit of a pink princess, and the soft furnishings in this room didn't disappoint. A queen-sized bed dominated the room, its buttoned satiny headboard soaring up to the ceiling. The bedcover depicted rose-coloured spriggy flowers, and the plumped-up pillows looked invitingly soft. Matching curtains hung at the picture window, and restful floral prints graced the walls. I could almost feel the bed calling to me, and suddenly felt a bit foolish standing in the doorway holding Josh's hand, like a lover full of anticipation. I don't know whether he read that last thought, but he diplomatically let go.

'Make yourself at home, Hattie.' He gave me a little prod and, after a moment's hesitation, I crossed the threshold. 'See you later.'

I nodded, not quite trusting myself to speak, emotion now well and truly lodged in my throat. Seconds later the door quietly closed. I was alone. Kicking off my trainers, and without bothering to undress, I crawled under the duvet. The cover was as light as a cloud and smelt comfortingly like a soap powder my mother had used when I was a small child. I pulled the quilt up to my chin, balling into the foetal position. Feeling strangely soothed, I closed my eyes. Seconds later, I was fast asleep.

# Chapter Eight

I don't know how long I slept but I was awoken by my mobile phone ringing. Opening one bleary eye, I saw the screen glowing away on the bedside cabinet. I wiggled my toes under the duvet and snuggled into a tighter ball, unwilling just yet to let the outside world intrude. To hell with it, voicemail could pick up the call. Like a steel portcullis, my eyelids clanged shut again. However, the caller wasn't to be deterred. Seconds later the mobile once again burst into life. Annoyed, I sat up and grabbed it. The display told me it was my mother.

'Mum,' I said, 'if you're ringing to persuade me to attend yet another accidentally-on-purpose event starring Mark Jackson, it's a no.'

'Hattie? Hattie are you there?'

'Yes, of course I'm here,' I said, stifling a yawn.

'I've just had a very alarming telephone call from my friend Edith. She said she was doing some shopping in Tesco and spotted you in aisle three, so she thought she'd trolley over and say hello, but apparently you started chucking cans of baked beans around—'

'What? I did no such thing! I accidentally knocked some tins off the shelf and tripped over and—'

Oh for heaven's sake, Mum wasn't even listening to me.

'—and it wasn't just one or two tins, according to Edith, it was loads and loads, and they were flying up in the air, and several of them landed in aisle four, and someone tripped over them, and apparently they smacked down hard on the floor and were out cold—'

'Mum, could you just listen to me for a minute—'

'—and Edith said it was pandemonium, and somebody screamed for an ambulance to be called—'

'Look, it must be a very bad signal because you don't seem to be able to hear what I'm saying—'

'—and, well, I'm just ringing to make sure you're all right, because that sounds very out of character for you, although I know you sometimes suffer premenstrual tension, but surely it's not so awful that you'd go berserk in Tesco, eh, love?'

'Mum, can I call you back, please, because this is a really bad line—'

'Edith said she couldn't see what happened after that because staff directed shoppers to stand back for the paramedics, who were there in a matter of minutes – whatever people say about the National Health Service, they do a marvellous job – anyway Edith lost sight of you after that, so could you ring me back just as soon as you pick up this voicemail because you know how I worry, and I'd really like to know what on earth possessed you to do such a thing—'

Oh for heaven's sake, this was ridiculous. And why was Mum referring to our conversation as a voicemail? Wasn't she aware I'd answered her call?

'CAN YOU HEAR ME, MUM?' I bellowed into the handset.

'—and if it *is* PMT you really *must* make an appointment with your doctor, because you can't make free with tins of baked beans,

Hattie, it's not good for your health, and clearly not good for whoever was strolling down aisle four. It would be awful if you got sued—'

'It was an accident!'

'—so don't forget to call me as soon as you get this message, darling.'

There was a click from the other end. Mum had hung up. I checked the number of bars on the mobile. Zero. A little message in the top left-hand corner of the screen read 'No Service'. I sighed and chucked the mobile back down, then flung back the duvet cover. A little puff of Buddy's hairs momentarily filled the air. It was high time that dog stuck to his basket instead of lolling all over my newly laundered bedding the moment my back was turned.

Swinging my legs over the side of the bed, I paused as a distant memory began to filter back. Oh yes. That's right. I'd been dreaming of being in another dimension. The Halfway Lounge that supposedly belonged to Him Upstairs. I snorted with contempt at such fanciful imagination and stared around my bedroom. Yes, *my* bedroom. I was back in my cottage, complete with faded duvet and – I sneezed – beagle hair. I felt ridiculously happy. Outside the bedroom door I could hear Fin talking to Buddy who was woofing joyfully, no doubt demanding his breakfast. I grinned, ramming my feet into my slippers. Standing up, I grabbed my comfortable old dressing gown hanging from the lopsided peg on the back of the bedroom door. As I wrapped it around me, tying the cord, I thought a decent cup of coffee wouldn't go amiss. In fact, forget using the bathroom. I'd go and put the kettle on right now!

I opened the bedroom door. And stepped straight back into the Halfway Lounge.

# Chapter Nine

The door shut behind me and I stared, open-mouthed, at Josh. He was sitting on the sofa I'd been laying upon when I first arrived in this place. He stood up to greet me.

'Hey! How do you feel?' he asked solicitously.

For a moment I was too angry to speak.

'How do I feel?' I eventually spluttered. 'How do I *feel*?' I strode over to him and waggled a finger under his nose. 'I feel absolutely outraged. Furious. Livid. How *dare* you trick me into thinking I was back home in my cottage? What sort of person are you? Actually, don't answer that. I'll answer it for you. You're cruel, that's what you are.'

I turned on my heel and stomped out to the veranda. My tatty trainers were back on my feet, and I was once again dressed in scruffy joggers and a hoodie. I stared moodily at the sylvan scene before me. I hadn't even had a chance to put the kettle on and make that longed-for drink.

'Here,' said Josh, coming up beside me. 'Drink this, and then I'll explain.' He passed me a steaming cup of coffee. Wordlessly I took it from him. The cup was exactly like the one I drank from at home, wittily captioned 'You're a Mug'. Oh, I was a mug all right, and there was nothing remotely witty about this situation.

A silence prevailed, broken only by the sound of me making unfortunate slurping noises.

'Sorry,' I muttered, after another two minutes of interminable silence had passed.

'Apology accepted.'

'You're not really cruel.'

'I know.'

'I just said that to annoy you.'

'I know.'

'Do you know everything?'

'Mostly.'

'Including the design of my cup?'

'I read your thoughts about wanting a coffee and provided it for you. But you're the one who turned the cup into a replica of what you use at home, just like you're the one who changed the bedroom I created for you into a copy of where you usually sleep.'

'Right,' I said flatly. 'And hearing Fin talking to Buddy was simply my imagination, eh?'

'Kind of. Let me explain something to you, Hattie. You might think it's complex, but it's breathtakingly simple. You manifest what you want by thinking it. Remember I told you that, on Earth, a shift takes place when intent is established? Well, here it is instantaneous. Your coffee is a "thought construct" put together by vibrational building blocks. On Earth, where vibrations are denser, it's not possible to pluck a cup of coffee from thin air. But it's still possible to *feel* the vibration… the intent. For example, how many times have you walked into a room and sensed an atmosphere? Plenty! That sensation is a diluted form of "thought construct". Thoughts might not be visibly tangible on Earth, but if they are dark enough they can be keenly felt, and still hurt those we love.'

'You're blinding me with science.'

'Okay, scrap the above. Change it to "wishful thinking". Except here, it happens!'

'Okay,' I said in a small voice, 'I'm understanding better how I subconsciously changed the pink and white bedroom into the human form of a dog basket that is my bedroom at home.'

'Good!'

'I'm sorry for having a pop at you.'

'You don't have to apologise for anything, Hattie. I appreciate this is wacko stuff for you to deal with.'

I smiled at him, liking his use of the word 'wacko'. It was typical of my own type of vocabulary, and I once again felt a sensation of being on the same wavelength as this guy. It wasn't just spine zingers he gave me – quite a few of my brain cells were doing a happy dance, too.

'Was my mother's telephone call wishful thinking?'

'Ah.' Josh inclined his head, whilst considering how best to explain. 'No, that was something different. She really *did* telephone your mobile, but answering her call in this dimension is outside the Law, and therefore not permitted. So her call went to voicemail which you "tuned into" whilst in a relaxed state.'

'I don't want her worrying about me.'

'Don't panic. Everything is under control back home.'

I shook my head, feeling more than a little befuddled.

'Mum mentioned that another shopper had been injured. Knocked out. I feel terribly responsible. Are they okay?'

'Yes. Again, everything is under control.'

'Thank goodness,' I said, relieved. 'Er, where's the bathroom?' Perhaps a nice hot shower, blasting a big fat jet of water over my body, would soothe my frazzled feelings.

'You don't need a bathroom here. Nor do you need to sleep, eat or drink. They're just earthly habits you're experiencing. But sometimes the soul needs to rest because it is processing a lot. There was a heap of that going on when you went to bed earlier.'

'Right,' I said, my tone morose. I swallowed the last of the coffee, welcoming its warmth. As I tipped back my head and drained the last drop, the mug vanished from my grasp. At the same time, something reared up inside me. An emotion. I recognised it instantly. A sensation of squaring one's shoulders. Facing up to a situation. Growing a backbone. I could only presume that my soul had done enough 'processing' while I'd been asleep to feel fortified enough to get on with the reasons why I was here. I'd had enough of this place. The view from this veranda might be stunning, but it was starting to make me feel like screaming. I wanted out. And if the exit door to this halfway place was via reviewing unpleasant chapters of my life, then so be it. Josh was now looking at me with both surprise and delight.

'Are you ready to begin, Hattie?'

I nodded, and gave him a determined look.

'Let's get on with this, eh?' I said. 'Where do we start?'

# Chapter Ten

'Okay,' said Josh. 'In a moment, we're going to walk through a door straight back into an old part of your life. We can't rewrite history, but we *can* change the way we deal with it – and that's in here.' He made a fist of one hand and tapped it against his heart.

I nodded, wondering what little gem of a scene was going to greet me.

'It's time to alter something relating to an event for which, it seems, you blame yourself. It's important you forgive others in this scenario, but ultimately that you forgive yourself.'

Forgive myself? I wasn't too sure about that. If Josh was talking about what I *suspected* he was talking about, then that would be a tough cookie. I'd spent years mentally beating myself up. Blaming myself. And still did. But I'd give it my best shot, because I was desperate to go home. Never again would I moan about Buddy rolling in fox poo, or Fin treading in it and tracking it into the house, or my mother plotting to marry me off to Mark Jackson and talking suitable wedding venues with Margery. I just wanted to get back to everything that was familiar and dear.

'Ready?'

I took a deep breath and nodded as Josh indicated the same door I'd walked through earlier. Last time it had led into a pretty pink bedroom. I speculated what room was awaiting behind the closed door this time. Josh stepped forward and pulled the handle down. As I moved over the threshold, I experienced a frisson of shock. This was no room. It was a car. More specifically, it was *my* car. And I was sitting in it, my hands trembling upon the steering wheel. The vehicle was stationary, parked in a very familiar road.

I exhaled shakily. I'd replayed this scene a thousand times before. But only in my mind. On such occasions, my brain had conjured up nasty implements… hot needles for sticking into mascara-lashed eyeballs, and a vet's emasculator for removing horses' testicles – or, in this case, the eyeballs of my ex-bestie and the testicles of my ex-husband.

'Those are dark thoughts, Hattie,' said Josh.

I looked across the handbrake in surprise.

'How come you're here with me?'

'To guide you. You don't really want hot needles and veterinary equipment, do you?'

I sighed. 'I guess not.'

'Good. Apart from anything else, you were making me nervous.'

I laughed. Despite the seriousness of what was about to unfold, Josh was keeping it light for me. I appreciated that, and once again felt a mental connection. He grinned, and immediately my heart began to pump, as if I'd just gone for a rather brisk walk. God, but he was handsome. I had a sudden urge to lean across the handbrake and snog Josh senseless. I wondered what the curve of his lips would taste like as I pressed my mouth against his. How would he react?

Would he be shocked, and shove me roughly away? Or would he welcome me with open arms, wrapping them around me, one hand momentarily breaking away from my body to feel its way around the edge of the passenger seat, releasing the catch that sent the seat reclining backwards with a whoosh, so that I landed breathlessly on top of him, the pair of us half laughing, but suddenly pausing as we greedily drank each other in, him raising his hands upwards, his beautiful long fingers pushing through my hair as he pulled me down on top of him, his hands moving back down as they urgently wandered inside my hoodie, burrowing under my t-shirt, walking up my spine to my bra strap and making me gasp with delicious anticipation as the hook gave way, me subtly shifting my body weight so he could catch my breasts in his warm palms as my own fingers began undoing all the buttons on that spotlessly white shirt and—

*Good heavens, Hattie, what's the matter with you? How can you possibly think such outrageously sexy thoughts at a time like this? And anyway, you swore off men forever, remember?*

'I'm not privy to know what you're thinking right now, Hattie, but I suspect you've moved on from the dark thoughts.'

'Er, yes,' I muttered. More like X-rated ones. I forced my mind back to the present situation. It was a dire one. For I was outside the house of my ex-friend Pippa Brown, who, right now, was having it off with my husband.

# Chapter Eleven

'Okay,' said Josh, 'just to recap, you're reviewing your past. This is only real to you. You're not rewriting history. What has gone before can't be altered. You can tinker with conversation, but not the essence of the scene. However, what *can* be changed is your mental and emotional response to these situations. Understood?'

'Yes,' I nodded, as a net-full of butterflies threatened to take off in my stomach.

'I'm going to have to switch frequency to become invisible,' said Josh. 'I've crossed a dimension here. This is your personal flashback, not mine, so I mustn't encroach upon it by being seen. I'll be talking straight into your head too, so nobody else will hear me other than you. Rest assured though, you're not alone and I am here to support and guide you. Okay?'

No, it wasn't okay. Nothing about this situation was okay. But I'd go along with it. Home was calling, and I so badly wanted to return. I nodded my assent at Josh, and then opened the car door.

Seconds later I was passing through Pippa's side gate and stepping hesitatingly into her utility room. As previously, laundry was swishing around in the washing machine, and the tumble drier was rumbling away. Once again, my footsteps went unnoticed.

My ears tuned in to the racket going on upstairs. It sounded like something out of a porn movie. Pippa was shouting her head off. From the utility room I could hear her voice, but not specifically what she was saying. As I crept through the hallway and put one foot on the bottom tread of the staircase, she became clearer and, indeed, more vocal.

'Oh, yeah, baby, do it like that, yeah, do it like that. Oh, oh-oh-oh! You naughty boy, I'm coming, ah-ah-ah, it's happening again… AHHH!'

My bowels once again lurched as I stealthily climbed Pippa's staircase, swallowing the bile that threatened to rise up as I made my way along the now familiar landing to Pippa and Brian's master bedroom. Except Brian wasn't here. He was safely out of the way, at work, tucked behind his desk, probably sipping a coffee his secretary had brought him while he studied the figures on his screen just as I, in Brian's home, now studied the figures bouncing around on his marital bed.

Nick's bobbing backside greeted me, Pippa's legs wrapped around his hips. A second later, with awesome choreography, the two of them changed position so that Pippa was now on top of my husband. He flung his arms across Pippa's sheets as she juddered about on him like a jockey trying to stay on a particularly frisky horse.

'I'm gonna whip you with my hair, babe!' she gasped, shaking back her long red mane before tossing it over her head so it gently lashed Nick's chest. 'I'm gonna do that again,' she panted. And she did. Forward. Back. Forward. Back. I felt motion sick just watching, so goodness knows how she felt. I clung onto the door frame as Nick grabbed hold of her hair, almost sending her nosediving onto his chest.

'You little bitch,' he gasped, 'you bloody cock tease.'

'Yes, I-am-I-am-I-AMMM,' Pippa wailed, as another climax began to take hold. Good God, how many orgasms could a woman achieve in one coupling? About three hundred, at the rate she was going. I wondered if it was possible to have a heart attack from such energetic sex? And whether, if I crept away and left them to it, Pippa would eventually scream, 'I'm coming, oh-oh-oh, now I'm GOINGGG', before slumping down lifeless over Nick's torso.

But I knew that wasn't going to happen, because I recognised what was coming, and it wasn't Pippa. Any second now… three… two… one…

'What the fuck?' said Nick angrily, as he spotted me clinging to the door frame.

Pippa's head turned an unattractive one-hundred-and-eighty degrees before she screamed again, but this time in shock.

'Oh, Hattie!'

'Ah, Pippa, ah-ah-ahhh,' I said, my voice dripping with sarcasm.

'Please,' she begged, jumping off Nick faster than an Olympic hurdler in reverse, 'don't tell Brian.'

As she scrambled for her clothing, I gave her a withering look, but it was fleeting, you understand, because Nick was getting up from the bed and walking slowly towards me. He still had an enormous erection, and I instantly averted my eyes, looking at his face. His expression was almost insolent. Any earlier contempt on my part was shrivelling by the moment, unlike Nick's privates, which, out of my peripheral vision, seemed to be waving at me.

'Don't just stand there, Hattie,' he sneered. 'Why don't you join us?'

The comment sparked outrage in Pippa. 'How dare you!' she shouted at Nick, as she pulled on her thong back to front and winced painfully. But Nick wasn't listening. His eyes were on me, seemingly boring into my soul, trying to prise away the layers to expose hidden secrets.

'I'm sorry, Hattie,' whimpered Pippa, not bothering with her bra and ramming a sweater over her head.

There was no apology from Nick, who remained defiant, his erection still full, as if goading me.

'You know why I do this, don't you, Hattie?' he mocked.

'Because you're a tart?' I queried, my voice sounding peculiarly calm despite the hideous circumstances being replayed here. Josh had told me I could tinker with the lines of past conversation, but my response to Nick's question matched the script from two years previously.

'Don't you talk to me about being a tart,' Nick hissed, 'Try taking the plank out of your own eye before you start complaining about the splinters in other people's.'

He stopped in front of me, his erection stabbing against my jeans. There was something horribly intimidating about the action and it brought back a bitter memory. My mind touched on another situation… but seconds later the shutter clanged down, blocking it from the fringes of my thoughts, and I was back in the moment. *This* moment. I was aware of Pippa, in the background, suddenly looking frightened. There was an ominous tension in the air that hadn't been apparent moments ago, and it was evidently shredding her nerves.

'Get out, Nick,' she bleated. Her order held no conviction. Unsurprisingly, my husband ignored her.

I looked at him with revulsion. Who needed this crap? Not me. A two-faced friend and a husband who didn't know the meaning of honour. I was done with them both, and finished with this marriage. I didn't need this man. In fact, did I need a man at all?

*Careful, Hattie.*

Josh.

*This is the point where you made a vow to swear off men forever, consequently blocking a destined relationship built on true love.*

He was talking inside my head. I found myself responding likewise.

*What exactly am I meant to be doing right now? Am I supposed to tell Nick I forgive him? Because I don't feel so inclined. In fact, I feel beyond angry!*

*No, forgiving him at this moment is not required, because as time moved on you actually did do that. The emotions you're currently experiencing are simply old programs that are running. What you failed to do, however, was forgive yourself for thinking that you drove him to behave in this way. But we will address that another time in the appropriate chapter of your life where you can absolve yourself. For now, the only thing that matters is opening your heart, so you can love again in the future.*

As I stood there, watching Nick, but listening to Josh, something deep within me seemed to shift, like a massive slab of ice cracking and fragmenting into little pieces. Two years ago, I had left Pippa's bedroom with tears streaming down my face, emotionally crippled by a double betrayal. But now I found myself heeding Josh's words, and subsequently rewriting the lines of the script that had previously played out. Empowered, I cleared my throat.

'I realise now, Nick, that our marriage only lasted as long as it did because I've stayed with you out of a sense of duty, a misplaced devotion that has neither been acknowledged nor respected. Whatever I've done, I don't deserve this. This time you've gone too far.'

'Good heavens, hark at the little mouse flexing her vocal chords and roaring like a lion,' he scorned. 'You won't divorce me. You haven't got the balls.'

'In which case, I'll borrow yours,' I smiled, and with that I grabbed Nick's testicles and twisted hard. As he let out an ear-piercing scream, Pippa's hand flew to her mouth. Nick's erection dwindled like a popped balloon and he staggered backwards, collapsing heavily on the bed.

Pippa regarded Nick warily, before turning her pale face to me. 'Is there any chance we can still be friends?' she grovelled, her voice full of hope.

'None at all,' I said cheerfully, before turning on my heel and walking out of Pippa's bedroom – and straight back into the Halfway Lounge.

# Chapter Twelve

Having apparently undone my vow to swear off men forever, I felt peculiarly elated. How strange. For the last two years – whilst time had done *some* healing – I hadn't been aware just how bogged down I'd been with anger and hurt. It had been most satisfactory twisting Nick's knackers. In fact, I was amazed I'd not done it sooner. Perhaps, when I was home, I should take out an ad in the local paper, offering my testicle-twisting services to other downtrodden wives.

*Ladies. Marriage in crisis? Husband a prat?*
*Contact Hattie Green on 01632 960532*
*Specialist in ball breaking that will leave him quaking!*

Oh yes. The scales were rapidly falling from my eyes. How had I unwittingly given one person so much control over my life? But how easily was it done! I'd given away my power for years, letting Nick demean me so much that I'd been left with zero self-respect and little self-esteem. But now… well, I felt so much lighter. It was an incredible sensation.

'Well done, Hattie,' said Josh, appearing by my side again, 'I'm so proud of you.' And with that he pulled me into his arms and wrapped me in a congratulatory bear hug. I was immediately over-come with another emotion. Not just sexual attraction – although there was plenty of that if the zingers going up and down my spine were anything to go by – but the fact that his arms felt so right. So perfect. Suddenly I felt confused. They couldn't possibly be the 'right' arms because he resided in a completely different world to mine. In a matter of seconds, I went from elation to despair.

*Get a grip, Hattie, eh? According to your Mr Bradley Cooper looka-like, there's a terrific guy that the universe just can't wait to deliver to you.*

'Hey, I'm sensing sadness,' said Josh. He held me away slightly so that he could peer down into my face. 'Hmm. You need a pick-me-up.' He led me over to the Halfway Lounge's sofa. 'Sit down.' I didn't need telling twice and sank gratefully into its squashy depths. 'Here,' he said, handing me a glass.

'*More* brandy?' I frowned. 'I'll be an alcoholic at this rate.'

'No, it's not booze,' he grinned, and his smile instantly turned my insides to mush. 'You won't have tasted anything like this before.'

I sipped cautiously. Nice. In fact, very nice. 'What is it?'

'Ah, now you're asking. If I said, "Essence of Rainbow", you'd think I was spinning a line straight out of a Disney movie.'

'Try me,' I said, taking another sip, and immediately welcoming the sense of fortification stealing through my body.

'Okay. See if you resonate with this explanation. Light is energy. A rainbow is spectral light. To put it simply, there is a way of transferring this energy from all those different colours into objects or liquids. In this case, all those different vibrational colours are revitalising you.'

'It once again sounds very scientific. How does your boss figure in all this?'

'What humans need to recognise, Hattie, is that when they explore science, they are actually exploring All That Is.'

'Right.' I drained the glass, none the wiser.

'Feeling better?'

'I am, actually.'

Josh gave me an evaluating look, and instantly the piercing blue eyes began wreaking havoc within me. I gazed up at him from my sitting position on the sofa, suddenly feeling rather awkward. Why had he stopped talking and, instead, was now staring at me? Did I have a bogey on my nose? My hand automatically fluttered upwards and did a discreet swipe. No. Or, wait! Good heavens, could it be that he was… I gulped… could he be giving me *that* sort of look? Was it possible? I could feel myself getting rather hot, bothered and flustered. Was something going on here? If so, I needed no encouraging. Whether it was the work of undoing a vow and then drinking an energising rainbow drink, or just feeling drugged with downright desire, *something* was happening here. Perhaps he wasn't sure about making a move on me? After all, I'd just revisited a harrowing chapter of my life and watched the multi-orgasmic Pippa in action with Nick. Perhaps Josh needed a little encouragement on my part, to let him know that I was perfectly willing, ready and able to road test my new-found broken-vow *joie de vivre*. I lowered my eyelashes coquettishly then looked up again in what was hopefully an alluring manner.

'What is it?' I whispered huskily.

'I was just thinking… no… no, forget it.'

'Forget what?' I said, subtly moving forward on the sofa, ready to spring into his arms upon being given the slightest encouragement. 'Tell me!'

'I'm not sure if you're ready.'

I fairly tingled at hearing those words. Ready? I was so ready I suspected that at any moment I might self-combust. Should I perhaps stand up, so he could once again wrap his arms around me, to aid any potential lip-locking? Or should I remain on the sofa, so he could sit down next to me, and then we could easily recline to a horizontal level? Either way, he needed encouraging… needed to be given the green light.

'I'm ready,' I quavered. My whole body seemed to be trembling. I hoped I didn't look like Buddy when he'd spotted a squirrel and visibly shivered with the anticipation of a chase.

Josh's response was to bestow me with a mega-watt smile which had me gripping the edge of the sofa with excitement.

'If you're sure,' he murmured.

'I'm sure,' I nodded, my head whipping up and down, 'I'm very, very sure.'

'Excellent,' he beamed. 'How's your diving?'

I looked at Josh in bemusement. Was this a euphemism for diving headlong into a new relationship – albeit an astral one? In which case, bring it on.

'It's been some time,' I said breathlessly, 'but I'm up for it.' *Oh heavens, Hattie, that sounds so crass.* 'I mean, my diving is good. I think so, anyway. I've never had any complaints, if you catch my drift.' I reddened.

'Is that right?' Josh murmured. 'Then let's put it to the test, eh?'

'Yes please,' I whispered, standing up. *No, no, don't say 'please', Hattie, good grief you'll be thanking him next.* 'Where do you want to go?' I asked, sotto voce.

'I think on the beach might be a good starting point,' Josh replied.

On the beach? Wasn't that a bit, you know, public? Not that anybody else was ever around, thanks to all these peculiar vibrational thingies, but even so. Personally, I'd have thought this wonderful large sofa was much better for a reintroduction to some horizontal activity…

'I'm not able to read what you're thinking,' said Josh, looking highly amused, 'but if you're game for this, then that's great. Hold onto me tight, Hattie.'

I didn't need telling twice, and grabbed hold of Josh enthusiastically. Instantly the earth moved. But not in quite the way I'd been expecting.

# Chapter Thirteen

It seems like a cliché to say that I was so overcome with lust, so heady with desire that the earth didn't just move but fairly shook as I wound my arms around Josh's neck. As he enfolded me in a tight embrace, it seemed like a trillion stars exploded in the surrounding atmosphere. I closed my eyes against their brightness and clung to Josh, my body immediately reacting to his proximity. In that moment I was unsure if my legs would ever be able to bear my weight again. My goodness, no man had ever made me feel like this before. But then again, this was no ordinary man. I wasn't even sure if he could be described as a man at all. After all, this place wasn't Earth. So presumably, Josh wasn't human. But before I had time to further dwell upon such thoughts, he was gently extricating himself from my grip.

'Open your eyes, Hattie,' he said.

I did, and looked around in amazement. The Halfway Lounge had disappeared, and we were standing on the edge of a sandy cove, shaped like an artist's palette. The water was so vibrant it was as if it had been injected with a bright turquoise dye. Light glinted off its surface creating millions of tiny diamonds, yet there was no overhead ball of fire causing this wonder. I glanced around, pondering where the brightness and warmth of the day was coming from, for there didn't seem to be a sun in this world.

'Light here is a little different,' said Josh, answering my thoughts.

'Where does it come from?'

'All of Creation,' he said.

'Are you going all religious on me?'

'Nope' – he shook his head –'just stating a fact.'

'I don't understand,' I sighed.

'You don't need to,' he smiled. 'Just enjoy it. So, what do you think?' He lifted one hand and gestured at the scenery.

'Breathtaking,' I replied, 'although that word doesn't do justice to what I'm seeing.'

From our vantage point, my eyes roamed along a range of mountains, their tops covered in glistening glaciers. Lower down, creeping right up to the water's edge in places, was a dense green forest of what looked like trembling aspen and balsam poplar. It was both beautiful and tranquil.

'Shall we sit down?' asked Josh.

I looked at the ground doubtfully. It was covered in shingle and didn't look particularly comfortable. Before I could make any comment, a huge squashy beanbag appeared at my feet.

'For Madam,' said Josh, his eyes twinkling.

'That is such a neat trick,' I laughed, sinking downwards and allowing the filler to mould itself around my bottom and thighs. Bliss.

'You're perfectly able to perform a "trick" or two yourself,' he pointed out, flopping onto a second beanbag. 'In fact, why don't you give it a go? I'll have an ice-cold beer, please, Hattie.'

'Oh,' I said, unsure, 'remind me how to do it?'

'Just *desire* it.'

Hmm. There were plenty of things I desired right now, and beer wasn't one of them. Nonetheless, I was anxious to please Josh, so gave it a whirl. I immediately thought about a tankard kept in my kitchen cupboard for my father, which he sometimes used if we went out in the garden to relax in the summer months. Mum and I would nurse a flute of Prosecco apiece, while Dad contentedly sipped his lager. The same tankard suddenly appeared in Josh's hand.

'Good effort,' he said encouragingly, 'but it's empty.'

'Oh, this isn't as easy as I thought it would be.'

'Keep practising,' Josh smiled, 'nice and cold, and not too much—'

'Oops, sorry,' I apologised, as froth poured down the side of the tankard.

'—head,' Josh added, watching with amusement as liquid dripped all over his glowing white jeans.

'Oh dear,' I said, leaning over and rubbing ineffectively at the wet patch, then instantly snatching my hand away. *What are you doing, Hattie? You look like you're feeling him up, for goodness' sake.*

'No worries, I've got this,' said Josh, as the foam immediately disappeared, and the trousers reverted to their former pristine appearance. 'Keep practising,' he said, chuckling.

'Right,' I muttered.

'You were thinking about Prosecco just now, so how about you keep me company and we'll drink companionably together whilst enjoying this perfect view.'

'Okay,' I nodded. This time I successfully produced a glass of pale gold bubbles and was privately pleased not to spill one drop.

'Perfect,' Josh nodded his approval, 'I'll make a cosmic barmaid out of you yet.'

I laughed, appreciating his banter and how easily we joked together, then carefully put the flute to my lips. Heaven. We sat on our beanbags soaking up the fabulous view, quietly enjoying our refreshments. I gave a contented sigh. This was all a far cry from my normal life. When had I last sat outside enjoying good weather and the company of a man? Last summer, if you counted Vigo Village's one month of decent sunshine. For the whole of July, the temperature had soared, rapidly drying out the lawn and bringing ants crawling to the surface of the baked earth. They'd driven Buddy nuts as he'd lain at my feet. On a couple of occasions there had been two men with me. My father, and my son. Three men, if you included a male dog in the mix. Sitting here now, with Josh, it felt very different. Very *right*. That word again. But it was true. Here, by the water, I felt like one half of a couple. Weird. I sneaked a look at him. He was gazing at the horizon, apparently lost in thought. I cleared my throat.

'Don't you ever get lonely, Josh?'

He turned and looked at me, his face instantly creasing into a smile. 'Never.'

'But you're here, all on your own.'

'Who says I'm on my own?'

'Well, aren't you? When I'm not around, who is with you?'

'Others who need helping. Lots of us do this, you know. Even you.'

'Me?' I asked, startled. 'I don't know this place.'

'Yes you do, Hattie,' he murmured. 'You know it in your dreams, you just can't remember it.'

'I come here in my dreams?'

'Not necessarily specifically here. This is a special place reserved for particular lessons. But hopping across *the veil*, yes. We all do it at night, we just don't remember it.'

'Why not?'

'Because we're not meant to. It would interfere in our daily lives otherwise. And as I said before, if everyone consciously knew about this place, they would be dropping in the moment things got tough back home. But at night, ah, that's a different matter. In sleep, the mind is released. It can go anywhere.'

'What, even to Jupiter?'

'And beyond. You'd be amazed how big Creation is.'

'You're making my brain boggle,' I said, taking another sip of Prosecco. 'So, you're saying I skip over here at night?'

'That's about the measure of it,' Josh grinned.

'In which case, why didn't you just summon me to the Halfway Lounge when I was asleep in my bed?' I frowned. 'Why go through that charade in Tesco?'

'Firstly, I didn't summon you. You responded to the universe's intervention. I'm just a co-ordinator.'

'You've lost me.'

'Secondly,' said Josh, ploughing on, 'the task in question couldn't be achieved if you'd been tucked up in bed. The circumstances weren't right. By contriving the situation in the supermarket, there is a better chance of you remembering things when you return.'

'Right,' I said, none the wiser. I tipped back my head and drained the glass.

'In the meantime,' said Josh, 'do you fancy going for a swim?'

I balked. What? Stripped down to my smalls in front of Josh? No thanks. The last thing I wanted was him catching sight of my jelly belly and cellulite thighs.

'Come on in,' said Josh.

I did a double take. Like a badly edited film, Josh had literally 'jumped' from his beanbag to standing up to his knees in seawater. The white shirt and jeans had been replaced with glowing white swim shorts, the hemline of which was rapidly soaking up the water as he turned his back on me and began to wade out. I felt myself go slightly hot as my eyes greedily roved over his broad back, but not before I'd caught a glimpse of an impressive six-pack. The water looked so inviting. Apart from anything else, I wanted to swim with Josh. Mind made up, I scrambled to my feet and was surprised to find myself wearing an itsy-bitsy bikini that, back home, would probably have cost a month's wages. Even better, my stomach was beautifully flat and – I craned my neck round – yes, no cellulite. Had I manifested this? The perfect body. Flipping heck. If only it was as easy in everyday life. But right now, I was going to milk this moment for all it was worth.

'Wait for me!' I called.

And then I threw back my head, felt my hair ripple over my well-toned shoulders, and followed the Adonis ahead of me into the water.

# Chapter Fourteen

Wading after Josh was pleasurable for two reasons. Firstly, I could study him without him knowing. Secondly, I'd never been in water like this before. As my eyes feasted on Josh's well-defined back, travelling across the biscuity-golden skin, another part of my senses revelled as water sprayed up and over me when I clumsily splashed after him. It also struck me that there was an awareness of every individual drop of water tickling and fizzing against my skin. Never had I felt so alive. Which was pretty bizarre, considering the real me was presumably still prostrate in a Sidcup supermarket.

'Come on, slowcoach,' Josh called, half turning and giving me the benefit of a chiselled chest covered in a smattering of dark-blond hair. I couldn't help noticing how it darkened and narrowed to a tantalising snail trail. I had an overwhelming desire to trace the line of it with my fingertips. Gasping at such audacious thoughts, I concentrated on the task in hand – bounding after those spotlessly white swim shorts.

The floor was shelving down now and, bit by bit, our midriffs disappeared below the waterline. The temperature was refreshing without being cold, and a sensation of bubbles made me feel like I was immersed in a giant glass of Alka Seltzer. Thrusting my arms out, I pushed forward, kicking my legs, and launched into a stylish front crawl that I'd never perfected back home but which, here, was wonderfully effortless. I streaked past Josh, then did a neat flip turn, twisting out of an underwater somersault so that I was facing him again. Surfacing, I tossed back a waterfall of wet hair and grinned at Josh's expression. He looked amazed. As well he might. I was gobsmacked.

'You're a good swimmer,' he said.

'Oh, it's nothing,' I replied modestly, 'you should see me in action at the local swimming pool.'

Josh raised an eyebrow. 'Future Olympic contender for the women's one hundred metres freestyle?'

'More' – I put my head on one side – 'certificate for achieving ten metres in the children's pool.'

Josh roared with laughter. 'I like your sense of humour, Hattie.'

*And I like you*, I privately thought.

'So, if the reality is that you're not long out of water wings,' said Josh, 'it must be safe to assume your efforts at manifestation are suddenly coming along in leaps and bounds.'

I grinned at him in delight. 'Yes, I guess they are.'

'Good.'

We were quite a way from the shoreline now and treading water, something I'd never achieved at Swanley's White Oak Leisure Centre. Nick had always loved hurling himself off the top board in the diving area, while I'd cowered at the side, watching him enviously as I clung to the tiled ledge, making sure the lifeguard was within shouting distance.

I noticed Josh giving me *that look* again… the one that set winged creatures flapping about in my stomach and gave me a delicious sense of anticipation. I gazed back at him, praying my pupils hadn't dilated to the size of giant clam shells.

'Do you have any regrets, Hattie?' he asked softly.

I blinked, unsure of his question. Of all the things I'd hoped he might ask, it hadn't been that.

'Do you mean in my life, in general?'

'Sure.'

'Well, er, you know' – I blew out my cheeks – 'yes, a few, but then no more than the average person. Why?'

'A person shouldn't go through life with regrets.'

I frowned. 'Sometimes it's unavoidable.'

'Hm, I disagree.'

'What do you mean?' I asked, aware that a tone of defensiveness had crept into my voice.

'Are there things in life that you still want to do, but haven't done?'

'Are you talking about a bucket list?'

'Yes and no.'

'You have a habit of contradicting yourself when I ask a direct question,' I said, feeling somewhat exasperated.

'I apologise. Okay, you mentioned a bucket list. Do you have one?'

'Um, well, since you ask, no, I don't. I've never given it any thought.'

'Is that because you've been too preoccupied with the past and *what might have been* rather than *what could be*?'

I opened my mouth to say something, but no words came out.

'You tell me,' I said somewhat tartly, 'after all, you're the one with the inbuilt encyclopaedic knowledge about me. Do those mind-reading skills go so deep that you actually know me better than I know myself?' I was aware of sounding petulant, but I didn't like the probing. Josh had touched a nerve, and I was reacting accordingly. 'I get what's going on here,' I said, narrowing my eyes. 'It's a softly, softly approach, isn't it? Let's get Hattie relaxed. Then I'll suggest she revisits a troublesome former part of her life. Put things right. Then whoopie-doo, she can have a nice rainbow drink, loll about for a bit on a beanbag, enjoy some recuperation, have a swim, and just when she's feeling like a cross between Tom Daley and a mermaid, I'll hit her over the head with a list of regrets and suggest she revisits another dark corner of her past. Well I don't appreciate it, Josh. And you can tell your boss, or whoever it is that appointed you as "co-ordinator" of my life, to bog off and keep his nose out.'

'That was quite a speech,' said Josh, looking astonished.

I could feel myself flushing with shame at being so outspoken, so unnecessarily rude, but was also petrified of Josh knowing secrets that were buried so deep that most of the time I conveniently managed to forget they even existed, until moments like this came along, where they rattled their chains, begging for release, demanding to be unburdened.

'Sorry,' I muttered, lowering my gaze to the watery depths beneath me, watching my feet distort in the ripples created as they constantly paddled backwards and forwards to keep me afloat.

'I've told you before, you don't need to apologise. I appreciate the fact that, despite this backdrop being something like *From Here to Eternity*, this whole experience is tough for you.'

'Do *you* have regrets, Josh?' I demanded, volleying his question right back at him.

'Only one,' he said wistfully.

I hadn't expected that answer. Somehow, I'd rather anticipated his response would be something of a lecture. How he'd gone through life fulfilling every desire, shoving obstacles – or even people – out of his way in order to achieve the holy grail of attainment… perfection… a halo… whatever the cosmic equivalent was for reaching one's goal.

'Which is?' I prodded.

His mouth twisted sadly, and for a moment he looked almost vulnerable.

'I've never fallen in love. Not properly. Oh, I've had a few relationships, don't get me wrong. I even lived with a lovely woman for a couple of years. But the moment she started talking marriage and babies, I knew she wasn't The One.'

'But you just called her a "lovely woman"? If she was pretty and kind and companionable and ticking all the boxes, why not spend the rest of your life with her?'

'Because,' he sighed, 'I knew, deep down, it wasn't meant to be.'

'How?' I persisted.

'She didn't make my heart sing.'

I stared at him. Was that what true love was all about then? Addressing your mundane everyday life, juggling the commute to work with the household chores and then, at the end of the day, yawning your way into bed with somebody who flicked on a switch inside your heart so that 'The Sound of Music' was being played at top volume?

'So' – I puckered my brow – 'why didn't you change your personal circumstances? Do a bit of manifesting – some of that cosmic ordering you were talking about earlier?'

'Oh I did all that, you betcha. The wheels were put in motion on more than one occasion, but it's been… tricky. Those wheels have had some stubborn brakes holding them firmly in place. But the intent has always been there on my part, so now I must be patient and let the universe respond in its own unique way.'

'If you don't mind my saying, Josh, there are easier ways to fall in love.'

'Really?' he said, looking mystified.

'Yeah, there's online dating.'

'No thanks.'

'Why not? You simply type into a computer and it delivers the perfect match. Give or take a few oddballs, sex maniacs and compulsive liars.'

Josh snorted with laughter. 'It sounds like a perfect nightmare, and definitely not for me.'

'By the way, that isn't any sort of reference to you,' I added hastily. 'I'm sure there are some very nice men – and women – on the internet, but it's rather like looking for the proverbial needle in a haystack.'

'Call me old-fashioned, Hattie, but there's something about meeting a girl in the moment that is far more romantic than tapping a keyboard and expecting it to come up with Miss Perfect Match.'

I shrugged. 'I'm sorry you've not met Miss Right. And I hope the universe delivers for you,' I said charitably, which I thought was quite generous on my part because frankly why the heck couldn't the cosmos deliver a man like this to *me*? I raised my eyes heavenwards and silently shouted at the strange light. *How about sending someone like Josh over to my part of the world? Are you even listening, Mr Creator of All That*

*Is? It's all very well chatting to Josh in this halfway place, admiring his marbles – and I'm talking about his mental ones, I'm not that smutty you know – and loving his looks, his physique, his charm, his perfection for heaven's sake, but haven't I just broken a flaming vow about never loving again? And here's a gorgeous man who wants to fall in love. Well, hellooooo?* But there was no reply from Him Up There, and given that I wasn't sure I even believed in Him, I didn't expect a response either.

'Hattie?'

I dragged my gaze from the weird golden sky. 'Yes?'

'Shall we carry on enjoying the moment? I'm here to help you. Not bully you.'

'I know. And I apologise again for my outburst. I didn't mean to rant.'

'It's fine. Honest. And I'm sorry for not being clearer when I asked you about having regrets.'

'I didn't mean to bite your head off.'

'And I didn't mean to provoke you. Let me rephrase that earlier question.'

I looked at Josh warily.

'While you're here and enjoying your new-found swimming prowess, how do you fancy taking it one step further?'

'Are you, by any chance, going to suggest we try walking on water?'

Josh threw back his head and laughed. 'No, I was going to suggest we go for a walk under it.'

'Eh?'

'There's a whole new world down here. Fancy exploring?'

'Um, I'm not sure, there's something about being underwater that makes me feel enclosed and a bit claustrophobic.'

'This isn't Earth, Hattie. Free the mind. Don't go home with the regret that you didn't explore a hidden paradise – you could never be as safe as you are right now.'

Some part of Josh's words must have penetrated my brain because I found myself seriously considering what he was saying. Here I was treading water, when back home I'd have sunk like a weighted body being thrown into the Thames.

'Do I need to manifest a wet suit and oxygen tank?' I said, half joking. But the answer popped into my head just as Josh replied.

'No. All you need to do is take my hand, and trust. Can you do that, Hattie?' He swam closer, reached out and entwined his fingers with mine. As the familiar zingers went up and down my spine, I knew that if I couldn't follow Josh to the ends of the earth, then I would at least follow him to the depths of an ocean. Creation hadn't delivered me a man back home, but right now I was here, in this halfway zone, with a heavenly guy. I wanted to make the most of it. To savour it. And yes, make sure I left with no regrets.

Josh must have been reading my mind again, because a second later he pulled me under.

# Chapter Fifteen

For one moment, as the water went over my head, rushing up my nose, filling my ears and blocking out sound, I experienced pure terror. Josh's fingers were still entwined with mine and, as panic began to consume me, I gripped them hard.

*It's okay, Hattie*, he said directly into my head.

*I can't breathe*, I mentally replied.

*You don't need to.*

*Yes I do… I do*, I gabbled, on the verge of shoving him away so I could claw my way back to the surface. Glancing upwards, the sky's strange light seemed so far away. I realised we'd stepped off an underwater shelf and were now plummeting downwards faster than a high-speed elevator. Josh tugged on my hands.

*Look at me, Hattie… I said LOOK at me!* His voice was both urgent and insistent.

I obeyed, regarding him with wide, frightened eyes.

*Breathing is an earthly habit. If you want to breathe, do so. You won't drown. It's not possible in this dimension. Likewise, if you want to hold your breath, that's fine too. There's no right or wrong way of doing this. The easiest way to deal with fear is to stay in the moment.*

*Apply that thought to 'the now' and then the individual breath won't matter, because it won't be required. You are totally safe.*

I nodded but was riddled with doubt, still too petrified to inhale, although a calmer and more detached part of me digested his words. It was apparently okay not to breathe if I didn't want to. I could just hold my breath instead. And actually, I thought, as I tore my eyes from Josh's face to glance around, hadn't we been travelling for well over a minute now? Ordinarily, in my life back home, I'd have expired by this point. As an ex-smoker, even holding my breath for twenty seconds was a challenge. It dawned on me that holding my breath had become effortless. My grip on Josh's fingers relaxed slightly and he responded with a smile of encouragement.

*That's it, Hattie!* he exclaimed with delight, *you've got it!*

I nodded imperceptibly, still getting acquainted with the weirdness of not actually needing to physically inhale and exhale.

*It seems so strange.*

*It is, and it isn't.*

*There you go again*, I sighed.

*What's that remark supposed to mean?*

*Giving me one of your ambiguous answers. You're very fond of saying 'yes and no' and now you're replying with 'it is, and it isn't'.*

The sound of Josh's laughter filled my head. *The thing to remember, Hattie, is that nothing is ever set in stone. You can change track whenever you want. Just like you've switched from breathing to opting to hold your breath.*

*Right*, I said dryly. I had a feeling there was a deeper meaning to that little gem of advice, and that Josh was feeling his way more carefully after my earlier mini explosion about having regrets. *Can I ask a favour?* I said, suddenly feeling a bit embarrassed.

*Sure. Fire away.*

*Can you keep hold of my hand?*

*Don't tell me*, he said mischievously, *it's been ages since a man held your hand so you'd like to make the most of it?*

*Idiot*, I responded, but not without humour. Little did he realise he wasn't far off the truth. *I would just feel more confident about the breathing issue if you remained holding on to me.*

*Sure*, he winked, *and I was only teasing.*

*I know*, I bantered back, although a part of me wistfully longed to hold his hands for reasons of romance rather than reassurance. My palm was enfolded in his larger one, and his grip was firm and almost proprietorial. Or was I being fanciful? Probably. But it was nice nonetheless, and I was also acutely aware of another sensation going on in my body. Around the heart region too. A feeling within my aortic chambers. They seemed to be pumping away in time to a hidden beat. It was almost like tapping one's foot whilst listening to a song. I blanched. Was this what Josh had meant by having someone in your life that made your heart sing? I strained to listen to my body, willing it to respond to my silent query. I sensed a response. But it wasn't belting out 'The Sound of Music'. More a frantic version of 'Waterloo' with lots of shrill whistles and waving flags. I gulped, which was nothing to do with the breath-holding going on. *Don't do this to yourself, Hattie, please. He's from one world and you're from another. Don't even think about it otherwise you'll end up possibly going mad.* But didn't this sort of thing make one feel somewhat mad? Wasn't that where the saying 'madly in love' came from?

As Josh gave me another reassuring smile and pulled me down ever deeper, I realised that it wasn't just the depths of this ocean I was falling into. I was pretty damn sure I was falling in love. And I had no control over it whatsoever.

# Chapter Sixteen

Confusion threatened to overwhelm me. It seemed to whirl in my head like the water around me. Was I really falling in love? *Oh, Hattie, don't be so ridiculous! You've known Josh for all of five minutes. And you don't need reminding that this whole situation is bizarre. It's total fiction. Even if he says it isn't. Reality is not discovering your heart has a sound system that plays Seventies disco music and… oh, hello… what have we here?*

I felt like a skydiver parachuting into a strange land and could now see, below, that all manner of plant life was rooted into the seabed, which was rushing up to meet us. As we gently landed, puffs of white sand clouded around our legs. The yellow light above was now so far away it actually resembled a sun to this watery world. Far from being in murky depths, a soft blue glow prevailed, making vision easy. We were standing on a wide path that meandered through a forest of underwater trees. I gazed slack-jawed at branches that moved as if caught in a soft breeze, the leaning boughs like arms reaching out to us. Instead of being bare, gnarled, or rotten from submergence in water, the trees were positively thriving, full of emerald-coloured leaves. Some bore fantastically shaped blossoms in a palette of colours I couldn't even begin to describe, while others heralded strange fruits, the likes of which I'd never seen before. As Josh led me by the hand, I felt like we were walking through The Garden of Eden. It was dazzlingly vibrant, and mind-blowingly overwhelming.

*What do you think?* said Josh.

*You tell me*, I retorted, *you're the mind-reader.*

*I can sense what you're thinking, but I'm not hearing it. Why's that?*

*Maybe it's because I can't put what I'm seeing into words.*

*You know, there are places on Earth like this, too.*

*Really?*

*Yeah. Some have been discovered. Man is busily exploring – read that last word as 'wrecking' – but there are so many places like this deep below the waterline they are virtually alien worlds within a world. There are caves so huge they could house a city. Some even have their own jungles and rivers.*

*A river underneath a sea?* I frowned. *How is that possible?*

*There are deep channels within the seabed. The water within those channels is denser than the surrounding seawater because it has a high salinity. It also carries a lot of sediment so, by its nature, it will appear as a river. In the same way, there can be the appearance of waterfalls too. They are full of nutrients, and a bit like arteries to the ocean.*

*You're going all scientific again.* I raised one hand and waggled a finger at him.

Josh laughed and squeezed my hand, and instantly a hidden part of me began to glow. One way or another there was quite a lot going on under my ribcage right now. As we moved through the strange and exciting landscape, I felt like I was walking through a fantasy world. And that was another thing. With every step we took, there was no sensation of drag. It was as effortless as strolling through a park.

*Are there any fish down here?*

*Sure,* Josh nodded.

*Where are they then?*

*All around us.*

My head swivelled from left to right. *I can't see any. Are they hiding in the trees?*

Josh chuckled. *Remember that you and I are on a different frequency in this place. There aren't meant to be any distractions.*

*Oh, c'mon, Josh, it's not like fish are people, for heaven's sake. I can loosely understand why your boss doesn't want other folk wandering up to me and saying, 'Hey there! My name's Frank. What sentence are you serving here until parole comes up and grants you escape?' But it's not quite the same with sea creatures, is it? I'm hardly going to be ambushed by an octopus demanding to know the intricacies of my life and why I married a man who wasn't—*

I felt myself grow hot at what I'd been about to blurt, and instantly shut up. Josh stopped walking and pulled me round to face him.

*Hattie, this place isn't jail.*

*It feels like it*, I said in a small voice, *albeit a very beautiful one.*

Josh tutted, but not unkindly. *You're here for a reason. This is a soul journey. It's not a sentence. Think of it as a kind of meditation, if you will. Right now, you're deep within yourself. Working on resolving past hurts. Forging new paths that haven't so much been shut off from you as blocked by ten-foot-high walls with barbed wire along the top. THAT has been your prison, Hattie. Not here. This place is the key that will set you free.* He wound an arm around my shoulders and gave them a little jiggle, as if trying to shake some sense into me. *Do you understand?*

I nodded miserably. There had to be an element of truth in his words because I was increasingly aware of another part of me busily sifting through the previous days and years of my life, looking for moments where, not to put too fine a point on it, the shit had hit the fan. Where my world hadn't so much as wobbled but rocked right off its axis. Some of those moments had been caused by other people. Like Nick. And Pippa. Others… I sighed gustily. Well, other episodes had been caused by myself.

*Hey, enough of all this self-analysing*, said Josh. *This isn't the time.* He squeezed my shoulders again. Without realising what I was doing, my free hand – the one that wasn't still linked in his – moved around his waist and I automatically leant into him, inclining my head. I later told myself that I'd simply reacted like a child wanting reassurance from a parent, so that when Josh dropped a fleeting kiss on my head sending my senses reeling, I reminded myself that his gesture had simply been a paternal reaction, like a father reassuring a child. Even so, the music in my heart was starting to turn into a nightclub with a plethora of anthems that, even now, were deliciously throbbing their way up and down my spine.

*You still want to see fish?* asked Josh.

*Yes please*, I gasped, trying not to stagger from the electric-shock effect his lips had given me when touching my hair.

*In which case, LET THERE BE FISH!* he bellowed joyfully, then burst out laughing when he saw the astonished look on my face.

The waters were suddenly teeming with aquatic life. Shoals of brightly coloured fish were bustling about, their different hues, shapes and sizes like stand-alone pieces of an enormous fluid jigsaw. But – wait – something wasn't quite right.

*Every now and again they fade in and out of my vision*, I said.

*Yup*, Josh nodded. *I had to tweak the vibration. Otherwise if a giant whale comes along you could accidentally get knocked over. This way, they can see you, but also swim right through you. Speaking of which, look straight ahead.* He jerked his head.

I looked, and nearly swallowed my tonsils, experiencing a sudden desire to climb into one of the nearby trees and hide amongst the thick foliage. A vast whale-like creature was swimming towards us, a calf hugging its underbelly.

*Stand still*, ordered Josh, his hand tightening on me so I couldn't bolt. *You're perfectly safe. She's not aggressive, but she is curious, and so is her baby.*

Seconds later the creature was swimming past us, although her baby momentarily hovered, its dorsal fin stabilising its body long enough for Josh to stretch my hand forward and let my fingers shimmer through its shape. There was a sensation of velvet passing under my touch. The calf seemed to enjoy the contact, rubbing against our conjoined hands like a cat weaving around chair legs. A moment later and it had swum on, leaving me both gobsmacked and thrilled.

*So, Hattie, on reflection would it be true to say that putting your trust in me and letting me take you down to this underwater world is something you don't regret?*

*Absolutely*, I nodded happily.

*Good. Hold that thought. Because it applies to everything in life. Never walk away from the chances life throws you.*

*Right-oh*, I warbled, stifling a yawn. I suddenly felt indescribably tired. Weariness washed over me like one of the waves on the surface of this vast water.

*You're flagging*, said Josh, *because you're starting to process things again. I'd better get you back, and you can have another sleep.*

*Will it take long to get back to the Halfway Lounge?* I asked, looking upwards at the faraway lemon light, and trying not to yawn again.

*Not even a second*, he smiled in answer. *Are you ready?*

*Yes*, I said, grabbing both his hands in mine in anticipation of a rocket-like movement propelling us upwards. Instead I found myself staggering slightly, as if stepping off a roundabout in a child's playground. I was back in the Halfway Lounge, dry, and dressed.

'Wow,' I said, blowing out my cheeks as I looked at Josh.

His eyes snagged on mine, drawing me in, until I felt like my whole body was smiling in response.

'That was something else, eh?' he murmured softly.

I nodded, whilst privately thinking *he* was something else.

# Chapter Seventeen

As I tottered through the Halfway Lounge's door to the sumptuous bedroom beyond, Josh caught hold of my hand.

'Before you nod off, Hattie, I want you to know that nobody here is forcing you to review any part of your life until you're ready. You are the one who is setting the pace here, and you are the one who decides when to review a chapter. Okay?'

'Sure,' I nodded, eyelids visibly drooping.

'And I'll be there, in the background, ready to help if you need it.'

'Thanks,' I said, yawning hugely.

Josh grinned. 'Go and get some shut-eye.'

I didn't need telling twice. Flopping down on the luxuriously soft bed, I wondered if, when I next opened my eyes, this plush pink and white room would still look as it did now? Or whether it would once again morph into my tiny but cosy bedroom in Honeysuckle Cottage. I felt a pang of longing and hoped I'd awaken to beams peeking out of old plasterboard, rather than this flawless white ceiling that seemed to shimmer and glow like Josh's jeans and shirt. I ached to hear Buddy barking comfortingly in the background and the soothing murmur of Fin chatting to a mate on his mobile.

When I next opened my eyes, I was in an altogether different bedroom. I recognised it immediately. Naturally it was from the past. The room bore all the markings of belonging to a single male with sky-high testosterone levels. The furniture was a mix of black and polished chrome, the walls a stark white, one of which held a framed cityscape hanging at a slightly crooked angle. A leather sleigh bed dominated the centre of the room. And I was lying upon it. A quick glance under the duvet revealed I was completely starkers. I hastily placed the cover over me again and wondered where Josh was. I presumed he was here somewhere, on a different frequency, and that I couldn't see him.

'Are you there?' I hissed.

No reply.

Hmm. I wasn't sure if Josh was just being diplomatic given my state of undress. I mentally concentrated on clothing myself, so easily done in the Halfway Lounge but, peeping back under the duvet, I could see the attempt to manifest garments hadn't worked. I was still in my birthday suit. Damn. Right, so it was only in the Halfway Lounge that one could manifest itsy-bitsy bikinis and a Hollywood body. I looked back under the duvet again. Actually, on closer inspection, the body didn't look too bad. This episode of my life was pre-Fin, so my belly was smooth and flat, the muscles taut. Even so, I didn't want Josh seeing me in the nuddy.

Clutching the duvet tight to my bosom, I leant out of bed and scanned the floor. A familiar pair of size eight jeans came into view. I stared at them. Size *eight*! Snaking out an arm, I scooped them up. My pants were still inside them, as were my socks, such was the urgency with which the garments had been shed. A moment later the pants were on – bugger, back to front from the feel of it – but there wasn't a moment to lose, so I ignored the discomfort and wriggled into the jeans.

I hastily averted my eyes, not quite ready to embrace the situation I was in, or the glaring clues that were telling me what this episode in my life was about. The faint smell of last night's takeaway hung in the air. My memory was piecing everything together. I remembered that takeaway – it had been shared on a Saturday night. Okay, so that would mean that, in review time, it was now Sunday morning.

Happily, my t-shirt was lying in a creased heap by the bedside cabinet, but I had no idea where my bra was. Hadn't I been wearing one? I went a bit hot at the memory of how I'd dressed on this particular occasion. Right, definitely no bra. Clearly I'd been dressed to thrill, willingly flashing my threepenny bits. I grabbed the t-shirt and disappeared right under the duvet, fighting my way into the garment, swearing when an armhole evaded me, finally surfacing with my hair mussed up so that I looked like Ken Dodd. All I needed was a red, white and blue tickling stick to complete the look. However, unlike Ken Dodd's famous catchphrase, there was absolutely nothing about this situation that tickled me.

# Chapter Eighteen

The bedroom door swung open just as I was emerging from under the duvet.

'Hey, babe!' said a familiar gravelly voice that, back in the real time of this moment, would have had me weak-kneed with longing but which, revisiting years later, simply left me cold. 'Why are you dressed? Never mind, I'll enjoy peeling those jeans off you again in a little while.'

I stared at Nick Green, the man who would eventually become my husband. Ten years older than me, he was in his prime at thirty-six. He was naked, apart from his Calvin Klein underpants, and had a body that showed he didn't waste a penny of his Gold gym membership when he wasn't wheeling and dealing and cinching deals. He was carrying a breakfast tray bearing tea and toast for us both and came towards me beaming a smile capable of melting the stoniest of hearts. Devastatingly good-looking and lethally charming, it was rumoured that his soft line in patter frequently charmed the knickers off women.

'H-hi,' I gasped, tugging my t-shirt down. I saw his eyes stray to my nipples pressing against the thin fabric and immediately let go of the cotton hem, slouching forward and rounding my shoulders like a hunched gnome.

He placed the tray on the bedside cabinet and then, in one swift move, kissed me full on the mouth.

'More of that in a minute,' he said, waggling his eyebrows.

*Dear Lord, please not.* My brain was struggling to remember what came next in this little episode of life. Had we abandoned the breakfast, pulled off each other's clothing – well, just the pants on his part – and then got down to it on this ridiculously vast hotbed of lust that had no doubt seen frenzied action with countless other women? I wasn't going to wait to find out.

'I'm starving!' I chirped, reaching for a piece of toast and shoving it between my lips. If my mouth was out of action, he wouldn't be able to stick his tongue in and wrap it around my tonsils. 'Mmm,' I groaned, in apparent ecstasy, spraying crumbs everywhere. 'Heaven.'

'Wasn't it just, Hattie?' he murmured, looking at me intensely, his eyes quickly moving off my face and flitting over my t-shirt again. 'I never expected this to happen between us, you know.'

'No, nor me,' I lied, swallowing the toast quickly, lest it stick in my throat. It came to me in a blindingly clear flash of recollection that this was the first lie I had told Nick. A second one would follow in the not-too-distant future.

I'd first met Nick Green temping. I was having a quarter-life crisis, not knowing what I was doing with myself. Having graduated from university with a degree in biochemistry studying cellular and molecular biology in cells and tissues, post-uni life had come as something of a rude shock. I'd waved goodbye to my friends and sailed off into the world thinking it was most definitely my oyster and that I'd land a pearl of a job. I'd naively believed I'd walk straight into a laboratory-based career in the dynamic pharmaceutical industry, only to discover that for every interview I attended, hundreds of other applicants were vying for that one position, too.

'Darling, you don't seem to be doing anything with your life,' my mother had said, puffing away on one of her perpetual ciggies after I'd drooped through the door, mouth downturned.

'Well I'd hoped, by now, I'd be peering down a microscope and discovering a cure for lung cancer,' I'd quipped, flapping my hands through the air in a quest to avoid having a passive smoke. At this point, I'd not long since given up the ciggies myself. However, almost overnight, I'd gone from craving the damn things to complete abhorrence.

'I don't know why you bothered with all that university malarkey,' Mum had mused. 'In my day a girl did a secretarial course, set her cap at a handsome boss, and then got down to the serious business of raising a family.'

'God, Mum, you sound so old-fashioned. And anyway, I'm not sure I ever want children,' I'd said, getting up and opening a window to let out the fug.

'Of course you will, Hattie. Your ovaries are programmed to do that. One day you will be scaling one of those ridiculous rocks you like climbing with Martin, then you'll stop dead in your tracks and listen to your body screaming to be impregnated. You will yearn for broken nights, dirty nappies and regurgitated milk.'

'I'm pretty sure my boyfriend has no plans to become a father for the foreseeable future.' At this point in my life, Martin was my long-term boyfriend, whom I'd met at university. The M word had never been mentioned as such, but everybody took it for granted that one day he would make an honest woman of me. But all that was way in the future, along with the broken nights, dirty nappies and regurgitated milk. I'd wrinkled my nose. 'And anyway, Mum, if that's your sales spiel for parenthood, you're definitely not selling it to me. Apart from anything else, I want to be my own woman and have financial independence from a man.'

'Take it from me, darling, all that burning your bra nonsense is very overrated.'

I'd silently gnashed my teeth. 'I'm sure Emmeline Pankhurst would spin in her grave if she could hear you talking.'

'Oh, I didn't know Mrs Pankhurst had burnt her bra? I just thought it was chaining herself to railings that she had a thing about.'

'Honestly, Mum, I can't believe the way you speak sometimes. Women burned their bras because they felt it made a statement when they were making a stand for Women's Rights. It was symbolic. It showed independence of men. And the women who didn't burn their bras often didn't bother wearing one at all, just to show their support.'

'Or lack of it, surely?' said Mum, with a shudder. 'Nothing worse than floppy tits.'

I'd sighed and written my mother off as a lost cause. But after nearly a year of trailing after job after job after job, finding myself shortlisted several times over but getting precisely nowhere, I'd arrived at a point of desperation. Many of my friends had also been on the receiving end of the same demoralising experience and ended up drifting into jobs that weren't degree-related. Some were even getting married. But all of them were independent of their parents. Apart from me. Martin had landed himself a prize job and, thanks to a massive handout from his parents, had got himself on the property ladder. He'd suggested I move in with him and submit my CV to the Co-Op around the corner who were looking for a shop assistant. I didn't know what was worse: seeing all that studying go to waste whilst accepting the charity of a roof over my head from my boyfriend… or being as independent as I could be from Martin, but remaining at home, sponging off my parents. Either one was a bitter pill to swallow. I opted for the latter, staying in my childhood home and having no desire to wash Martin's socks and underpants. And anyway, lately I'd had some doubts about Martin being someone I wanted to spend the rest of my life with. If he honestly thought I'd be happy working at the Co-Op, what did that say about him truly knowing me? I was aware that things needed to change in this relationship – maybe even end – but I wasn't quite sure how to go about it, especially as I didn't know who would be the most upset, Martin or my mother. For now I was taking the coward's way out and doing nothing.

Meanwhile, I found myself turning into my mother – doing exactly what she had done as a young woman and enrolling at a local college for a secretarial course. I'd told myself it was just a means to an end. That it would be a springboard to a job which would catapult me into joining the workforce and, from there, I would eventually find my niche – if not in the pharmaceutical industry, then maybe the agrochemical sector. Secretarial work was simply a stepping stone to rest upon until the right job came along, something to put money in the purse and fill the days until I *finally* got to take part in clinical trials, or even patenting. I had a brain, damnit! There simply *had* to be loads of fabulous opportunities waiting for me somewhere.

Meanwhile, after dipping my toe in the clerical waters, I eventually opted to become a temp. I told myself it would be easy to extricate myself quickly from a temporary working situation when that *real* job came along.

It was at this point my intellectual brain did a total bunk, along with all the common sense I'd ever possessed. Emmeline Pankhurst would have been horrified, and no doubt supporters of Women's Rights might have felt compelled to strangle me with the straps of their abandoned bras. Little had I known, on this particular Monday morning, as I'd slipped into my cubicle at Shepherd, Green & Parsons, turned on my monitor, and tapped in the password for a six-month maternity cover stint as Mr Nicholas Green's assistant, that life was about to dramatically change.

# Chapter Nineteen

The moment Nicholas Green, Director, strode through the open-plan office with a 'Good morning, Caitlin', my fingers had paused over the keyboard and my jaw had been overtaken by gravity. I'd gaped after the vision that had whizzed past my desk knowing I was in serious trouble. Nick had reversed backwards, peered at me in horror and said, 'You're not Caitlin.'

'N-no,' I'd stammered, suddenly overcome with shyness. 'I'm H-Hattie. Your temp. Caitlin is on maternity leave.'

'Of course she is,' he'd nodded.

I'd looked up at those dark brown eyes knowing that all thoughts of going to a previously scheduled interview for a coveted position at Jones Pharmaceuticals were flying right out of this office's floor-to-ceiling windows.

'Until Caitlin returns, you've got me,' I'd added timidly, hoping in my heart of hearts that Caitlin would fall so madly in love with her new son that she'd ring the office, weeping into the telephone that it was absolutely imperative she never leave her baby's side until the day he married, and that therefore it was impossible for her to ever return to Shepherd, Green & Parsons. And then Nick would summon me into his office and ask if I would step in permanently because, actually, I was far more efficient than Caitlin had ever been and frankly, he didn't know how he'd ever managed without me.

'Coffee-making skills up to scratch?' Nick had asked.

'Definitely,' I'd nodded enthusiastically. If this man had asked me to go to Guatemala and personally pick the beans for his morning fix, I'd have gladly taken the next jumbo jet to Central America to do his bidding.

'Excellent,' he'd smiled, 'so grab yourself one too and then pop along to my office with your notebook.'

This had set the pace for a morning ritual, and over the following few months of the booking I had come to love the next bit that followed. I'd sashay into Nick's office, heels click-clicking on the polished floor, two mugs of coffee held aloft, notepad tucked under one arm, biro clamped like a rose between my teeth. Setting one cup down on his desk, I'd take the other and retire to the sit-soft area reserved for clients, crossing my legs and unashamedly flashing a bit of thigh as I sipped my coffee companionably with him. Unlike my boyfriend Martin, Nick was a real charmer. He was prone to banter which was full of comical innuendo, and there was a relentless flirty undertone. He was careful not to cross boundaries in the workplace, but would nonetheless push it right up to the line. We got on so well together, and I'd become increasingly smitten. One or two female employees of the Mrs Pankhurst mould disapproved of Nick's waggling eyebrows and smooth patter, but I wasn't one of them. In fact, I lapped it up, so much so it had started to put some definitely non-PC visions in my head. Flashing a bit of thigh was nothing compared to my thoughts.

It was at this point of the mundane morning routine that I'd conjure up the most unspeakably outrageous visions of him locking the office door, then loosening his tie before growling, 'Hattie, you're playing havoc with my heart and bedlam with my Dictaphone.' In two huge strides, Nick would then cover the distance between the door and sofa and roughly pull me to my feet, all the while gazing lustfully into my eyes, which would cause me to swoon prettily before he kissed the life out of me. Needless to say, I'd also taken to reading a lot of Mills & Boon romances where women were maidens and men were… well… men. Sexual harassment in the workplace didn't exist, and nobody had any desire to burn their bras or chain themselves to railings. That said, one particularly lurid reverie had featured chains, but not in any way that Mrs Pankhurst would have approved of…

In reality, of course, the coffee break comprised of a ten-minute pleasant chat about everything and nothing, before the day got well and truly underway with Nick alternatively barking into either the telephone or his Dictaphone, while I sat in my cubicle typing at one-hundred-and-twenty miles per hour. Sometimes Nick asked me to work late. On these occasions I'd be in heaven, with my imagination conjuring up all sorts of improbable scenarios. Like leaving the office late but, just as the lift doors closed, there would be a power cut, and nobody around to come to the rescue. We'd be forced to spend the night together, hugging each other for warmth. Naturally one thing would lead to another. Nick would pin me against the defunct lift buttons, kissing me deeply as his hands came up and cupped first my face, then my breasts, then down a bit more and… oh, it was the work of a moment imagining myself in so many sizzling situations.

The fact that Nick was married was neither here nor there.

# Chapter Twenty

Ah, yes. Unfortunately, there was a Mrs Green. His *second* wife by all accounts. This was most definitely a blot on my Mills & Boon landscape. When I wasn't daydreaming about my romantic life with Nick, another goodly part of my time was taken up with the fantasy of Mrs Green conveniently clearing off. In my head I magicked up a vast number of reasons for her packing her bags that included falling madly in love with the gardener, her tennis instructor, and even becoming a lesbian and eloping with her best friend. Anything that would enable me to give a discreet cough and step into the empty void, whereupon Nick would say, 'Good heavens, Hattie, whatever did I see in her? How could I have been so blind to what was so obviously under my nose all along?' True love, albeit, heavily rose-tinted on my part and disappointingly colourless on his part. I was pretty damn sure that, flirty banter aside, outside the office I didn't register on Nicholas Green's radar.

Meanwhile my own boyfriend was wondering why I was so distracted. We'd been seeing less of each other by this point – mostly by design on my part – but Martin hadn't been ringing me as often either. But the next time we did hook up, maybe I gave the impression of being elsewhere. It caught his attention… my glow of secret happiness… occasionally hugging myself… and even making the odd excited squeaking noise. It was then that Martin raised his eyebrows in suspicion and asked me outright if I was having an affair. Which I was, of course. In my head. In fact, there was so much going on in my head back then that if I'd dared to share it with a bestie, no doubt I'd have been given a stiff talking-to and told to take a reality check. Instead I prayed a lot. Not for redemption, you understand. Oh no. I prayed for quite the opposite. That Mrs Green would look at Nick over their evening meal of lamb chops and vegetables and say, 'I have a confession to make. I've fallen in love. With God. I'm going to become a nun. Don't ever contact me again.'

God featured on almost a daily basis in these fantasies, not least because I found myself praying so fervently to Him and making the most ridiculous bargains.

*I'll give up my seat on the train to anyone and everyone, if you grant me Nick Green.*

In the office I became Miss Helper Extraordinaire.

*I'll help everybody with their workload when I've finished this bit of typing, if you let me have Nick Green.*

Once home again in the evenings I would practically hustle my mother out of her own kitchen as I took over with the dinner. On other occasions I'd shoo her away from the ironing board.

*I'll never let my mother lift a finger again if you'd just be so kind as to give me Nick Green.*

It was the same with my father.

*I'll never again let my dad do all the gardening without assistance, but only if you promise me Nick Green.*

Charities were another bargaining point with God.

*The next time I see a tin being rattled outside Sainsbury's, I promise to donate all my change. Okay, delete that last word. Cash. In exchange for Nick Green.*

A tiny part of my brain knew that even though I wasn't physically cheating on Martin, mentally it was another story. And wasn't that meant to be just as bad? My conscience kept trying to vocalise this, but I'd squash it into silence, insisting it was perfectly acceptable and simply harmless daydreaming. After all, nothing had actually happened between Nick and myself. And anyway, what woman hadn't fantasised at some point in a stale relationship? There couldn't be a female on the planet who, as her pot-bellied partner peeled off his socks and turned out the light, hadn't pretended it was Poldark lying next to her in order to make the sparks fly. Was that cheating? Of course not!

Meanwhile I continued bargaining with God. At one point I nearly bankrupted myself donating to ten different charities in one month. The last straw came when I pounced on my mobile phone following a televised appeal to house abandoned animals. As soulful eyes in a mournful face filled the TV screen, the camera panning to canine ribs jutting like a xylophone, I hurriedly texted away the last of my salary, all the while fervently praying to Him Upstairs. *You see? You see what I'm doing, God? This is how much I want Nick Green. I'll do anything. Anything at all. Even impoverish myself.* I was subsequently hounded by the charity's marketing team to head over to their online probate solicitor and bequeath all my worldly goods to their cause. It was at this point that Martin stepped in and asked what the hell had gotten into me. He had good reason, because lately it hadn't been him.

My final prayer of the day was last thing at night. I'd fall into bed, exhausted from so much mental bargaining, and meditate to calm the mind. Except it wasn't long before the meditation would feature Nick Green. As I listened to softly playing pan pipes on my iPod, suddenly Nick became the flautist. I'd be sitting at his feet, cross-legged, hands together as if in prayer, the two of us engulfed in a soft violet haze, when suddenly he'd cast aside the syrinx and sit down opposite me, leaning in to gently brush my lips with his mouth. Obsessed? You bet I was.

But one day, one *gloriously* fantastic day, God was listening and answered my prayers. My request was granted. But sometimes you need to be careful what you wish for.

# Chapter Twenty-One

I'll never forget that day. Nick arrived at the office but, instead of flying past my desk in a whirl of energy, he'd walked by without his habitual sunny greeting. His eyes had been blank, his expression bearing all the hallmarks of a person in deep shock. Wordlessly, I'd stood up and headed off to the kitchen to make our usual morning coffee. Minutes later I'd gone into his office minus the notepad – having sensed this wouldn't be required right now – and shut the door after me.

'Hattie,' he'd said, as if coming out of a trance.

'Are you all right, Nick?' I'd asked.

'I think so. Actually, no. I'm not sure I'll ever be all right again.'

I'd set the coffees down on his desk, and lightly touched his forearm. He still had his coat on.

'Let me hang this up for you. Sit down, Nick. Here,' I'd said, as he obediently slid out of his coat, 'have this coffee. I've put in an extra sugar. It's good for shock, and you look like you've had one.'

'Yes,' he nodded, 'yes, I have. Something very unexpected has happened.'

I'd put the coat on a hanger. The fabric was still warm from his body, and I'd let the garment half envelop me, for a split second kidding myself that it was *Nick* hugging me. It had taken all my willpower not to wrap the coat right around me. Looping the hanger over the peg on the back of the door, I'd then sat down on the sofa opposite his desk to await hearing whatever catastrophe had befallen him. To my surprise he'd not collapsed on his leather executive chair behind the vast mahogany expanse, instead opting to sink down next to me on the sofa. Our legs had never been so close. If I'd moved my thigh just a couple of millimetres, it would have touched his. I'd felt the heat coming from him, and been almost dizzy with longing. There was also a sensation of warmth near my neck, and I'd experienced a frisson of delight upon realising he'd flung one hand carelessly along the back of the sofa, just an inch or so from my hair.

'I won't beat about the bush, Hattie.'

There was something about his tone that had fingers of cold dread coiling around my heart. Oh no. Caitlin was coming back. A nanny had been employed and Nick's regular secretary couldn't wait to roll up her sleeves and get back to the grindstone, meaning Yours Truly wasn't just out of a job but would never see Nick Green again. No. It couldn't happen. I wouldn't *let* it happen.

'Wh-What is it?' I stammered.

He'd sighed deeply before replying. 'My wife's left me.'

For a moment I'd simply stared at him, not quite believing what I'd just heard. So... nothing to do with Caitlin then. Not yet, anyway. I'd been granted a reprieve on that score. Meanwhile... meanwhile, oh my goodness! My eyes rounded as his words properly registered. Mrs Green had upped and left Nick. He was still married, but now separated. Which meant, as far as I was concerned, he was now available and definitely up for grabs. It was simply down to me to do the rest. I was overjoyed. Delirious.

'Your wife's left you?' I gasped, hoping that I looked stunned and not ecstatic.

'Yes,' he said, his expression bleak, eyes momentarily flitting away from me to stare at his trousers, as if the navy pinstripe might yield answers to his predicament.

'Oh my God!' I exclaimed, not sure whether I was talking directly to the great man himself, or speaking to Nick.

'You see, I fell in love with someone,' he murmured. 'Someone who wasn't my wife.' He tore his eyes away from the Savile Row tailoring and looked directly at me. 'I fell in love with someone I shouldn't have. Someone who was out of bounds. In this office,' he added, his voice now so low his last sentence was only just audible. But those three whispered words had a momentous impact upon me.

My heart began to pound like a bongo drum, chasing away all the months of despair, weeks and weeks of angst, its steady beat now a throbbing pulse that put my whole body on red alert for the words that were surely about to tumble from his lips. It was more than I'd ever dared hope for. He was going to confess he'd fallen in love with me. I was suddenly very aware of his hand so close to my neck, the fact that the office door was shut, that it was just the two of us, here on this sofa, sitting side by side, our bodies so thrillingly close. I nodded at him encouragingly, knowing that it was important I remain seated and calm, not leap up and punch the air, or whoop like an extra in a film full of cowboys and Red Indians. Instead I arranged my features into a hopeful mix of sympathy and compassion, and gazed back at him, waiting for those magic words. And still he stared.

'Who?' I eventually croaked, unable to bear it any longer. 'Who, in the office, have you fallen in love with?'

# Chapter Twenty-Two

Waiting for Nick's response was agony. It could only have been seconds before he replied, but sitting there, on that sofa, so close to him, it felt like centuries. I waited, heart thudding, hardly daring to breathe, for his response. But when he finally answered, the breath whooshed out of me for all the wrong reasons.

'Erin,' he said.

I'd stared at him stupidly. 'Erin?' I repeated, not understanding.

'Yes, I've been seeing Erin. In Accounts.'

'B-but, Erin's married.'

'Yes, Hattie. I know she's married. Just like me.'

'So… so you've been having an affair with Erin.' Nothing like stating the obvious.

'Yes. For the last three months.'

'Three months?' I'd gasped. I'd been at Shepherd, Green & Parsons for *four* months. If he'd wanted an affair, well, not to put too fine a point on it, why not with me? *You cow, Hattie! Fancy even thinking such a thing. Shame on you for even daring to voice that you'd be willing to be 'the other woman'. A mistress, no less. That's not your style. Apart from anything else, what about Martin? He's your boyfriend. Remember him? I know you don't see much of him these days, but you haven't officially ended it, have you!*

But the truth was, back at this point in my life, whilst my conscience had sent off klaxon-like warnings to my brain, which had sensibly nodded in agreement, those cautions weren't being heeded by my heart which was defiantly sticking two fingers up to both the conscience and the brain.

'Right, so let me get this straight,' I said, frantically trying to collect my fragmented thoughts and kick away my own peculiar feelings of betrayal, 'you and Erin are an item.'

'Nooo, Hattie,' Nick sighed wearily. 'We were never an item. It started out as a bit of fun, then got out of hand. She has a husband who works away from home a lot. Consequently, Erin has felt lonely and neglected.'

Well, stroll on down! And what about me? Sitting here day after day, stuck in a world of dreams that nobody else could access? *Erin* was lonely? She didn't know the meaning of it! She *had* a hubby. A lovely one at that. I'd met him a couple of times at after-work gatherings, and he'd been such a sweetie. She didn't need another man when she already had one! The fact that I had a sort-of man too, of course, was neither here nor there.

'Well,' I said, scratching my head in bewilderment, 'are you and Erin going to *become* an item?'

'Definitely not.' Nick shook his head again.

'But I thought you said you loved her?'

'Yes. I do. Well… did.'

'Did?'

'In hindsight I think I muddled love with lust.'

Understandable. Erin was nearly six feet tall, a doppelgänger for Lisa Snowdon and had a voice like Jessica Rabbit.

'So what's happening now? Is she not leaving her husband for you?'

Nick had laughed mirthlessly. 'No, Erin has made it quite plain that she's now out of bounds. Her husband knows nothing of the affair, and she isn't about to confess all. Erin told me that whatever we'd had, it's over. Apparently, her husband has been posted to a different office closer to home, so will hardly ever have to go away on business and she will no longer be lonely. Everything is now hunky-dory for her. It's just *my* marriage that has hit the rocks and smashed to smithereens. I'm sorry, Hattie. You're my secretary. I don't know why I'm telling you this.'

'Of *course* you can confide in me,' I said stoutly. 'We work together, so can't avoid each other, and it was so plainly obvious from the moment you walked through the door that something was very wrong… and rest assured, you can trust me not to repeat this to anyone.'

'Thanks,' he said gratefully.

'But,' I said, shaking my head and still not understanding, 'you said your wife has left you. I take it she found out?'

'Oh she suspected I was having a fling, all right. She just didn't know who with. She won't go after Erin though. Apart from anything else…' he trailed off uncomfortably.

'What?'

'She's not bothered about knowing who it was.'

I stared at him incredulously. What woman didn't want all the details of her love rival? If it had been me I'd have been out there, tail up, nose down, sniffing out clues and wanting every bit of minutiae, right down to her shoe size. Which was enormous in Erin's case.

Her feet were so big she practically skied down the corridor. I tried not to gnash my teeth together or hyperventilate.

'Why doesn't your wife want to find out who you were seeing?' I asked, my breath now coming in quick snatches.

Nick shrugged, his expression somewhat sheepish. 'I suppose she's seen it all before. She can no longer be bothered to know the particulars.'

'All before?' I echoed incredulously. 'What… you mean… Erin hasn't been your first infidelity?'

'Nope. Not the first. Not by a long shot.'

I gaped at my boss – the man I loved. Oh yes, despite hearing that Nick had a propensity to being unable to keep his todger in his trousers, my body was taking no notice at all and still sending out cartoon hearts in his direction.

'If you,' I gulped, unsure whether to ask such a blunt question, 'if you are a serial adulterer, why bother getting married in the first place?'

Nick gave a wry smile. 'Why indeed, eh? I believe that is what's known as a sixty-four-thousand-dollar question, Hattie.' He looked briefly upwards, contemplating the ceiling. 'I like being married,' he said simply. 'It's nice to have someone who is meant to be the summer to your winter… the missing piece of a jigsaw… the one who makes you feel whole.'

I caught my breath at his audacity and suddenly felt inflamed with anger.

'Then why on earth would you cheat on your wife if she is all those things?' I demanded.

'Because,' he said, bringing his eyes back to me and smiling disarmingly, 'I guess she wasn't those things after all. I suspect you have the same thoughts about marriage as me, Hattie. That it is to be treasured. Nurtured. It's a wonderful union – for those who get it right. But if it's not perfect on every level, flaws show up. Cracks appear. Some couples row. Gin bottles at dawn, and all that. Or else they cohabit in silent resentment. Which we did. And that's when the marriage becomes incredibly vulnerable to some extra-curricular activity, if you see what I mean.'

'Right,' I nodded, trying to make sense of what he was saying. In which case, if he was right, then one could point the finger at Mrs Green and say, somewhat conveniently, that *she* was to blame for Nick's wandering eye. My heart leapt at this thought, even though my brain was shaking its head in despair. 'Okay, I get it,' I nodded, 'you're saying your wife was never the right woman for you in the first place, and that had she been, none of your affairs would ever have happened?'

'Correct,' said Nick.

The cynics would have rolled their eyes and said Nick's explanation was simply moulding the truth for his own purpose – that what he really meant by 'a good marriage' was having an unpaid housekeeper providing hot dinners, washing his underpants, darning his socks, and efficiently running the marital home. He wasn't bothered about whether wifey was too tired to later pull off her pinny and morph into a sexy little minx who swung her bra around her head like a football rattle, because he could get the naughty side of things elsewhere. But I wasn't one of those cynics. Put simply, I was me – young, inexperienced, hopelessly blinded by love, and willing to overlook any flaws in both his explanation and his character. Mrs Green had gone, that was all that mattered.

It was only much later I found out that the second Mrs Green had once been 'the other woman' and that the first Mrs Green had been divorced to make way for the second Mrs Green. And even if I'd known that right at the start, would it have stopped me? I doubt it. Because apart from being madly in love, I had a new goal… aim… ambition. Call it what you will. And that was to become the third Mrs Green.

# Chapter Twenty-Three

It's easy in hindsight to spot things that, at the time, go right over your head. When Nick had come into the office looking so shocked prior to confiding his marital indiscretions, I'd automatically assumed he was in a daze because his wife had upped and left. After all, he'd used those very words, 'My wife has left me.' Much later, he let slip the facts, which were a little different.

Without warning, Mrs Green II had unceremoniously chucked Nick out of the marital home. Having done her own detective work and arrived at the foregone conclusion that her husband was, yet again, having a fling, she'd bided her time to neatly exact revenge. Without Nick suspecting anything was up, she'd secretly removed the house key from his key fob, waved him off to work, then rung in sick to her own place of employment. She'd then methodically set about divesting all the wardrobes and drawers of Nick's belongings, packing them up in several suitcases. A reservation at a local hotel had been made in her husband's name, and a taxi had been called to deposit all the luggage at the hotel. She'd then opened a new bank account in her own name and transferred the entire contents of the joint account across. Finally, she'd messaged Nick, timing the communication to ping his mobile whilst on the evening drive home. Nick had illegally picked the text up whilst behind the wheel of his car, and nearly ploughed into the vehicle in front of him.

*Nick. We're finished. You know why. Don't bother coming home because you'll find you no longer have a key. I'm keeping the house and have closed the joint account. Consider it compensation for the hell you've put me through. If you want to fight me for it, I'll see you in court.*

Needless to say, Nick hadn't waged war to keep anything. It transpired that the second Mrs Green had paid the lion's share of the marital home because of Nick not having much in the way of spare dosh after his first divorce. The original Mrs Green had been allowed to keep *her* marital home because there were two young children, and the house had formed part of her divorce settlement. Afterwards, there had been steep monthly maintenance payments for two daughters, both of whom were in private schools, had ponies, enjoyed ballet lessons, had violin tutors, belonged to a weekly swim club, and outgrew children's designer clothes faster than you could say Dolce & Gabbana.

Starting again – *again* again – had initially seen Nick looking very stony-faced, but he'd quickly rallied and got on with his lot. Fortunately, there had been no children with the second Mrs Green, so there were no maintenance payments to make. She'd taken what she wanted at the time of disposing of him. Nick had spent the first few days in the hotel whilst quickly sorting out the next stage of his life – renting a bachelor pad. Somehow, it hadn't seemed strange when he'd asked me to accompany him on a few viewings, to give an opinion, and simply keep him company. Afterwards, it had seemed perfectly natural to walk across the road to that invitingly cosy restaurant and have dinner together.

When Nick had finally made a decision about which property he wanted and picked up a set of keys from the lettings agent, he'd been overjoyed.

'I've moved on,' he said, 'and now I need to move in. The only trouble is, I don't have any furniture. Fancy coming out with me after work and helping me choose stuff?'

Was he kidding? I didn't need asking twice! My backside was off my typist's chair and sitting in the leather bucket seat of his sports car quicker than Lewis Hamilton completing a circuit at Brands Hatch. There was something marvellously couple-like about going shopping for furniture together. *I* knew it was Nick having a spending spree for his top floor abode for one, but the shop assistants didn't. It gave me a secret thrill when they bantered with the good-looking man and the young pretty girl standing shyly by his side.

'Oh no, you're not going to let him buy a big black leather settee are you, love?' said the guy in the furniture department. 'Aren't you going to march him off to Laura Ashley and choose something twee covered in spriggy stuff?'

It was the same when Nick ordered a sixty-five-inch flat screen TV for the living room.

'Don't forget your lovely missus here, Sir,' said the salesman in Electricals. 'She'll want her own wall-mounted telly in the kitchen while she's cooking your supper. We can't have you missing *Corrie*, can we, darlin'?'

We'd all laughed, and I'd inwardly glowed, basking in the assumption that we were an item. After all, what was wrong with pretending and indulging in a little more make-believe, when most of the time I wasn't in the real world anyway.

When we'd strolled into the bed showroom, I'd salivated at the sight of an elegant four-poster with an overstuffed mattress that looked like something out of 'The Princess and the Pea' fairy tale, whereas Nick had headed straight for a black leather sleigh bed practically the size of a football pitch.

'You'll need acres of bedding if you buy this one,' I cautiously advised.

'I absolutely *have* to have loads of space in a bed, Hattie,' he replied. 'There's nothing worse than turning over and finding yourself tumbling onto the floor, or flipping the other way and having a nose-to-nose encounter with your bedfellow who, prior to snuggling under the covers, had minty-fresh breath but, at four in the morning, reminds you of your parents' dog's halitosis.'

I'd giggled, immediately imagining myself lying by Nick's side, spooning dead centre in this massive bed, a huge expanse of mattress to the left and right, with a discreet Gold Spot spray on the bedside table to avoid early-morning kisses reminding him of Shep's breath.

From there we'd chosen bedding, towels, a dinner service, cutlery and by the time we'd strolled towards the pay point I'd nearly linked my arm with his, quite forgetting for a split second that we weren't really a couple at all. *Yet*, my heart had piped up, much to my head's despair. Oh yes, make no mistake about it, my brain was working overtime to penetrate the layers of rose-tinted mist obscuring Nick's faults. Anybody with an ounce of common sense would have told me I was beyond gullible. I did pause briefly – for all of five seconds – to wonder at the sanity of pursuing this attractive older man with a bad-boy history, but my heart swatted such thoughts away as if they were a dirty black cloud spoiling a golden ray of sunshine. I so badly wanted to feel that heat and refused to think about getting burnt. Yes, I had the hots for my boss, but it wasn't just that. It was love. It had to be. Why else did I want to not just share this man's life, but also look after him? I'd certainly never felt this way about anyone before.

Everything was duly delivered to the apartment, and Nick properly moved in. On his first night he asked if I'd like to join him there for dinner to celebrate, and also to say thank you for all my help. It was a Saturday evening, and he said he'd cook. He made a complete hash of it, setting off the smoke alarms and stinking out the open-plan kitchen-come-lounge. He'd gone on to order a takeaway and we'd headed off to the bedroom to escape the fug hanging in the air along with the stench of cremated food. We'd sat companionably on the vast bed together, eating, chatting, laughing, perfectly at ease with one another as we'd tucked into our respective curry dishes. He'd even put a piece of chicken tikka on his fork and held it out to me to try.

'Taste this, Hattie, it's absolutely delicious.'

*Like you*, I'd privately thought as I'd leant forward, opening my mouth. He'd popped the morsel between my lips and I'd closed my eyes in ecstasy. Not so much from the taste of the food – which was sublime – but because, somehow, it had seemed like such an intimate gesture… to feed me. I'd immediately reciprocated, spearing a piece of tender lamb and gently placing it on top of his tongue. He'd rolled his eyes appreciatively and declared it wonderful. And then, quite suddenly, we'd lost our appetites. Nick had gazed at me, and whatever I'd been about to say had gone unsaid. He'd given me the sort of look I'd spent so long hoping – indeed praying – for. The look of love. Well… that's what my heart had whispered. My brain had said something else, blowing lots of frantic whistles and waving red flags, screaming that it was simply lust on Nick's part, and that this man wouldn't know the meaning of love if it was parcelled up and delivered to his flat in a John Lewis van. But I didn't care. If lust was the only thing on offer, then I'd take it. And I did.

As Nick removed the tray of abandoned curry and set it down on a nearby chest of drawers, I'd felt my body thrill at what was coming next. And when he'd pulled me into his arms and we'd tumbled backwards against the new William Morris bedding, there was nothing on my mind other than finally claiming this man and letting his body blend with mine.

We'd spent the entire weekend in bed. It was only when I'd finally tottered home, sated and drunk with love, that I'd realised I'd overlooked something. Or, more to the point, some*one*. My boyfriend, Martin.

# Chapter Twenty-Four

'Where have you been?' cried my mother, as I walked in through the front door – all starry-eyed – late on Sunday afternoon. 'Dad and I have been worried. You didn't even telephone to say you wouldn't be home. Not very thoughtful of you, Hattie,' she added, shaking her head.

'Sorry,' I grinned, 'something came up.' My mind instantly wandered back to the bedroom and smuttily went over exactly what had come up and what had been ripped off.

Mum paused in wiping up the dishes, putting down the tea towel to regard me with rather knowing eyes.

'What's going on, Hattie?' she asked quietly. 'You usually spend your weekends in something of a mood, mooching around the house, getting under my feet, watching re-runs of Bridget Jones getting in a lather over Daniel Cleaver whilst not knowing what to do about Mr Darcy. Which reminds me, Martin rang, asking if we knew your whereabouts. Why didn't you answer your mobile phone?'

'Battery died,' I said, grabbing another tea towel to help with the dishes.

'I hope you know what you're doing,' she hissed, flicking the kitchen door shut with her foot so Dad couldn't hear us chatting.

I feigned surprise. 'I simply spent the weekend with a friend,' I replied, vigorously polishing some damp knives and forks.

'Yes, it's *which* friend that's bothering me,' she muttered.

'I had a last-minute invitation to spend time with a pal from the office,' I shrugged, rattling crockery into the drawer. 'It's no big deal.'

'I see,' said Mum, opening another drawer and deftly putting away a stack of clean saucepans. 'And who is this bosom buddy that you had such a great girly time with? Because, let's be frank, I've only ever heard you talk about half a dozen women, all of whom are married with children, and usually beyond weary by half past five in the evening. Indeed, from what you've previously told me, they long for the weekend so they can exchange their exhaustion for something else – being frustrated and frazzled as they drag their protesting offspring around the supermarket, nagging their equally knackered husbands into taking part, before doing some compulsory family time at the local park. Which of these women, Hattie, is suddenly your new bestie, hmm?'

I rolled my eyes. 'Oh, give it a rest, Mum.' I buried my head in the cupboard as I stacked plates onto a shelf, my hair falling across my face, so Mum couldn't see my blushes. The trouble with my mother though was that she had an inbuilt lie detector. Jeremy Kyle could have used her on his show and caught out every guilty guest without the need for a polygraph.

'Don't lie to me, Hattie.'

See? Told you.

'I'm not lying to you,' I replied, 'I honestly did spend the weekend with someone from the office.'

Mum paused to eye me beadily. 'Yes, that much is true. But it wasn't a female, was it?'

I ignored her and carried on with my wiping, cups tinkling together alarmingly as I shoved them onto a shelf.

'It's that boss of yours, isn't it?' she continued. 'Don't think I haven't had my suspicions about your feelings for him, Hattie. Apart from anything else, ever since you started working for him, you've had acute mentionitis. Nick this. Nick that. From everything you've told me about him, I think I could go on *Mastermind* and win with Nicholas Green as my specialist subject, and yet I've never met the man.'

I shut the cupboard door and spun round to face her. 'Yes, okay, it's my boss. I spent the weekend with Nick. Is that a problem?'

'Are you *mad*?' she demanded. 'He's married.'

'But not for much longer,' I countered.

'*And* he's been married before,' she said, ignoring me and sweeping on.

'So what's wrong with that?' I said crossly. 'It's no crime to have been married more than once. Celebrities do it all the time.'

'He's not a celebrity.'

'Oh right, so ordinary folk aren't allowed to cock up a couple of times in their pursuit of true love?'

'True love?' Mum sneered, her lip curling with disdain. 'Is that what *this* is then, Hattie?'

I opened my mouth to say something but bit back the words. Well, on my part it was true love. Of that I was sure. But I couldn't speak for Nick. At no point, between giggly tussles under the duvet, had he uttered those three magic words. In fact, when Monday morning rolled around, I just hoped he didn't call me into his office and tell me that the whole thing had been a small diversion on his part, a bit of fun while he dusted himself off from his last marriage, and that our relationship would immediately revert to a professional one. Was I destined to watch him go off to his meetings leaving me to stroke his desk lamp and furtively sniff the aftershave on the collar of his coat? I could feel my bubble bursting as the doubts set in. Damn my mother for doing this to me.

'Look, Mum,' I sighed, 'I didn't know anything was going to happen between us.'

'Oh don't give me that,' Mum snorted. 'You've been dripping around this house these last few weeks looking like Cinderella lusting after Prince Charming, slow-dancing with the vacuum cleaner when you think I've not been looking, crooning love songs into the nozzle. You know perfectly well that you've been waiting in the wings for something to happen with this man, and suddenly – bam! – it has. You've jumped in head first without pausing to consider the repercussions.'

'What repercussions?' I asked, brow furrowing. 'He's as good as single, and so am I.'

I knew, as soon as I'd uttered those last words, that I'd let Mum provoke me to the point of falling into her trap. I shut my eyes as she looked at me triumphantly.

'Forgive me if I'm wrong, Hattie,' Mum crowed, 'but I seem to remember you have a boyfriend. Just to remind you, his name is Martin. I'm aware he's not been in touch much lately, but I would presume that he still believes *you* are *his* girlfriend.'

'We're like brother and sister,' I said dismissively.

'But you haven't actually finished with him, have you?' Mum cried.

'No,' I snapped, 'because I haven't had the chance.'

The kitchen door opened, and Dad peered around it. 'Why all the raised voices?' he asked. 'Are you two having a barney?'

Before either of us could answer, the telephone rang. Mum snatched it up, eyes not leaving my face.

'Hello?' she said, glaring at me. 'Yes, she's right here. I'll put you on, just a sec.' She passed me the handset. 'For you,' she said, smiling sweetly, as my heart sank. 'It's Martin.'

# Chapter Twenty-Five

'Hi,' I warbled into the mouthpiece, watched all the while by Mum. My father frowned and went out again, shutting the kitchen door after him. There were far more pressing things to do than listen to a mother and daughter bicker in the kitchen. A football match beckoned.

'Hey!' said Martin.

Mum put her hands on her hips, clearly waiting to hear what I was going to say next. I glared at her. Ah yes, she wasn't the only one who could do meaningful things with her eyeballs. Nor was I having her earwigging on this conversation with my boyfriend. Correction. Ex-boyfriend. I gave her a defiant look and marched out of the kitchen, up the stairs to my bedroom and shut the door firmly after me. No doubt she'd tiptoe along behind me, creep along the landing, was doing so even now, pressing one ear against the door. This was the downside of still living at home. A definite lack of privacy. Undeterred, I slid back my wardrobe door, climbed in and settled down amongst the shoeboxes, pulling the door shut after me. Ha! Try listening now, Mum.

'Hey,' I said, attempting to make my tone light.

'Hattie, we haven't seen each other for ages.'

'Yeah, I've... er... been a bit busy.'

'Me too,' said Martin quickly. 'But I thought I'd catch up with you and, well, when I rang you didn't pick up on your mobile. So I called your parents, and they had no idea where you were. I was starting to worry.'

'Sorry,' I said, feeling guilty, 'something came up at work.'

'You've been working all weekend?'

'N-No, just, um, it was a work colleague's leaving do and, you know, we all got a bit plastered, so I stayed over at... hers.'

'Right,' said Martin, doubt evident in his voice. 'It must have been one hell of a bash to have stayed the entire weekend.'

'Oh it was,' I said quickly, spotting a handy excuse and swimming frantically towards it.

'Well never mind, you're home now. We should catch up with each other.'

'Mm,' I said, taking the coward's way out and trying to be non-committal.

'Do you fancy coming out tonight? I thought we could go to the cinema. Check out that new Tom Cruise film and afterwards, well, you know...' his voice trailed off and he chuckled naughtily. '...go back to mine. You could bring your toothbrush and go to work from here.'

I wriggled uncomfortably, and it wasn't just because I was sitting on a pair of spiky stilettoes. Whatever had happened between my boss and me, and whether we became a couple or not, there was one thing I knew for certain. I no longer wanted to be an item with Martin. My passion under the duvet with Nick had most definitely seen to that. I'd never be the same again. If I couldn't have Nick,

then I didn't want anybody. And I certainly didn't want Martin.
We'd hardly seen anything of each other lately anyway, so I should
have properly let him go weeks ago, instead of chickening out, not
knowing how to end things. I wasn't the sort of person to dump by
text. That wouldn't have been kind or fair, given the length of our
relationship, not forgetting the assumption by everybody – especially
my mother – that at some point we would live the rest of our lives
together. It was time to behave responsibly and end this face to face.
The fact that I felt like a total bitch for waiting until sleeping with my
boss made me feel two inches tall. It would have been so much better
to have looked Martin in the eye and said, 'Look, it's not you, it's me.'
Whereas now it was a case of, 'Look, it's not you, it's someone else.'

'Yes,' I croaked, before coughing and clearing my throat. 'I'd
like that.'

'Great, I'll book the tickets now. It's Sunday night so we should
get a seat without any problem. You can buy the popcorn,' he said
happily.

'Sure,' I said, putting a smile into my voice. 'But, er, I'm really
whacked after my weekend with the girls so, ah, if it's all right with
you, I won't stay over.' My mind mentally raced ahead on how to
deal with the break-up. Already I was envisioning us watching the
film, and me being a bit aloof. Keeping my hand in the bag of
popcorn, rather than resting it on his leg. Putting some emotional
distance between us, so to speak, so that by the time the credits were
rolling and we were heading out of the cinema, he'd have sussed
something wasn't quite right and be primed for the moment when
I pulled him aside as the late-night audience streamed past, and
told him face to face that I didn't think it was working any more.

*In front of all those people, Hattie?* my brain gasped.

Oh. Good point. Right, so not at the cinema then. Perhaps it would be better to go back to his flat after all? I wouldn't stay the night, but I'd talk to him there. It would be private. Somewhere to quietly say, 'Look, Martin, I'm terribly sorry, there's no easy way to say this, but you bore the pants off me.' Oh no, no, too unkind. 'Sorry, Martin, but I no longer find you attractive.' Nooooo, that wouldn't do either. 'Martin, darling! Listen, I'm madly in love with my boss, and we spent all weekend in bed behaving like oversexed rabbits.'

Oh GOD! Why wasn't there an easy way of doing this without causing pain… hurt… upset? I heard a floorboard creak and knew Mum was eavesdropping. I needed to end this call, and quickly.

'Right, let's do this!' I said, the determination in my voice unfortunately being misinterpreted as enthusiasm by Martin.

'Fab, babe,' he crooned into my ear, 'and even if you don't stay overnight, I trust you'll still come back to the flat for a little while, eh?'

'Yes,' I said reluctantly. But it wouldn't be for the reason he was thinking.

'I can't wait to have you all to myself and show you a time you're *never* going to forget.'

'We'll see!' I twittered nervously. 'Catch you later.' I abruptly hung up, heart pounding, just as my mother yanked open my wardrobe door.

'Well?' she demanded.

'I'm going out,' I said, scrambling out of the closet and plonking the handset in Mum's hand.

'Again?'

'Yes. To do what I should have done ages ago.'

'You're ending it with Martin?' said my mother, looking aghast.

'I don't love him any more, Mum.'

'I hope you know what you're doing, my girl.'

But I wasn't listening. I was too busy mentally rehearsing what I was going to say to my soon-to-be ex. Minutes later, I was out the house, heading off into the night, all the while preparing my speech which, no matter how many times I tweaked or changed it, still sounded awful.

Even now, revisiting this memory, I couldn't tell you what the film was about. I do know that we had a couple of drinks each before the film started. I sat stiffly in the auditorium, my body tense, staring at the screen, not taking in any of the action or drama. Afterwards, I allowed Martin to take me back to his place, shut the main door after me, lead me up the stairs to his flat and then walk me across the living room to his sofa. We had a few more drinks as I delayed the inevitable. It was only when I realised that Martin was drinking doubles to my singles and getting a gleam in his eye that I snapped to. I sat down, back ramrod straight, and began burbling out the words that had been floating around for the last few hours in my head.

'Martin, you've been my boyfriend for… well, it seems like forever… and, well, the thing is… the thing *is*…' I trailed off helplessly, looking at the ceiling, the curtains, the carpet, anything for inspiration. But then he did something unexpected. He'd been sitting next to me, but now he moved himself, so he was sitting at my feet. He leant forward and took both my cold hands in his, rubbing warmth into them, holding them tightly.

'Don't, Hattie,' he said quietly, 'don't say another word. I know exactly what you're trying to say.'

Relief flooded through me. 'You do?' Oh, thank goodness. Call me a coward – which I was – but it was so wonderful not to have to say the dreaded words that he'd sussed.

He nodded, his expression one of understanding, and then his face broke into a banana grin. 'But it's wrong for you to be the one to ask.'

'Eh?'

'It's a man's job. Hush,' he said putting one finger over my lips, still grinning away. 'I know we seemed to drift apart for these last few weeks, but I've given this a lot of thought. I want things to change. For the better.' Seconds later he'd shifted his position, so that he was now down on one knee. 'Darling, Hattie. My heart has been yours ever since we met at uni, and it will always be yours. You're the love of my life, and I want to grow old with you.'

And then he said the four words I'd been dreading.

'Will you marry me?'

# Chapter Twenty-Six

I stared at Martin in horror. His heart had always been mine? I was the love of his life? I'd *never* felt that way about him, even before Nick had crashed into my life playing havoc with my emotions. I *had* loved Martin, once, but in the way one might love a dear friend. Even now, I was still fond of him. But, shamefully, I'd always regarded him a bit like a favourite bobbly cardigan. Reassuring. Familiar. The fact that we'd sometimes slept together was just something that had happened. It was like going to bed with a cuddly teddy bear, or a comfort blanket. It was pleasant, but not mind-blowing. And if that sounds heartless, I don't mean it to. There was a time when I'd thought him fascinating, but that had been when we'd studied together which, now that I'd met Nick, seemed another world away. My mother had often reminded me that Martin was 'a good catch'. Despite repeating her mantra to myself many times over, I'd remained unconvinced that he was *my* good catch. And anyway, you can't marry a person just because your mum longs to go shopping for a mother-of-the-bride outfit and a big hat. Sooner or later, the relationship would have floundered. But now I had two things to contend with – extricating myself from this relationship *and* turning down a marriage proposal. Somehow it felt like I was about to be doubly cruel.

Martin laughed. 'I can tell you're ab-sho-lutely gob-shmacked.' He was slurring slightly from the alcohol. 'Why? After all, isn't that what *you* were going to ask *me*?'

I stared at him with huge, apprehensive eyes. 'N-No, actually, I was—'

'No?' Martin interrupted, his brow furrowing. 'You weren't going to ask me to marry you?'

'Er, no. I wasn't.'

There was silence for a moment, as he regarded me thoughtfully. 'You mean, I've just made a dick of myself for nothing?'

'Not at all,' I said, my voice sounding placating. 'It was a lovely proposal. Lovely.'

He looked at me uncertainly, the cogs in his brain almost audibly whirring. 'Right, okay. Well, never mind,' he said, recovering his composure, 'I was going to ask you anyway, on your birthday. I had it all planned out. A trip to a Toby Carvery – no scrimping on the roast beef for my girl – a nice shandy with dinner, maybe have your parents there with us, and then somewhere between the ice-cream and coffee, I'd have popped the question right there in front of the entire restaurant.'

'S-Sounds splendid,' I whispered, as a part of me started to wonder what I'd ever found attractive about this man. A proposal in the local carvery? What, packed out with screaming children, oblivious parents, Nan and Grandad's mobility scooters blocking the aisle, while a harassed waitress sprayed sanitising fluid across the next table before rearranging and banging down the salt and pepper pots?

Martin shrugged. 'I can still do the formal proposal on your birthday. But having asked you the question here, you might as well give me your answer now.'

I gave him a frozen smile. 'Right.'

'Right? Is that a "yes" then?'

'It's… it's a…' I gulped, 'maybe… not.'

'A maybe not?' he frowned. 'What do you mean?' he said, his brow knitting together. 'What's a maybe not?'

'It's… it's a no.'

'No?' he repeated, his expression turning to one of confusion. 'You mean… hang on, let me get this straight, you mean—'

'I mean I don't want to marry you.' I hadn't realised I'd been holding my breath until those words tumbled out of my mouth, leaving me gasping slightly. Feeling stressed about it didn't help. I'd be hyperventilating in a minute.

A mixture of emotions played out across Martin's face. From shock, to disbelief, to horror, and finally anger. When he next spoke, his voice was like a pistol shot.

'Why not?' he demanded.

'Because,' I said, quaking, 'I'm not the marrying kind.'

'What are you talking about?' he demanded. 'Are you trying to tell me you're a lesbian?'

I nearly laughed, except it wasn't funny. Nerves were taking off in my stomach like a shoal of leaping salmon. Indeed, one appeared to have shot up into my oesophagus and entangled itself with my tonsils. I tried and failed to find the right words to placate and provide some sort of damage limitation as Martin's face went from pink to puce.

'Bloody well talk to me, Hattie,' he demanded, giving me a little shake. 'It's the least I deserve. Do you mean you don't want to get married *yet* or, more specifically, you don't want to marry *me*?'

It would have been so easy to have opted to answer the former question, followed by lots of soothing words, 'Yes, I meant later of course, obviously I want to marry you one day in the future', and then administering a reassuring peck on the cheek before getting the hell out of there. Once home, I could have then reached for my mobile phone and done what thousands of other people do. Texted and got straight to the point.

> ME: *I don't want to go out with you any more and I definitely won't be marrying you.*
> MARTIN: *Are you dumping me?*
> ME: *Yes.*
> MARTIN: *Oh, okay. You bitch…*
> ME: *Really sorry…*
> MARTIN: *Cow. Tart. You were frigid anyway. Oh, and yes, your bum does look big. In everything. We're talking larger than Lidl.*
> ME: *\*presses block button and heaves a huge sigh of relief\**

However, regrettably, that option wasn't available. I was in Martin's flat. And something so hideous was about to happen that I couldn't stay with the memory of it for a moment longer. Suddenly I felt like I couldn't breathe. I clawed at my throat, screwed my eyes up and screamed out loud. It was the most piercing primeval sound I'd ever made in my life. Abruptly, Martin's flat disappeared, and I sat bolt upright in the pink and white bedroom of the Halfway Lounge, hot tears pouring down my face.

'It's okay, Hattie,' Josh said, holding me tight. 'Shh, everything's fine.'

'I can't relive what happens next, Josh,' I cried, snorting attractively and wiping snot from my nose with the back of my hand. A tissue instantly appeared in my palm. Pulling away from him, I trumpeted into it.

'You don't have to relive it, Hattie,' he assured me, 'you just have to *review* it.'

I regarded Josh with bloodshot eyes, desperately trying to push down the feelings of panic. 'And you?' I demanded. 'You said you'd be right there with me, but I didn't see you.'

'You won't see me, Hattie. I explained that to you previously. There are vibrational changes involved. But you're not unsupported, or alone. It was me who brought you out of the memory. I could see from your aura colour that your stress levels were rising.'

'And that's another thing,' I rounded on Josh furiously, the unhappiness of it all making me angry, and regrettably he was now right in the line of fire. 'I don't want you seeing private stuff… situations where I'm… ' my voice trailed off.

'I told you before,' said Josh gently, 'circumstances that are sensitive, just like your thoughts, are kept private from me. But I'm still able to read you. It's like a finger marking a page in a book and therefore knowing the exact place you're at in a memory, all down to frequency patterns and, well, I won't bore you with the quantum physics of it all. Just understand the screening of personal stuff remains private to you, okay?'

I nodded, reassured a modicum.

'The important thing to remember,' said Josh, 'is that you don't have to relive what happened next. But, as I said, you *do* have to review it. So, when you're ready, Hattie, you will have to return to that moment. You made a vow, remember?'

I tutted disparagingly, dabbing at my eyes with the now soggy tissue, gratefully taking another that hovered in the air like a small flag fluttering in a breeze. 'All these vows, Josh, that I'm supposed to have made—'

'There's no suppose about it.'

'Well I'm fed up of them. People go through life wagging their fingers at other people, at the situations they've created whilst muttering all sorts of dark threats and oaths, but they get by. They don't end up having surreal experiences like this.' I reached up and briefly tore at my hair. 'I feel like I'm going blooming mad.'

'Who's to say they don't experience this but just don't remember it?' Josh pointed out. 'You're not going mad, Hattie. There's more chance of you going mad if you *don't* revoke the pledges made. And right now, you need to deal with Martin. What he did left a black mark on your soul. These things, if left to fester, not only cause resentment, they can make you ill. How many times does someone say that a situation, or a person, "makes them sick"?' And if they say it enough, it manifests. The soul is like the most beautiful flower you can ever think of. It's also like a sponge. When anchored to the body it absorbs the emotions that filter through the human layer. If the soul becomes too darkened from the power of words, it will eventually shake itself like a wet dog and spray everything back into the human body. In turn, that can cause illness.'

'I don't believe I'm hearing this,' I spluttered. 'That's a shocking thing to say.'

'But unfortunately true,' said Josh. 'Listen to me, Hattie,' he said, gripping me tightly and forcing me to look directly into his eyes, 'everyone has the ability to heal themselves. It's just knowing *how*. It must come from within. That is the starting point.'

I shook my head wearily. Some of what Josh said rang true. I knew I was sick of carting all the secrets around with me. Sick of feeling weighted down. Sick of a deep unhappiness that went way beyond feeling fed up or disgruntled. And then I noticed the language I'd just used whilst mulling it all over. *Sick of*. It made me question if that was why, in my ordinary everyday life, I was always the first to succumb to coughs and colds, the first to develop a tooth abscess on a bank holiday, and the last to get over a bug. But it wasn't just my physical health that sometimes seemed a bit off, my emotions very often felt skewed too. In the corners of my mind, I often felt haunted by the past, and there had been private moments where I'd seriously wondered about the state of my mental health.

'You don't have to do this now, Hattie,' said Josh. 'We can take a break. Go and have some fun. Ride a rainbow or something.'

'Ride a rainbow?' I gasped, half laughing. Whatever next?'

'Sure. It's exhilarating. Want me to show you?'

I nodded slowly. 'Yes… yes, I'd like that. But—' I hesitated, as another part of me weighed things up. I was all for playing hooky and avoiding the situation with Martin, but on the other hand I wanted to go home and get back to my normal, gloriously boring and mundane life. Putting off the inevitable wasn't helpful. 'I want to return to Martin first,' I said. 'I need to get this sorted out.'

Josh nodded. 'Sure?'

'Yeah. Do I have to lie down, like previously? You know, go back to sleep?'

'Only if you feel a need to rest and gather your energy.'

I considered. 'Nope, I don't feel tired at all. In fact, if anything I feel energised. I guess now that you've reassured me, I'm eager to get this piece of the past addressed.'

Josh squeezed my hand encouragingly and gave me one of his blowtorch smiles. Despite the seriousness of what was about to happen, it didn't stop the all-too-familiar zings whizzing up and down my spine.

'Now just remember, Hattie, you are reviewing this scenario. You will remember how you felt, the facts of the situation, and see yourself acting them out as such, but you won't be living it, although you can step in and change the script anytime you like to serve your purpose.' I nodded. 'And,' Josh continued, 'the crucial point here is that you find it in your heart to forgive.' I momentarily closed my eyes, and then nodded again. Ready?'

'Ready.'

# Chapter Twenty-Seven

Just like an audience watching Act One end for the interval, suddenly the curtain was back up ready to continue with Act Two. I was back in Martin's flat, and everything was as it had been before I'd screamed, and Josh had yanked me back to the Halfway Lounge. The only difference was that I was now both *in* the scene *and* observing it, from a detached place that I can't properly describe. In some respects, it was a bit like watching a programme on the telly and being so thoroughly immersed in the drama that I was right there with the protagonist. However, it was also like having my backside superglued to a seat, making it impossible to leave the room, whilst at the same time discovering the remote control was missing so the channel couldn't be changed.

It was a revelation to revisit this chapter of my life with fresh eyes, because so much had been deliberately blocked from my mind over the years, thus distorting facts and blaming myself. Only in my darkest, loneliest moments had snatches of memory ever filtered back to haunt me, and even then, like strands of annoying hair around one's face, I'd irritably pushed them away, sweeping them back to the recesses of my mind, whilst continuing to believe everything to be my fault.

'Bloody well talk to me, Hattie!' Martin demanded, giving me a little shake. Anger had stopped him from slurring, but the booze had heightened his emotions. 'It's the least I deserve. Do you mean you don't want to get married *yet* or, more specifically, you don't want to marry *me*?'

'I don't want to marry you,' I said. My voice was calm but more assertive now.

'But why?'

I stood up, picking up my handbag, getting ready to distance myself from the flat, from him, indeed the situation. But Martin wasn't prepared to let me leave without an angry exchange of words.

'WHERE THE BLOODY HELL DO YOU THINK YOU'RE GOING?' he shouted, jumping to his feet and blocking my exit.

'Home, Martin,' I said, my voice quavering slightly. 'I'm tired. It's late, and I have work tomorrow.'

'So do I, but I'm not letting you go leaving things like this. I deserve some answers, Hattie. If you don't want to marry me, should I also presume you no longer want to go out with me either?' He gave a mirthless laugh. 'Not that there has been much in the way of going out together recently. I know that's been as much my fault as yours but' – he nodded his head slowly – 'now that I stop and think about it, you've not phoned me once to ask why I've not been around. Were you hoping we'd just fizzle out? Is that it?' His eyes pinned me to the wall, boring into mine, searching and finding the truth. His mouth set in a thin line, and he gave a snort of derision. 'Of course,' he nodded, 'what a fool I've been. The writing has been on the wall for ages, hasn't it? I've just been too busy elsewhere to stop and read it.'

'I'm sorry,' I said quietly, starting to edge around him.

Like a popped balloon, Martin's anger suddenly evaporated and, to my horror, his face crumpled.

'Don't do this to me, Hattie,' he begged.

Instantly I felt consumed by guilt. Guilt for making him feel so miserable, and guilt that I'd cheated on Martin with Nick, even though Martin didn't know about that. I knew in my heart of hearts this break-up was necessary, but I so wished I'd done it before I'd slept with Nick. The tears were pouring down his cheeks now, and he was openly sobbing. I found myself choking up at his visible distress. This was awful. Terrible. To cause a person such angst wasn't in my nature, and yet it was happening right in front of me. And it was my fault.

*Careful*, said Josh inside my head. Without speaking, I acknowledged that I'd just blamed myself, and then mentally retraced my steps away from some of those words regarding culpability. Yes, Martin was upset. He was crying. But then tears are natural when a couple break up. After all, it could so easily have been the other way around – Martin falling in love with someone else and needing to extricate himself from *me*. Break-ups happen to everyone at some point in their lives, sometimes several times over. And whilst the person on the receiving end might have a meltdown and a bad case of the screaming heebie-jeebies, it doesn't mean that it's acceptable for them to—

*Correct*! said Josh, interrupting my train of thought and once again speaking into my mind. *You're doing really well, Hattie. Keep it up. Do not waver from these thought processes while you are reviewing.*

'Hattie, please,' said Martin, 'I can't bear it.' His arms were around me in a trice and he was sobbing into my hair, gulping like crazy. Even from my safe viewing point I could feel my heart squeezing with compassion at his suffering. I watched as my other self patted Martin's back absent-mindedly, as one might do when trying to soothe an upset child. Pat, pat, pat, there, there, there. I was murmuring soft words now, trying to comfort him, and for a moment it seemed to be working. His heaving chest was settling down to a more regular rate, the sobs quieting. Reassured that he was over his initial angst, I made to move away. Except I couldn't. Martin's grip upon me had tightened, and he was now speaking urgently into my ear.

'Don't go, Hats,' he said, abbreviating my name to a short form I hated. 'Stay a little longer. Don't leave me yet.'

'I really think I should go,' I said, gently attempting to extricate myself from his grasp.

'In a bit, after I've made love to you.'

I recoiled in horror. 'No,' I said, wriggling in his enforced embrace, the flat of my hands moving to his shoulders, ready to push him away.

'Please, Hats, just for old time's sake. One final bit of rumpy-pumpy so I have a lovely memory to look back upon.'

'No,' I said again. 'We've made memories for you to look back upon.'

'Please.'

'I said no.'

'But I *want* to,' he insisted, his boozy breath hot upon my ear. Too late I realised that the previous chuggy gasps of upset had changed to those of desire. I went to shove him away, but in a flash his hands had grabbed my wrists.

'Playing hard to get, Hats?' he said, a gleam in his bloodshot eyes.

'Like heck,' I hissed, fists flailing helplessly. 'I bloody well said *no*.'

'Don't give me that,' he puffed, attempting to push me back down on the sofa. 'You *love* sex… you love everything about it… on the odd occasion we got it together,' he added. His breathing was getting more laboured now, and, Christ, I'd forgotten how strong he was. 'Oooh, you naughty girl, you're taking playing hard to get to the next level!'

'I'm really not!' I squeaked, alarm well and truly setting in.

'Yes, you are! You wicked little creature, you're teasing me. It used to be one of our things, remember? I once chased you round and round my bedroom with you shrieking, "Come and get meeee!" and you're doing it now, aren't you?'

'Don't be ridiculous,' I spluttered, wondering what – or who – he was talking about. 'You've never chased me round your bed—'

But my protest was cut off as I crashed backwards on the sofa, with Martin's full weight on top of me, his mouth coming down hard on mine. It was like kissing the bottles of pub empties. Wet lips and smelly breath. God, I could hardly breathe, and panic was now well and truly consuming me. One thing was definite. He meant business. This was a man who liked to remove himself from his desk at one o'clock and head off to his employer's on-site gym. How many times had he bored me to tears talking about the weights he'd lifted in his lunch hour? And then there was the squash. Three times a week he socked balls at a wall with various workmates. Martin wasn't physically strapping, but he was very wiry and, right now, it was like wrestling with a lump of iron. Just when I thought my lungs might burst from lack of air, he pulled away.

'You scrumptious thing. Such a little temptress. Keep playing hard to get, Hattie, it's really turning me on.'

'Martin, there is no playing about this. I'm deadly serious. Do you hear?'

'Oooh, this is so exciting, I had no idea you could be so assertive, you wicked tease.'

'That's because I really don't want to *mmmmmm*—'

He was kissing me again, bruising my lips, and grinding his hips against mine.

'Lovely,' he gasped, as he came up for air again, 'but don't resist me quite so much, my darling, otherwise I might have to spank you for being such a naughty girl.' One hand was pawing at my dress now, rucking up the hem, and I squealed in anguish. Dear God, things were getting seriously out of hand. I bucked under his weight, but to no avail. As his hand reached my pants and began yanking, I filled my lungs and let out an almighty scream. This was a flat. We were on the top floor, but people lived below. I just hoped they were in and would hear my cry for help. I was just revving up to make another bloodcurdling shriek when Martin clamped his other hand over my mouth. 'My, my, Hattie, you are being a mischievous minx, aren't you! But, darling, be a little more considerate of the neighbours, eh? Meanwhile carry on playing hard to get. It's thrilling. Wonderful. I love it.'

I whipped my head to the side, momentarily loosening his grip over my mouth.

'You're not listening to me, Martin,' I gasped, 'please stop. I'm not up for this, but you're not taking on board what I'm saying.'

'Ooooh,' he cried, 'you're getting all prissy now, when I know that really you're gagging for it.' His hand clamped over my mouth again, and for a moment I really did gag. My pants were down, and he was lifting his hips to undo his zipper. I wriggled frantically, desperate to shake him off. His hand momentarily shifted on my lips and, without missing a beat, I clamped down hard, like a Pit Bull, right on the fleshy bit between the thumb and forefinger, hanging on for all I was worth. Martin bellowed at me to let go, but I didn't dare, shaking my head from side to side like a dog refusing to give up a bone.

'FUCKING HELL!' he screamed, momentarily removing his weight from me. I rolled off the sofa and onto the floor, shaking like an aspen caught in a gale-force wind. I half-scrambled to my feet but my legs gave way as he kicked one foot into the back of my knees. Suddenly I was nosediving onto the floor.

'Oooh, you're wanting to play really rough now, eh, my darling!' he panted, grabbing my hands and twisting them behind my back. 'That's fine by me, Hattie. I love it. I'm loving it all.'

As the carpet rushed up to my face, I found myself once again unable to move, spitting out the taste of blood from where I'd bitten his hand. I went to scream again but my face was pushed into the Axminster as, with a cry of triumph, Martin finally did what he'd been determined to do.

# Chapter Twenty-Eight

When it was over, Martin collapsed on top of me, hugging me hard.

'Oh my darling,' he moaned, 'Thank you.'

I couldn't believe my ears. Shuddering and jerking uncontrollably, a part of me wanted to burst into tears, but the waterworks wouldn't oblige. Instead I was silent. Wide-eyed. Numbness enveloped me like a blanket. Presumably it was shock. I'd bitten my cheek where his weight had slammed me down onto the carpet, and my whole body ached as if I'd gone ten rounds in a boxing ring.

'Why are you trembling?' he crooned, stroking my hair. 'You must have had a sugar crash from expending all that energy. I'll get you some chocolate in a minute. When I've got my breath back. I must admit, Hats, I never had you down for wanting a bit of the old rough and tumble. That was quite a nip you gave my hand. For one fleeting second, I almost thought you wanted me to stop, ha ha ha! But then I realised it was all part of your exceptionally cunning act.'

'No,' I croaked, 'I wanted to hurt you.'

For a moment, Martin looked at me uncertainly. He was sweating heavily, and his eyes were bright and glassy from the booze, but something in my tone had sent a moment of doubt flickering across his features. A second later he waved his hand, as if in dismissal of such thoughts.

'Of course you didn't mean to hurt me,' he said, half laughing. He released me to prop himself up on one elbow, peering at the injury with mild consternation. 'Hmm, I might have to put a plaster on it. Actually, maybe not. It seems to be more bruised than anything.' He wrapped his arms around me again, squeezing me with what I can only presume was affection on his part. He gave a sigh of contentment. 'Anytime you want a re-run, I'm more than happy to oblige.'

I was so gobsmacked I momentarily couldn't speak. My body was still quivering, presumably from spent adrenalin. At that precise moment I couldn't have got up and run even if someone had yelled, 'Fire! Evacuate the building!'

Martin rolled me over and peered at me intently. 'My goodness, you look quite pale. Let me get that chocolate.' He hauled himself up and padded off to the kitchen. 'Shall I put the kettle on and make you a tea?'

I didn't reply, and instead curled into the foetal position, hugging my knees, shivering all the while. Martin returned a few minutes later and seemed surprised that I was still on the floor.

'Hattie, you don't look very comfortable down there.' He placed a steaming mug on the occasional table. 'Come on, let's get you onto the sofa.' He hauled me up, then tossed a bar of fruit and nut into my lap. 'There! Sugar for my sugar,' he grinned, 'although I know you're not really my sugar any more. Don't worry, I have taken on board that you and I are over. I'm not completely thick, you know. And now that we're no longer an item, well, I don't mind telling you something. A little confession. There's been a reason that you didn't hear from me for a while. You see, I was getting the glad-eye from Carol at work. She's had the hots for me for some time and – gosh, I don't know why I feel so guilty telling you this, Hattie; after all, you've been cooler than the proverbial cucumber for such a long time now – but Carol asked me out for a drink a few weeks ago, and I said yes. You were always working late for that awful boss of yours, Nick the Prick, and I thought, "Hey, Martin, why not? Carol has the best legs in the office, and your own girlfriend isn't really up for it on the odd occasion you see her." I mean, what's a bloke to do?' He looked at me, eyes wide, palms raised in a gesture of helplessness as he flopped down on the sofa beside me. 'So I said, "Yes, all right, you're on, Carol. I'll sink a pint while you sip your gin and tonic." She turned out to be very good company. Got a good brain on her' – he tapped the side of his head, as if to underline Carol's supreme handle on intelligence – 'and a damn fine pair of tits too,' he sniggered, still the worse for drink. 'Er, well, sorry to tell you this, Hattie, but it really isn't an issue now as we're both free agents, although I don't mind telling you that – at the time – I felt incredibly guilty when she took me by the hand and led me back to her place. I didn't get a wink of sleep that night. Turned out she was a right goer. Never be fooled by the quiet ones, Hattie.' He laughed uproariously. 'There she was, a veritable warrior in the workplace, always dressed in navy blue pleated skirts and prim pearls, her specs looking like they belonged to Woody Allen, barking orders in a voice like Theresa May, but the moment she kicked the bedroom door shut with one sensible lace-up shoe, she turned into Miss Whiplash.' He rubbed his chin thoughtfully, eyes glazing at the memory. 'She made *our* little farewell performance on the floor just now seem as boring as three quick thrusts in the missionary position.'

'You cannot be serious?' I croaked, finding my voice. Was this the same man who, only twenty minutes ago, had been in floods of tears begging me not to ditch him? The booze must be addling his emotions, as he'd seesawed from crying to laughter very quickly.

'You sound like John McEnroe, ah ha ha ha! Oh, don't look at me like that, Hats,' said Martin benignly. 'A man has needs, so don't blame me. Blame yourself. You were never around. I was getting a bit fed up taking matters into my own hands. It's okay now and again, but it gets a bit boring going solo with Dick all the time. You're not going to get all cross with me now, are you? Here,' he said, picking up the mug of tea he'd made and holding it in front of me. 'Drink this and calm down.'

'Calm down?' I gasped, automatically taking the tea but not finding the strength to raise the mug to my lips. I still felt as weak as a kitten. Which was a shame, because I'd have liked to tip the hot liquid straight into his groin.

'Oh dear, you *are* angry. Look, it was a one-off. I wouldn't have bonked her again. But you've made it abundantly clear *you* don't want me, so surely you won't object to me taking up with someone who does? It would be jolly unfair of you, Hats, to start laying down the law about Carol. I didn't have you down as being one of those women. You know, the type that gets all huffy and starts ranting. All that' – he posted quotation marks in the air – '"I may not want you, but I don't want anyone else to have you either" nonsense. That's really bang out of order. I'm disappointed in you, Hats. I thought you were a reasonable sort of girl.' He tutted, adopting a pious expression. 'How incredible. You read about this all the time, on the problem page of the newspaper… in magazines… online. "Dear Agony Aunty, last year my girlfriend dumped me, but then she inexplicably turned into the stalker from hell. Now, whenever I open my front door, I have to look up and down the street to make sure she's not around before I venture out. However, the moment I'm fifty yards along the pavement, she steps out of a phone box and shouts abuse, or pops out of a neighbour's wheelie bin and starts chucking empty curry cartons at me. Now I'm too scared to venture out of the house. Please help. From Agoraphobic Adrian of Aberdeen." You mustn't become all bitter and twisted, Hattie.'

The shock of my ordeal hadn't yet passed, but from somewhere deep in my belly a tiny fire was igniting. Like kindling sticks that splutter smoke, threaten to die out, and then are finally coaxed into life, the tiny flame suddenly burst forth, and my voice roared back into life.

'You just forced yourself on me,' I said accusingly. My voice sounded odd. Like it belonged to someone else. 'How *dare* you sit and deliver a patronising lecture purporting me to be bitter and twisted, when you ignored my cries to stop!'

Martin looked as though he'd been slapped. '*What* did you say?' he gasped, his mouth dropping open in astonishment.

'You heard,' I said, my voice becoming high and reedy.

'Don't be so bloody absurd,' he spluttered, suddenly outraged and rapidly sobering up. 'I can't believe you just said that, Hattie. What a disgusting thing to say. You damn well take that back.'

'I damn well won't!' I shouted. 'You completely overpowered me—'

'And didn't you love it,' he snarled, his eyes ablaze. 'You were screaming your head off, begging for it.'

'Yes, I *was* screaming!' I cried. 'Screaming at you to stop. And you took no notice.'

His eyes narrowed dangerously. 'Wow. You really are a nasty bit of work, aren't you? My God,' he hissed, 'not content to turn into a jealous ex-girlfriend, or even become a stalker, you're prepared to go the entire whole hog and turn everything on its head taking this to the next level.' He glared at me. 'This isn't even a matter for an agony aunt, is it? It's one for the police.'

'Going to report yourself, are you?' I sneered.

'No,' he said, scooping up his mobile phone from the floor where it had fallen out of his trouser pocket earlier, 'I'm going to report *you*. I shall tell the police exactly what's happened here before you blacken my name and press all manner of fabricated charges against me. You,' he said, pointing a shaking finger at me, 'are going nowhere, until the boys in blue arrive, and a female sergeant examines you and confirms you were perfectly willing to sleep with me as evidenced by the fact that you have not been beaten black and blue, nor are you covered in grit and scrapes where you've been dragged down some dark alley and, in fact—' he paused and pointed the mobile at me, quickly capturing the image of me sitting quietly on the sofa. 'Perfect! Here you are,' he flashed the screen at me, 'enjoying a post-coital cup of tea and bar of chocolate, both thoughtfully provided by muggins here. You're not even crying, are you? Hardly a picture of distress.'

His finger swiped the mobile's screen, switching it from camera to numerical keypad. As his finger hovered over the number nine, a whole host of thoughts barged their way through my brain. The police would interrogate me. I'd respond, explaining that up until an hour ago, he'd been my boyfriend. That I'd accepted an invitation to the cinema. Gone out on a date. Indeed, I'd been seeing the accused for the best part of four years. Would they believe my side of the story if they knew I'd accepted a cinema invitation and willingly gone back to his flat afterwards? How did that square up with my purporting to end the relationship? In my head, I then saw Martin giving his explanation to the police: that he'd confessed to infidelity with a colleague, and the angry girlfriend had dumped him on the spot and was so mad she'd decided to wreak revenge in the worst way imaginable. I could imagine some thin-lipped female DCI, a dead ringer for Helen Mirren, listening to Martin who, even now, was looking self-righteous and full of indignation, informing me that it was women like me who gave genuine victims a bad name. Martin was right. There was no overturned furniture in his flat. No one had come beating down the door to see what the hell had been going on. I didn't have a mark upon me. Not one bruise. Not even a scratch. My tongue prodded the graze on my inner cheek where my teeth had made contact as we'd crashed onto the floor, but that wasn't evidence of a tussle, was it? Many people bit their cheek, simply by eating a sandwich. And he'd just taken a picture of me looking perfectly calm, cuppa in hand, choccy bar on lap, the photographic evidence – complete with digitally recorded date and time – very much at odds with the allegation from a supposedly distressed woman.

I gulped. Watching myself sitting there, I could easily read my body language and private thoughts: Perhaps it *had* been my fault, after all? Perhaps I'd sent out the wrong signals? Worn the wrong outfit? Maybe earlier, when I'd been getting ready at home, I should have tossed aside my favourite fire-engine red lipstick and opted for pale pink instead, so he'd not thought I was giving him the come-on?

All these thoughts played out in a nanosecond. Martin had already pressed the keypad's number nine twice. As he went to press it a third time, I leant forward and lightly touched his arm.

'Forget ringing the police,' I said quietly.

He stared at me, for a moment not saying anything, then slowly lowered the phone.

'Sudden change of heart?' he snapped. 'Why's that then, Hattie?'

'It's my fault,' I said quietly.

'How awfully good of you to say that,' he said sarcastically.

*Take care, Hattie*, Josh was suddenly speaking urgently into my head, *because this is most definitely not your fault. Remember, you can edit the script and rectify those words to move on with your life. Do it. Now.*

'It's my fault for coming to your flat,' I corrected, 'and making myself vulnerable to you taking advantage of me, but understand one thing, Martin. If I ever hear a whisper of another woman claiming that you did the same thing to her, I'll be crawling out of the woodwork faster than a termite.'

'Get out of here,' he hissed, snatching back the tea and chocolate.

'Don't worry,' I said, just about managing to stand up on still-wobbly legs. 'I'm going.'

'Go to hell,' was his parting shot.

At the time, I'd wondered if there really was such a place as Hell and, if so, had secretly wished with vehemence that Martin would be delivered there forthwith to spend all eternity in a place full of burning brimstone. Such had been the anger behind that thought, I'd even blamed myself for what had happened next. Because hours later, Martin was involved in a fatal car crash. His vehicle had become a fireball, and he'd exited this world in the devil's own flames.

# Chapter Twenty-Nine

*Can you find it in your heart to take back that secret desire about wishing Martin an afterlife of brimstone and fire, Hattie?* said Josh, speaking inside my head. *All these years later, do you still hope that Martin is in some cavernous place, shovelling red-hot coals whilst confined in chains?*

I sighed, suddenly dog-tired from reviewing this piece of high drama. *No, not any more. Not after knowing what happened afterwards.*

*Good. Because despite the outcome of what happened to him, it was nothing to do with your secret desire to have him banished to all eternal Hell. You can't change someone else's destiny, only your own. So please finish this episode in a way that is positive for you, allowing no stain to be imprinted on your soul.*

*Okay, I'll do my best.*

I returned with a whoosh to the scene with Martin, watching as the younger me hauled herself up from his sofa and shakily walked to the apartment door. Martin was walking with me, almost hustling me along. He was probably still over the limit booze-wise, but his manner was as sober as a policeman's as he practically escorted me off the premises. He leant across me and released the security catch, letting the door swing wide open.

'I never want to see you again, Hattie.'

'I have a feeling you won't,' I said, pausing on the threshold to look back at him, 'but nonetheless, I wish you well.'

A flicker of surprise crossed Martin's face. Had he, in that moment, privately acknowledged that he *had* been in the wrong after all? That he *had* deliberately misconstrued my protests for playing hard to get, just because his ego had been dented at my refusal to marry him? Some people can go through life lying to everyone but, ultimately, can you spend a lifetime lying to yourself? Once, I'd certainly thought so. After all, I'd done the same thing. But ultimately, you must own up. Not to others. Not even to a priest in a confessional with a hotline to God. But to yourself. As I turned away from Martin, I knew that my good wishes had jolted him into reflecting upon his drunken behaviour. And as I took myself off into the night, all I knew was that somewhere deep within my body another layer of heaviness was suddenly lifting itself up and being cast aside. I closed my eyes and sucked in a deep breath of sweet night air. When I opened them again, I was back with Josh.

'You are putting right the past just perfectly,' he said, giving my hand a quick squeeze. 'How are you feeling?'

'Different,' I said slowly. 'Lighter. Like I've just emerged into full-blown sunshine after living in a dark cave.' I was astonished at how skippy my soul felt just seconds after reviewing such serious trauma. It was beyond liberating. 'You know,' I said teasingly, 'I'm starting to feel like you're my own personal therapist. Is that what you do here? Counsel lost souls?'

He laughed. 'Nope. Believe it or not, you are counselling yourself. Although I'd prefer to change that word to "healing". I'm merely a tool that's giving you a little cosmic guidance,' he said with a wink. 'Now then, Hattie. Having shaken off a huge blanket of negative energy, how about we soup-up your soul with a high-voltage dose of fun?'

I gazed at the man before me, so unlike any other I'd known, and not for the first time found myself wishing he resided on the Earth plane, instead of this halfway place. Why was life sometimes so unfair?

'Well?' he prodded.

'Yes please,' I said eagerly. God, did he even have to ask? I didn't care what we did, just so long as we were doing it together.

'Then come with me, Madame,' he said, sweeping low in a mock bow before taking me by one hand, 'because I do believe your taxi is on its way as we speak.'

'My taxi?' I laughed, allowing him to lead me by the hand, out of the pink and white bedroom, across the lounge and out to the veranda, all the while relishing the fizzy tingles enveloping my hand, shooting straight up my arm, and setting my entire being aglow.

He glanced upwards, searching the skies. 'Here it is.'

I followed his gaze, staring into the lemony light, my jaw slowly being overcome by gravity as an enormous fluffy white cloud zoomed over the horizon and practically skidded to a halt by the veranda. If I lived in this place forever, I'd never quite get used to the bizarreness of it all.

'Sometimes,' said Josh, 'the bizarre can be quite normal.'

'You must be kidding,' I snorted, as we stepped on the cloud and sank into billowing, slightly shifting seats. 'I can't quite see myself with one of these parked on my driveway, or ringing up the DVLA and asking how much road tax to pay on something that moves without sound and is a zillion times faster than a Ferrari.' I settled back in my super-soft seat, secretly thrilled to be experiencing such weirdness.

'Enjoy the ride, Hattie.'

I did just that, privately telling myself not to keep questioning yet another surreal experience, and that the only thing that mattered about being whisked away upon this cloudy vehicle was to enjoy the experience with my gorgeous travelling companion. We were rising upwards now, thankfully at a far steadier speed than the one at which the cloud had arrived. Despite the ever-increasing altitude, neither my breathing nor my feeling of wellbeing was affected. The temperature remained pleasant, although a slight wind was evident. I shook my head, enjoying the breeze lifting my hair, feeling it ripple down my back and tickle the sides of my face. I couldn't remember the last time I'd felt so carefree. It was invigorating.

Higher and higher we soared, until this strange world was spread below like a vast tablecloth, the trees and mountain range looking like threads of green and white embroidery flanked by the occasional blue strand as rivers, here and there, twisted through the landscape. I was so engrossed in the vista below, that for a few moments I failed to notice the elevated scenery – and light changes – going on around us.

'I know you're enjoying the view, Hattie,' said Josh, interrupting my reverie, 'but look to your right.'

I tore my eyes away from the ground and gasped. 'It's a rainbow,' I said moronically.

'And not just any old rainbow,' Josh smiled. The spectrum of colours reflected on his skin, and bounced off his clothing, distorting his glowing white jeans and shirt into undulations of red, orange, yellow, green, blue, indigo, violet, and every shade in between. I looked down at my hands folded in my lap and saw that they too had become a myriad of shifting colour. How strange. And very beautiful.

'On Earth,' he said, 'the arch of colours visible in the sky is caused by the refraction and dispersion of the sun's light by water droplets in the atmosphere.'

'Are you about to go all scientific on me again?' I teased.

He grinned. 'Possibly. The job of a pilot is to watch his instrument gauges and not to listen to his own heartbeat, as someone once famously said. But what you're witnessing here is the heart vibration of the seven-plus billion people who inhabit Earth. And each of those vibrations are, just like a pilot's instrument gauges, being monitored by every Earth individual's personal spirit guide.'

'Uh oh, forget the science, you're going all religious on me instead.'

'I promise you I'm not. Just keep an open mind for a moment. Everything is made of waves – which includes thoughts. You cannot see or touch a thought, but you know it exists. But here, in this place, it is possible to see all those collective thoughts in all their glorious colour. From this perspective they appear as a constantly moving, shifting and flickering light that registers to the visual senses as a rainbow. But if you were to pluck one piece of gold or red or violet from this enormous structure in front of you, and put it to your ear, you would hear the very thoughts passing through an individual's mind. Assigned guides do their very best to assist the hearts of everyone. Why are you looking at me like that, Hattie?'

'I've asked you before, but I'll ask you again. Are you my guide?'

Josh smiled. 'No, but I *am* a co-ordinator, although that's not quite the same thing. You have a guide – but it's not me,' he added. 'Your own guide has been having a tough time.'

'Oh?'

'Yeah – trying to get your life, and thoughts, back on an even keel. Back to a place where you feel happy at a soul level. But because you were out of kilter with yourself at a much deeper level and had erected huge emotional barriers around yourself making your guide's job a very tricky one, that's where I came in to give some temporary assistance.'

'Right,' I said, not liking the word 'temporary' at all. I didn't want Josh to be transitory. I wanted him to be permanent. Even though I knew it wasn't possible to stay here forever – and nor did I want to anyway, such was the longing for my family and child, even my nutty dog – but if only I could somehow blend this place with my more usual habitat, so that Josh was part of my other life. The real life. The one that was full of wind and sunshine, hail and snow, and where rainbows were rarely glimpsed, and definitely didn't manifest like this one.

'You're looking sad, Hattie,' said Josh pensively.

'I don't mean to be sad,' I said, my voice wistful with longing.

'I can't read your thoughts, but I can read your heart's desire, and I know you've been without love for a long time.'

'You're starting to sound like a gypsy with a crystal ball,' I said flippantly, hoping to goodness my 'heart's desire' was being discreet and not blabbing its mouth off to Josh.

'You crave love.'

I flushed. 'Don't we all?' I muttered.

'Yes,' he said simply.

'Actually, I'll take what I said back. After all, a nun or a monk can spend very solitary lives not having the love of anyone.'

'They have the love of God,' said Josh, softly, 'and that's the purest love of all.'

'I'm out of my depth here,' I said, feeling like I was something of a failure in not grasping all this love business.

'No, you're not a failure,' said Josh, reading my thoughts again. 'Love is multi-stranded, Hattie. Just like this rainbow. The love you have for your parents is not the same as the love you have for your child and that isn't the same as the love you feel for your dog or the love you have for your home. Do you understand what I'm trying to say here? Love can be so many things… gentle, like when we care for a frail parent… or savage, as we roar like the lion protecting its young. There are many shades of love, and many colours of us.'

I boggled silently at the rainbow, feeling like I was skirting around the edges of something terribly profound but couldn't quite put my finger on it.

'This conversation is getting too heavy,' said Josh, standing up. My thoughts instantly scattered like skittles being knocked down by a bowling ball. 'Come on, I didn't bring you here to get all maudlin and confused. Take my hand.'

'We're getting off the cloud?' I asked, suddenly feeling panicky. What, up here, goodness knows how many miles above sea level? Not that I could see any sea, but still. Josh was obviously reading my mind again because he answered immediately.

'Are you already forgetting everything so recently learnt? What happened to believing the unbelievable? And allowing yourself to trust? It's not that long ago you were checking out underwater worlds without drowning, remember?'

I nodded, and took a deep breath. 'Right,' I said, sounding a hell of a lot more confident than I felt. 'So, we're getting off this cloud and, er, then what?'

Josh tutted. 'I told you back down there,' he jerked his head, 'we're going to do some fun stuff and ride a rainbow.'

'Okay,' I said uncertainly, 'and how do we do that?'

'You're in one of the universe's best theme parks,' said Josh, giving a mischievous grin, 'and in a moment or two, we're going to slide down this rainbow.'

I stared at him, my eyes widening with alarm. 'Slide down it? You mean… all the way back to the ground?'

'Where else?' he quipped.

'B-but what if I fall off?'

'Come on, Hattie, I've already told you. You *think* yourself back on again. Just like when we levitated off the veranda. If you're worried, hang on to me.'

I didn't need telling twice. I grabbed hold of Josh's arm, clinging on like a limpet as we stepped off the cloud and stood on the rainbow's apex. I had a bizarre moment of déjà vu, as if a part of me was travelling back in time to the days when I used to go to discos with my school mates, thrilling at the sight of the huge spinning mirrored mosaic ball over the dance floor. It had always twinkled and flashed with a million colours from the DJ's special-effect strobe lights.

'A disco, eh?' Josh chuckled. 'Well, why not!'

Suddenly the heavens were filled with the sound of 'Stayin' Alive' as Josh danced me across the rainbow, his white jeans and shirt instantly transforming into Tony Manero's famous white three-piece suit complete with flares. I threw back my head and laughed uproariously.

'This is too cheesy for words,' I hooted, as the familiar rhythms of the bass guitar sent my feet tap-tapping across the shifting colours, and the sound seemed to echo joyfully a million times around me. I couldn't remember the last time I'd felt so ridiculously happy. They say one should dance like nobody was watching. Well, Josh was watching, but as he didn't seem to mind making a total tit of himself, then neither did I. Which was exactly what we did whilst executing an impressive series of knee-drops, splits and finger pointing. Josh was laughing with me, not at me, and we were still laughing when he swept me into his arms and spun me round and round and round, until I was dizzy and completely out of breath.

'Hang on to me tight now, Hattie,' he said, 'because we're about to do something that John Travolta and his leading lady never did.'

Suddenly we were speeding, like skiers on the steepest black run, travelling over the crest of the rainbow and plummeting down the arch as the Bee Gees sang in their falsetto voices about wings and heaven and shoes. I was behind Josh now, arms wrapped around his waist and clinging on for dear life as our bodies blended together, swaying in time to the harmony of music, light and colour. I couldn't remember when I'd ever felt so terrified – or exhilarated. As we went into an almost vertical freefall down the rainbow, Josh spoke directly into my head.

*In this world, we have a saying. Want to know what it is, Hattie?*
*Sure.*

*That when you fall down a rainbow, you will fall in love.*

I didn't reply. After all, what was there to say? I was already doing just that.

# Chapter Thirty

'You're very quiet,' said Josh.

We were back in the Halfway Lounge, the pair of us having flopped down on a sofa apiece.

'I guess I'm just catching my breath,' I said untruthfully. The ride had indeed left me breathless, but breathless with joy. Whereas now… well, now I suddenly felt unbearably morose. *Good heavens, Hattie, what's the matter with you? One moment you're more buoyed up than a hot air balloon, dancing on rainbows and wrapping your arms around Heaven's answer to Mr Hunk of the Month, and then you're carrying on like a two-year-old who's had its sweets taken away.*

'You need something to perk you up,' said Josh. 'After all, you've been expending a lot of energy again – and emotional energy at that.'

I knew he was referring to Martin, and the trauma of what had happened in my ex-boyfriend's flat, culminating in his abrupt and shocking death, but in all truth that little bit of drama review suddenly seemed light years ago.

What was really upsetting my emotional applecart was Josh's little homily. The one about falling down a rainbow straight into love. Because I now knew, without a shadow of doubt, that I was falling in love with Josh. Even though I'd only been in the Halfway Lounge for what seemed like three or four days – I'd lost track of the precise time lapse – a part of me peculiarly felt that I'd known Josh for so much longer. Not days, not weeks, but years. And the growing feeling of love that I had for him went beyond attraction – of which there were pulsating high levels on my part. Indeed, this feeling of love even exceeded my desire for him to get off his sofa, stride manfully across the room, and roger me senseless – the thought of which suddenly made me feel quite faint. But sweeping all that to one side, I now understood that this feeling was one of those other shades of love. One of those other colours that Josh had touched upon when he'd been talking of love being multi-stranded. There seemed to be many layers to the way I was now feeling about him. Yes, I wanted to kiss him and spend an entire year in bed with him without any external interruptions, but I also wanted to do other things with him. Like, watch a sunset together. Take Buddy for a walk. Stroll hand in hand. Cook together. Eat together. Wash-up together. I wanted to sit on the other side of my French doors watching him mow the lawn while I sewed a button on his shirt. Me, who could hardly thread a needle. But he brought out all these emotions in me. Feelings that I wanted to do things I knew I could do, but also things that I had no idea how to do, but was willing to learn, to try, so I could do them both with him and for him. I didn't just want to be his lover, I wanted to be his best friend. His everything. Forever.

'Forever is a long time, Hattie,' said Josh quietly.

I stared at him, appalled that he might have read the torrent of emotions cascading like a waterfall through my mind. 'Did you just catch everything I was thinking?' I gasped.

'No. Just that last word. Forever. Do you want to tell me about it?'

I shook my head slowly. 'I'd like to. But I can't.'

'No such word as can't,' he said, eyes twinkling. 'Here, drink this.'

'Ah, Essence of Rainbow,' I said, giving a small smile as the familiar drink appeared in a tall glass on an occasional table in front of me. 'Very apposite after our fun ride.' I picked it up and sipped gratefully.

'So, you were telling me about forever,' Josh prompted.

'No, I wasn't. You were being nosy.'

'Indeed. Nothing wrong with being nosy,' he teased. 'Human beings adore being nosy. It's a favourite pastime, along with a good old-fashioned gossip.'

'I thought gossip was something only women did.'

'Don't you believe it,' Josh chuckled. 'Men love a bit of tittle-tattle, too. They just chinwag about it in a different way to the female side of the species. Men prefer to do it with a pint in hand, ideally in their local pub with an enormous plasma screen on the wall televising a football match. But if you can hear over the din of roaring encouragement to their team, and shouting at the ref for not picking up a foul, you'll catch an in-between conversation going on, and it's nothing to do with the football and everything to do with how Steve has blown three thousand pounds on a heap of junk masquerading as a car that his darling fiancée knows nothing about, indeed would hit the roof if she found out about, given that Steve is meant to be saving up for his wedding; or how the other guys admire Steve's bravado at paying rent on a garage in the next town on account of him being unable to take the car home, not to mention the thrill his mates are getting dreaming up excuses to their own wives in order to disappear for a few hours to visit Steve's secret garage, getting oil under their fingernails as they try and breathe life back into the knackered engine, all the while gossiping about the new barmaid and the size of her big—'

'Careful,' I warned.

'—blue eyes,' Josh finished. 'Whatever did you think I was going to say?' he asked innocently.

'So men like to gossip, too,' I said, arching an eyebrow. 'And thanks for the tip-off that you're actually all a thoroughly dishonest bunch blowing the housekeeping on tatty bangers whilst discussing the attractive barmaid's big—'

'Careful,' he warned.

'—blue eyes,' I finished.

'Well, we're not all like that, but you get the picture. Men just choose not to chinwag sitting round their bestie's kitchen table nursing a coffee and munching their way through packets of chocolate biscuits.'

'Ah, you've sussed me out!' I giggled. 'It's true. I've spent many a happy hour putting the world to rights with my neighbour, Jo, munching too many bickies and drinking so much caffeine my nerves end up jangling like an armful of bracelets.'

'And, as I said before, men are also remarkably nosy.'

'You did say.'

'But *you* still haven't.'

'Haven't what?'

'Told me why you were thinking about "forever".'

I drained my glass and set it down carefully on the occasional table. I cleared my throat, then shifted my weight on the sofa. A regrouping gesture. 'You mentioned that, here, in this place, there's a saying that if you fall down a rainbow, you will fall in love.'

'Yes, that's right.'

'Does that mean I'll fall in love?'

'Maybe,' he replied, looking mysterious.

'So what about you?' I asked. 'You were on that rainbow with me. Will you fall in love, too?' Rather brave of me to ask that question, I thought.

'Oh, I fell in love ages ago,' he answered, his voice so matter-of-fact he could have been discussing how he enjoyed eating eggs on toast, sunny side up.

'You're in love with someone?' I squeaked, my pulse cantering off before my heart was ready, causing an unpleasant ten seconds of palpitations. Please, God, no! My brain made a mental dinging noise as a high-speed memory pinged back. 'Hang on, when we went swimming in the sea, you told me you'd never fallen in love.'

'True. I did say that. And, if you recollect, you asked me why I didn't change my personal circumstances and do a bit of cosmic ordering. But you might also remember me saying that the wheels had been put in motion on more than one occasion but, unfortunately, it's all been a bit tricky. However, the intent has been established and I'm playing the waiting game… waiting for the universe to respond in its own unique way.'

'But… but… who is she then?' I asked, confused.

'I'm not allowed to talk about me.'

'Why not?'

'Because, as a co-ordinator, I have to remain neutral at all times. And anyway, you're here to investigate the finer details of *your* life. Not mine.'

'You're being deliberately evasive, Josh.'

'Absolutely,' he grinned. 'I've already told you that love is something we all need in our lives. Every single one of us, including me. So yes. I love someone – indeed, am *in* love with someone.'

I felt crushed. Well of *course* he had someone waiting in the wings. How could I have been so stupid as to presume otherwise? Just because I couldn't see her – because of all this vibrational frequency thingy-bob stuff – didn't mean that she might not be right here in this very room! I blanched. Perhaps she was over there? On the veranda? Invisible to me, but keeping a beady eye on the tall dishevelled woman in the scruffy clobber who got herself in such a tizzy every time *her* man innocently took her hand. I looked down at my clothes in dismay, and instantly transformed them into a long floaty dress. Moments later the tatty trainers had disappeared, and my feet were encased in strappy gold sandals. Another second passed, and my toes were now pedicured and slicked with shiny red nail varnish. *There, dear*, I silently said to the empty space on the veranda, *I may not be able to ravage him, but I'll at least try and look ravishing if nothing else.*

Josh looked faintly amused at the sudden transformation. 'Nice outfit,' he commented.

'Thanks.'

'Why do you keep looking at the veranda?'

'No reason,' I said, tearing my eyes away. 'So, you were telling me.'

Josh scratched his head. 'I do believe I've lost my train of thought.'

'You were telling me about the lady you're in love with.'

He laughed. 'No, you were asking nosy questions.'

'Only because you asked the nosy question about why I was thinking of forever.'

'Touché, Hattie, but I'm still not meant to tell you about me. However' – he leant forward on his sofa, as if confiding a secret –'I will share with you that I'm in love and very happy about it. Anyway, never mind my love life, you worry about your own.'

'I don't have one,' I said sadly.

'You will,' he assured me, 'in time.'

'How do you know?' I asked, yawning again, but this time failing to hide it.

'Because I'm your co-ordinator and have to make it my business to know these things.'

'You're incredibly mysterious,' I said, feeling irked. Why was his private life such a secret when mine was an open book for him to read? It wasn't fair.

'You're tired,' he said, watching me yawn widely again.

Suddenly, everything caught up with me, from the exhaustion of reviewing the chapter of life with Martin, to the adrenalin-pumping ride down the rainbow with Josh. My eyelids drooped. Sleep was calling. I didn't even have the energy to stagger through the door to the bedroom beyond. Josh stood up and swiftly crossed the room. A pillow materialised in one hand, a folded duvet in the other.

'Come on, get those feet up on the sofa,' he said, tipping me sideways like an ironing board, and popping the pillow under my head. It was as fluffy as the cloud I'd sat upon earlier. Moments later the duvet fluttered over me, softer than silk. I snuggled down with a contented sigh.

'Are you going to give me a goodnight kiss?' I asked, keeping my tone deliberately playful.

'If that's what you want,' he said gruffly. Leaning over me, his lips softly brushed my temple. I squirmed with delight, as did my eyebrows. Indeed, they felt like they might swoon right off my forehead. I was just trying to muster up the courage to light-heartedly ask if another kiss might be forthcoming, but this time on the lips, when everything went black.

# Chapter Thirty-One

When I next opened my eyes, it was with the feeling that I'd slept for a hundred years. I stretched, luxuriating in the cosiness of the covers over my body, frowning slightly as I observed the unicorns galloping all over a faded duvet from my secondary school years. I was back in my old bedroom at Mum and Dad's.

I looked at the clock on the bedside table. It was a little after seven in the morning. In the kitchen below, my mother could be heard humming along to the radio. Every now and again there was the sound of muffled conversation as my parents spoke to each other.

It was Monday. A work day. It was also the morning after that unspeakable night before.

My parents had already been in bed and asleep when I'd crept into the house after leaving Martin's apartment. I'd quietly made my way to the family bathroom, shut the door softly behind me, and started running a bath, tipping copious amounts of Mum's luxury bubbles under the tap. The writing on the plastic bottle had claimed to relax and rejuvenate in seconds. As the waters had started to foam, I'd found myself hoping that the manufacturer's promise wasn't just marketing hype.

Stripping off my clothes, I'd tossed them into one corner. Later they would find themselves bundled into a black sack and tossed into the wheelie bin outside, along with the shoes I'd been wearing. The physical distancing of what had happened was now firmly in motion. I wanted no reminders, including *that* set of clothes and footwear. Likewise, I was also now distancing myself mentally and emotionally. As I stepped into the boiling water, it was with only one thought. To scrub myself clean.

I must have stayed in the water for nearly an hour, until Mum tapped on the door, wanting to spend a penny.

'Are you all right, darling?' she stage-whispered, on the other side of the wooden panels.

'Yes,' I lied. In fact, numbness had descended and everything that had happened was buried deep within. I was reminded of Russian doll trinket boxes. The smallest now contained something hidden. And it had been placed inside another trinket box. Then another. And yet another. Over and over until it was unreachable. But I knew it was there. A tiny particle embedded somewhere deep within me.

'Will you be much longer?' Mum asked. 'Only I shouldn't have had that last cup of tea. I knew it would disturb me later.' I could hear her tutting at herself, out on the landing.

'No, I was getting out anyway,' I answered. Which was true. The water had long since cooled. Shivering slightly, I pulled the plug and then dripped my way across the floor, wrapping one of Mum's soft mismatched towels around my body before releasing the bolt on the door.

'You're bathing late,' said Mum. She looked bug-eyed as she stepped from the dark landing into the harsh glare of the energy bulb dangling on its flex from the ceiling. 'I thought you had a wash before you went out?'

'I fancied another one,' I said.

'Don't mind me,' she said, whisking up her nightie and sitting on the loo, 'we're all girls together.'

'Of course,' I said, towelling myself off rigorously. Mum and I had never had any inhibitions in front of each other.

'So, er, how was your evening with Martin?' she asked tentatively. 'Did you tell him you no longer wanted to be his girlfriend, or did you see sense and not tell him about that boss of yours? I hope you kept schtum,' she said, not pausing for breath, 'and realised the error of your ways, because nice young men like Martin don't come along every day of the week, Hattie.'

I sighed. This wasn't the time, the place, or hour for my mother to be asking inquisitive questions.

'Martin who?' I asked, my voice neutral, but my mind screaming with protest at voicing his name, instantly retreating and putting up steel barriers, padlocking them too before throwing the key away.

'I see,' she said, lips pursing. 'You've let Martin go in favour of Nicholas Green. Let's hope you don't regret it.'

At the mention of Nick, I felt my body relax. 'I have no regrets,' I said.

'Your skin is very red,' she said, whipping up her knickers and flushing the chain.

'Is it? I must have stayed in the bath too long.'

Mum leant over the side of the tub and washed her hands in the draining bathwater, ever conscious of water meter costs. I immediately felt a pang of guilt for having washed twice a few hours apart, the second time in a bath so deep it must have almost used up all the hot water.

'Good film?' she asked, attempting to sound less hostile, despite knowing her dream son-in-law was no longer on the scene.

'Yes,' I replied, although already I couldn't remember what film I'd seen. Everything was blurring around the edges now. Even the person I'd watched it with. The mind is a marvellous thing. Sometimes anyway. And certainly, after saying goodnight to Mum and having a few hours of sleep, the events of the night before felt far removed. Like it had happened to an acquaintance, rather than a friend. Thus was my state of mind when I walked into the kitchen the following morning, dressed for work.

'Morning, love,' said Mum. 'Are you feeling all right?' she asked, her brow furrowing.

'Absolutely fine,' I said, reaching for the loaf of bread on the worktop and slotting a couple of slices into the toaster.

'You look shattered. Not coming down with anything, are you?'

'No,' I said, shaking my head.

'I'm sure our girl is fine, Penny,' said Dad, from behind his newspaper. 'If you're making a cuppa, Hattie, stick one in here for your old pa.' He tapped the mug beside him, and I moved across the kitchen to take it. 'Ready for the office I see. Mum and I have taken the day off to tackle some outstanding chores together. We'll go back to work tomorrow for a rest, ha ha! How's that boss of yours? Still making you work late?'

'Oh, er, yes, sometimes.' My father didn't know too much about Nick. Certainly nothing about me hoping to become Nick's new girlfriend. He knew *of* him, obviously, mainly due to the aforesaid 'acute mentionitis' I'd suffered ever since stepping through the doors of Shepherd, Green & Parsons, but Dad had never put two and two together. It was only my mother, with her female intuition, who'd finally joined up all the dots. I could tell from her body language she was itching to get me on my own, so she could grill me further about what had happened with Martin.

As it happened, that conversation never took place. Not that day anyway. Instead a very different one occurred. When the telephone rang…

# Chapter Thirty-Two

'Hello?' said Mum, picking up the handset. 'Oh hi, Joy. Heavens, you're ringing early.'

I watched my mother from the chair I was perched on at the kitchen table as I mechanically chewed my toast. Mum tucked a strand of hair behind one ear as she listened. Joy was Martin's mother, but there was nothing untoward about her ringing my mum. She and my mother often rang each other up for a gossip, although quite why my mother found Joy good company was beyond me.

I turned back to the headlines I'd been reading from my father's newspaper as he sat opposite me, screwing my eyes up myopically to read about Tony Blair visiting Libyan leader Colonel Muammar al-Gaddafi in return for the dismantling of Libya's Weapons of Mass Destruction programme.

'Joy, what's the matter? Can you slow down, I don't understand—'

My concentration on the leading story fragmented. As I watched myself in this ethereal review time, the young Hattie sitting at the table in her parents' kitchen had paused, an anxious look upon her face. Had Martin told his mother about my accusation on our final night together? Had Joy been outraged? Was she, even now, bending Mum's ear and telling Mum exactly what she thought of her despicable daughter?

I froze, listening carefully as Mum talked to Martin's mother, a woman who was nothing like her given name. Like Blair and Gaddafi, she had the ability to smile to your face whilst stabbing you in the back. Today, as it turned out, Joy had valid reasons to be joyless.

'Oh my God, *what*?' Mum shrieked. Such was the volume of this last word that Dad lowered his newspaper, a frown upon his face, and I paused in taking another bite of my toast. Mum had spun round to face both Dad and me, colour draining from her complexion faster than last night's bath water. She looked stricken.

'What's happened?' asked Dad.

Mum shook her head at Dad. 'I can't take this in, Joy.' And with that she burst into tears, one hand fluttering up to her mouth.

Dad abandoned his paper, noisily scraping back his chair as he hastened over to Mum, placing an arm around her shaking shoulders, taking the phone from her with his free hand.

'Joy? Penny's gone to pieces. What's—?'

From the ethereal safety of my viewing platform, I now watched myself watching my parents. Dad's brow puckered with both puzzlement and then incredulity, his face visibly paling, as had my mother's moments earlier. His eyes widened with horror.

'I see,' he said quietly. 'There are no words, Joy. No words.'

My mother had put her head in both her hands and was openly sobbing. Dad held her away slightly, so he could better hear what Joy was saying. It was obvious to the observer that, at the other end of the phone, it wasn't just my mother who had gone to pieces and that Martin's mother was in emotional bits. Dad was coaxing information from her, encouraging her to form sentences, put stuttering words together, so he had the full picture of exactly what Joy was trying to tell him. His tone was gentle, prompting her to keep talking, and the interim silence this end was only broken by my mother's sobs and the occasional 'I see' from my father. At length though, his back stiffened. 'Now then Joy, that's not fair. At the moment, I don't think you know what you're saying – which is perfectly understandable. No, that's not true. No, Joy. I understand you're distressed, but I won't have Hattie blamed.'

I regarded myself sitting at the kitchen table, my own face becoming pinched upon hearing my father's words to Joy. At this point I didn't know for certain what Martin's mother was blaming me for, but was pretty damn sure it was going to be along the lines of me daring to sully her son's integrity. However, I didn't have to wait long to find out. My father's expression was grim as he briefly glanced my way, but upon seeing me hunched over the table, eyes wide and fearful, he quickly looked away again. At length, he solemnly thanked Joy for her call and hung up.

'Come on, love, sit down,' he murmured to Mum, guiding his distraught wife over to the table and pulling out a chair for her. She sat down heavily, swiping her hands across her face to stem the flow of tears. Dad pulled out the chair next to Mum and slowly lowered himself down, before his eyes came to rest on me. 'That was Joy.'

'Yes,' I said, my voice small and uncertain. 'I gathered.'

'You're going to have to be very brave, darling.'

I saw myself regarding my father ominously, still unaware of the news he was about to deliver to my younger self.

'What's happened?'

'Martin has died.'

'Oh,' was all I said.

The words went straight over my head. I couldn't take it in. On a scale of one to ten, it didn't even register. Was there something wrong with me? Was I some sort of emotional cripple? Was my father talking about the same person I'd been out with last night, a man who only a few hours ago had... My brain instantly swerved off in another direction. Far away. Protecting me. As I said before, the mind can be a marvellous thing.

Mum promptly collapsed over the table, her head sinking down on its wooden surface, a few strands of hair falling across the butter dish.

'I appreciate this is a hell of a shock,' said Dad, peering at me intently. 'I can't take it in myself. Understandably, Joy is distraught.'

'Obviously,' I nodded, my face emotionless. 'What happened?'

Dad took a deep breath, suddenly looking as if he'd aged twenty years.

'Apparently, after you left him last night, he rang his parents, and was in a state. Joy said he woke them up. It was late. Martin told her you'd ended your relationship with him, and you'd accused him of something unspeakable, although he didn't say what, but Joy gathers you had a row. Did you, darling?'

'Did I what?' I whispered.

'Tell him that you and he were over?'

I gulped and nodded, as Mum continued to sob, still prostrate across the table. So that's why Dad had told Joy that it was unfair to blame me. I could almost hear Martin's mother in my head, ranting in her grief, pointing the finger at me. A part of me shrivelled within, mentally throwing up my hands to ward off the accusation, but failing dismally. Oh, I felt guilty all right and spent years afterwards weighed down by it. From the moment the news of his death had broken, I had worn my culpability like a concrete cloak around my shoulders.

'Why did you end it, love?' asked Dad gently.

'I didn't love him any more,' I mumbled, 'but I don't think he loved me any more either.'

'Not according to Joy. She said he was preparing to propose to you on your birthday.'

I shook my head, my mouth suddenly dry. 'Whatever he said… whatever he'd planned… that was never going to happen. He told me he'd been having a fling with someone at his office. Recently they'd gone back to her place and… well, you know.' I wasn't used to having conversations like this with Dad, about sex and infidelity. We were close, but there are some topics you don't share with your father.

'Maybe telling you about this other woman was simply bravado on his part,' said Dad, thinking aloud, 'a bit of getting his own back and trying to hurt you, because you'd hurt him by ending it?' When I didn't reply, Dad carried on speaking, carefully picking his words. 'The thing is, love, whatever he told you, the fact remains that he was distressed enough to wake up his folks in the middle of the night. Joy told him to come on over, that he could sleep in his old bed. He told her he would sling a few things in an overnight bag and be on his way. Except he never turned up.'

I realised that Martin would have still been over the limit when driving.

'He had a collision with a lorry,' Dad continued. 'The car went up in flames, as did the HGV. The lorry driver jumped clear. But unfortunately, Martin didn't. Witnesses phoned the emergency services. Apparently, Martin's car was still registered to his parents' address, so a couple of policemen turned up on their doorstep a little while later.'

'I see,' I said quietly. 'I'd better ring Joy back. Offer my condolences.' Even as I said the words, a part of me marvelled at how detached I sounded. But nothing was registering on an emotional level.

'I wouldn't do that just yet, love,' said Dad, shaking his head, clearly wanting to protect me from Joy's venom. 'She's understandably not herself right now, and I don't think you are either, Hattie. You might be composed at the moment, but this is going to hit you hard later. Mark my words.'

Whereupon my mother, who had remained weeping quietly into the table throughout this exchange, suddenly reared up like a sea monster, her face blotchy and red, and pointed an accusing finger at me.

'Joy's right. This is all your fault!'

I shrank back in my seat, appalled.

'Now, Penny, that's not fair,' said Dad.

'But it's true,' Mum cried. 'Our daughter tossed Martin to one side. And what for? Or should I say' – her puffy eyes narrowed – '*who* for?'

'What are you talking about?' asked Dad, sounding both confused and frustrated.

'Hattie dumped Martin last night because she's got the hots for someone else. Isn't that right?' Mum demanded, through her tears.

I stared at Mum in dismay. Why was she doing this to me?

'Hattie is having an *affair* with her boss,' said Mum, her tear-streaked face now a mask of anger.

'Nicholas Green?' said Dad, looking at me, his previously grave expression turning to one of bewilderment. 'But he's a married man.'

'Yes!' shrieked Mum. 'Our daughter tossed Martin away like a tatty old slipper, casting him aside for some Lothario, when instead she should have been getting engaged to Martin. I can't bear it,' Mum cried, 'that poor boy. He should have been our son-in-law. We'll never see our daughter walk down the aisle to Martin waiting with open arms—'

'Mum, that was never going to happen anyway,' I muttered.

'—or see the children you would have raised together!' she wailed.

Which wasn't true either. Because although I didn't yet know it, Martin had left a legacy. And it was growing inside me.

# Chapter Thirty-Three

Needless to say, the rest of the day was blanketed in depression. Under the reproachful eyes of my mother, I took my guilt and shuffled off back to bed, ringing the office from my mobile. Nick wasn't yet in, but I spoke to Reception, leaving the message that a family bereavement meant I would be absent today.

I pulled the unicorn quilt up to my chin, wishing with all my heart the mythical creature would materialise in front of me, let me climb upon its back and that we'd gallop off into a fairy forest together, my very own twirly horned mount tossing his head at anybody who dared to hurt me – physically or verbally.

An hour later there was a tentative knock on the bedroom door and Dad stuck his head around.

'Ah, you're awake, love.'

'I've not been asleep,' I mumbled.

He came into the room, a cup of tea in one hand which he set down on the bedside table. 'Thought you could use a brew.'

'Thanks,' I said, giving him the ghost of a smile. Sitting up, I plumped the pillows behind me, gratefully taking the tea.

'Don't take any notice of your mum, Hattie. She was distraught. Still is, of course, but a bit calmer now.'

I nodded and took a sip of the hot liquid. 'Even so, she said some pretty awful things down there.'

'Yes,' he said tentatively. 'Look, love, tell me it's none of my business, but do you know what you're getting into with this married boss of yours?'

'He's not married, he's separated.'

'Right, but he still hasn't actually got the certificate to prove it, eh?'

I sighed. 'No. But he has his own place and there is definitely no Mrs Green living there.'

Dad contemplated the carpet for a moment. 'Are you serious about him?'

I didn't initially reply. How could I explain that my feelings were deadly serious, but that on Nick's part it could possibly be nothing more than a light-hearted diversion? After all, who wanted to come out of a marriage which – as my father had pointed out – had yet to officially end, only to immediately shack up with someone else? And not just any old someone else, but the secretary, no less. It was such a cliché. Nick's previous wives had both been highflyers. *They'd* been the ones with personal assistants and secretaries, the ones to scrawl with a flourish their signatures on company letterhead notepaper, not the one who merely typed it up and presented it for signing. At this moment in time I had no idea how Nick felt about me. It was all too new. I'd only spent one weekend with him, after all.

'I like him a lot,' I said, somewhat lamely. I was reluctant to elaborate. It would have been different if it had been my mother sitting on my bed. Indeed, we'd had many a girly gossip about the mysteries of men. But currently Mum was incommunicado.

Later in the afternoon, Joy telephoned, asking to speak to me. Passing me the handset, Dad hovered anxiously, his parental role coming to the fore, anxious to protect his little chick if the wolf in sheep's clothing so much as bared her teeth.

'Joy,' I said, gripping the phone. 'How are you?' Stupid question, in hindsight.

'Hello, Hattie,' she said, her tone brisk. 'I won't deign to give your ridiculous question an answer, but since you ask,' she added, immediately contradicting herself, 'I'm bone-tired. Understand-ably, I've not slept since the police knocked on my door.' The processing of her own devastation and loss was still in its infancy, but she'd managed to switch to auto-pilot. 'Rather than being at work and having the luxury of deciding whether to have a chocolate biscuit or shortbread on my morning tea break, instead I'm on compassionate leave' – her voice momentarily caught, but she immediately coughed and righted herself – 'planning my son's funeral.' The waves of grief coming from the handset were almost palpable.

'I can't begin to imagine what you're going through,' I whispered.

'Clearly,' she said, 'because I don't even detect tears in your voice, Hattie. How incredible is it that you went out with my boy for the best part of four years, but don't even cry when you hear the shocking news of his sudden passing?'

'Joy, it's not like that, you don't understand—'

'You're right,' she said, cutting across me, 'I don't understand. And I don't think I want to either. All I know, Hattie, is that you are one cold-hearted woman. Indeed, I suspect your veins are full of ice, not blood.'

I gasped, stung by the hatred in her tone. 'Just because I didn't want to marry your son, Joy, didn't mean I wished him dead.'

'Spare me the excuses,' she snapped. 'Right now, the only microscopic bit of comfort I'm getting is deep gratitude that a wedding will never happen. Thank God I haven't ended up with you as my daughter-in-law, because you are a wicked woman.'

Wicked? Bloody hell, that was a bit strong. For the first time since I'd heard the news of Martin's dreadful demise, tears stung the back of my eyelids. My voice, when I found it, came out as little more than a croak.

'Please let me know the funeral arrangements.'

'That's one of the reasons why I'm ringing, Hattie,' she said, her voice taking on a strangely triumphant note. 'Your parents are invited, but you are most definitely not. Stay away from my son and his send-off. If you couldn't love him in life, I will not have you squeezing out crocodile tears by his graveside in death.' From the other end of the line came the sound of a receiver crashing down.

'Are you all right, love?' asked Dad, putting an arm around me and hugging me tight.

'N-no,' I shook my head, 'I don't think I am.'

And with that I sobbed and sobbed and sobbed.

# Chapter Thirty-Four

From somewhere far away, I heard Josh's voice speaking to me.

*Tears are good, Hattie. Crying waters the soul. Refreshes and renews.*

Having started to cry, I found I couldn't stop. I was aware of Dad slipping out of my bedroom, the giveaway being the creak on the landing as his slippered feet took him away, down the stairs to Mum. Moments later he was back, but this time the protesting floorboards bore testament to two lots of footsteps.

'Darling?'

Mum. The mattress shifted as she perched.

'Sorry I was such a bitch,' she said.

Hearing her apology made me cry even harder.

'I didn't mean it,' she said, starting to sob herself. 'I was shocked at the news, and lashed out, as did Joy on the phone earlier. She doesn't know what she's saying at the moment, and I guess I didn't either.'

I had a feeling Joy knew exactly what she'd been saying – was still saying – but Mum was different.

'And whilst I had hoped,' she said, choosing her words cautiously, 'that Martin would one day be my son-in-law, it goes without saying that you are your own person, darling, and I wouldn't want you to have married him out of any sense of duty. You're young. You have your whole life ahead of you—'

She paused to blow her nose as we both realised the enormity of those last words. I did indeed have my whole life ahead of me, but someone else no longer did, and his entire family had been plunged into darkness because of it.

'—but what has happened has happened, and can't be changed,' she said, hastily ploughing on. 'However, what *can* be changed is the unkind words I said earlier. I love you, Hattie, and I want what's best for you. And whether my daughter chooses to be single or otherwise, is entirely her business and for nobody else – least of all me – to say or judge.' Her hand reached out and tucked a strand of hair behind my ear. 'Do you accept my apology, sweetheart?'

I sat up and flew into her arms, nearly knocking her off the bed.

'Of course I do,' I said, snuffling into her neck. 'I didn't mean for that to happen to him, Mum.'

'I know you didn't. I know, I know,' she nodded her head frantically. 'It was an accident. A dreadful, dreadful accident.'

'Joy has banned me from the funeral,' I gasped.

'She's crazy with grief right now. She doesn't mean it.'

'Oh but she does, Mum.'

'We'll talk to her. Of *course* you must go to the funeral. It's unthinkable for you not be there. Let things settle for now, love.'

Actually, Mum had misunderstood my shock at Joy's nastiness as upset that I'd been banned. In fact, I didn't want to be there at his graveside. Not after… my mind automatically moved away from what it had been about to voice. A coping mechanism.

Instead I said, 'It's fine. Don't push it, Mum. She and I were never exactly close anyway. I know you liked to natter to each other from time to time, but I found her hard work. I was never good enough for her precious son, and she never failed to let me know that, with her back-handed comments and snide remarks. If things *had* been different and I'd married Martin, she would probably have been the mother-in-law from hell.'

Mum nodded. 'I know what you mean, love,' she said sadly. 'She can be a very outspoken person.'

I didn't go to the funeral. I had the perfect excuse, because Joy was adamant she didn't want me there. Mum didn't go either. She was angry with Joy for banning me. However, Dad went, leaving a spray of flowers from us all on the newly dug grave. We later found out that Joy had picked them up and tossed them to one side in disgust.

*Can you forgive Joy, Hattie?* asked Josh from afar.

I felt my heart squeeze with pain. Anger too. I had been furious with Martin before he died, and livid with Joy for not knowing the whole story about her 'saintly' son.

*She called me wicked*, I cried, *and anyway, did she ever forgive ME?*

I knew, from the moment the words sounded in my head, that the question sounded petulant.

*Joy's forgiveness is neither important nor relevant. This is about you, Hattie. Your feelings… your ability to move on in life. So, I'll ask you again. Can you forgive Joy?*

I imagined myself in Joy's shoes. What if something like that had happened to my precious son? At the very thought of Fin not being in the world with me, I felt something in me claw its way to the surface screaming in protest, my throat automatically constricting with tears. It didn't bear thinking about. Would I lash out at the first person who might, in the loosest possible way, have put in motion the steps that lead to another's death? It had been dreadful to be on the receiving end of Joy's backlash, but understandable. It was human nature. Joy had never found out what Martin did. There had been no point in telling her, for it would have served no purpose, and I'd had no desire to ruin the memory of her son. No way. Joy had simply responded as any fiercely protective parent would react.

*Yes. Yes of course I forgive Joy.*

And the moment those words were mentally uttered, I felt my body sigh with relief, as if stretching after being bound with tight ropes. The viewing platform blurred, and I was suddenly back in my old bedroom again, the funeral yet to take place. I hugged Mum, as she did me, the pair of us crying into each other's hair as she apologised for her own unkind words. It was at that point we were interrupted by the doorbell.

'I'll leave you girls to it, and see who that is,' said Dad, clearly feeling a bit helpless with all this female angst emoting everywhere.

Two minutes later he was back, looking nonplussed.

'Hattie, love. There's a chap here to see you.'

Mum and I disentangled ourselves and looked at Dad questioningly.

'Who is it?' I asked, but I knew the answer almost immediately. For downstairs in the hallway, was Nick.

# Chapter Thirty-Five

'Let's take a break, Hattie,' said Josh.

I was back in the Halfway Lounge, on the sofa, and still wearing the floaty dress and strappy sandals I'd manifested earlier.

'How are you feeling?' he asked.

'Strange,' I said thoughtfully. 'For years, I've been angry at Joy for blaming me for Martin's death' – I shook my head slowly – 'but, peculiarly, it's gone.'

'There's nothing peculiar about it, Hattie. You've been dragging the resentment around for such a long time, but now it's been cast aside. Bit by bit you're shaking off the emotional shackles that have thwarted, stifled and imprisoned you in a self-built cage of misery. One by one you are removing the prison bars. Eventually the entire cage will collapse, leaving you free to take your life in a direction you've never dared dream about.'

I stood up and stretched, noting and relishing the difference within my body. Joy had once accused me of having ice flowing through my veins. Now it felt like a fizzy drink was whooshing through my arteries. Indeed, my entire circulatory system seemed to be sparkling with new-found freedom. It was such a liberating feeling it was as if, somewhere deep within me, a party was going on.

'That's what I like to hear,' Josh grinned, reading my thoughts. 'Let's prolong the party mood by doing something freakily fabulous.' Josh caught hold of my hand, and his touch instantly had the inner party bursting out through the very pores of my skin. I gave a shiver of deliciousness.

'What have you got in mind?' I asked.

'Ah ha, something that you had in *your* mind earlier!'

'You've lost me.'

'Shall I tell you, or do you want it to be a surprise?'

'Definitely a surprise,' I said, as a frisson of excitement had me catching my breath with anticipation. I wondered what he had in mind. 'Give me a clue,' I added, suddenly feeling like a five-year-old on Christmas Day, full of excitement at the first glimpse of presents under the tree.

'Okay,' said Josh, eyes twinkling mischievously, 'it involves nuzzling.'

I nearly swooned there and then at his feet. The only nuzzling I knew about was the lips-on-neck kind… hot breath whistling in one's ear, followed by gently spoken sweet nothings. Oh yesss! Gimme, gimme, gimme. I was up for some nuzzling all right. I batted my eyelids coquettishly at Josh.

'Sounds like my sort of thing,' I said, lowering my voice to what I hoped was a seductive level. 'So, er, where is this *nuzzling* going to take place?'

'Definitely not here.'

This was getting better and better. Perhaps this halfway place had a fabulous candlelit restaurant somewhere, full of atmosphere and romantic *je ne sais quoi* where Josh would manifest the perfect dinner *à deux* before leading me over to a leather sofa, the sort that was incredibly soft and squashy, and so low to the ground it was impossible to haul yourself up, in which case you might as well stay in it and, well, lie down. Horizontally. Together. Naturally. And then… my eyes glazed at the thought… and then we could get down to the serious business of *nuzzling*. I could imagine it now, his lips brushing mine, then softly moving their way across my jaw, stopping at one ear, gently nibbling on the lobe before moving around to that spot just behind your earring, that patch of skin that was super-sensitive, made your heart quicken, your breath go a bit faster, and your body squirm with delight, so that before you knew it your hands had taken on a life of their own and were moving up, up, up a bit more and I'd suddenly find myself grappling with Josh's snow-white shirt, unfastening all those glowing neon-white buttons, once again revealing the well-defined chest that I'd lusted over when he'd dragged me down to the underwater world and—

'Ready?' asked Josh, interrupting my reverie. 'You look awfully flustered, Hattie. Everything okay?'

'Yes,' I answered, trying not to gasp. But if he could get a move on, that would be brilliant. I was feeling quite faint with longing.

He led me to the door that had previously opened into the pink and white bedroom. Okay, looked like we weren't going to a restaurant with the squashy sit-soft area, but that was fine. I knew from experience that the Halfway Lounge's chamber had an extremely comfortable bed that I was more than happy to starfish upon with Josh by my side. He gave my hand a little squeeze, instantly causing havoc with the inner party so that a few metaphorical burly bouncers had to be despatched to rein in the mayhem. I steadied myself against the doorframe.

'Are you sure you're okay?' he asked, brow puckering with concern.

'Never better,' I murmured, looking up at him under my eyelashes.

'As long as you're sure. I don't want to rush you.'

Rush me? Was he kidding? It was taking all my self-control not to whip my hands up to the top of that shirt, rip it apart and send all those buttons pinging off the fabric and scattering around the lounge like a split bag of frozen peas.

'Seriously, let's do this,' I said hoarsely, 'I can't wait another second, or else I might self-combust.'

'Ah, a whole new meaning to *being too hot to handle*,' he laughed.

Blimey, flirtatious banter, or what?

'Yes,' I said, my breathing now in serious trouble. Enough of this suspense. It was killing me. 'Open the door, Josh,' I gasped.

He stared at me, as if considering whether this was a good idea or not, although I preferred to interpret it as a lingering look – certainly my eyelashes were doing the same thing because they felt as though they were melting under his gaze. But Josh must have concluded that it was fine to proceed, because he pushed down the door handle. It flew back on its hinges, but the pink and white bedroom was nowhere to be seen. I rocked back on my heels in surprise at the sight before us. But there was no time to take stock and reflect, for Josh was pulling me through the open door. A moment later and we had stepped into a huge grassy clearing edged with woodlands. The trees stretched up to the same strange lemon sky, their branches seemingly going on forever. I was reminded of a favourite childhood book about an enchanted forest full of magic. It was here that an enormous tree could be found, possibly the largest in the world, with boughs that touched the clouds and which, if you climbed it, took you to a magic land. And we were going to nuzzle here? I blew out my cheeks in surprise.

'What do you reckon?' Josh asked, giving me a few more twinkly looks that almost liquefied my legs, but not enough to send my body sinking to the ground. It wasn't muddy, but nonetheless I didn't particularly want to lay down upon it. Not for nuzzling or… well, anything else. I was just wondering whether to manifest a four-poster bed with a floaty fabric canopy for privacy, when Josh put a finger to his lips, indicating that I should be quiet.

A snap of twigs confirmed we weren't alone. I was suddenly beset with nervous tension, and my heart rate was speeding up for an entirely different reason. In a matter of seconds my ardour had done a bunk, and the only thing I was experiencing now was fear.

I huddled into Josh, seeking protection from whatever was hiding in these woods, which my overactive imagination was deeming more unfriendly with every passing moment.

*There's nothing to fear*, said Josh, reading my thoughts, *except fear itself.*

*That's all well and good*, I mentally squeaked, *but I'm not used to all this weird stuff. My heart is doing acrobat—*

But I didn't finish my sentence because two hidden beings suddenly stepped out into the clearing, revealing themselves in all their glory. They were both beautiful and terrifying. Beautiful because of their incredible size, majesty and elegance. Terrifying because they had, sprouting from their foreheads, the tallest, sharpest, deadliest-looking horns I'd ever set eyes upon. Tentatively they walked towards us. My fingers entwined tightly around Josh's, like a woman in labour grabbing hold of her midwife's hand.

*What are they doing*? I squealed.

Josh gently shook me off and pressed his palms together.

*Copy me, Hattie*, he instructed.

I eyeballed his hands nervously, then quickly put mine together, resisting the urge to cross myself, or even prostrate myself upon the floor and beg for mercy.

The creatures snorted, nostrils flaring dramatically, eyes rolling suspiciously as they checked us out.

*Josh, I really don't think I can stand another moment of this. Can we—*

*Bow your head, Hattie. As if in prayer.*

That bit was easy because, funnily enough, I had a sudden overwhelming urge to pray – mainly for my life. As both Josh and I lowered our heads, hands still firmly pushed together, the creatures extended one leg forward and bowed their heads low. Their horns missed us by millimetres, and I had to stifle the urge not to scream.

*They like us,* Josh murmured.

*Thank God for that*, I gasped. *What do we do now*?

*I'm amazed you're even asking.*

*Eh*?

*You have a very short memory, Hattie. Hang on. Let me do a bit of cosmic rewinding here. Watch this.*

Suddenly a film was playing in my head. I could see myself back in my old bedroom at Mum and Dad's. It was that fateful Monday morning not long after hearing the shocking news about Martin's demise. I was under my quilt wishing with all my heart that a certain mythical creature would materialise in front of me, let me climb upon its back and whisk me away through a fairy forest, its twirly horn poised to warn off anybody that dared to hurt me.

*This is what you have manifested, Hattie.*

Inspired by the images imprinted on my old duvet, somehow I'd plucked the very same thing from the ether, because standing before us were two enormous unicorns.

# Chapter Thirty-Six

*I thought you said we were going to do some nuzzling*, I quavered. My whole body was rigid with tension.

*We're about to*, Josh replied. *Keep your head bowed, and hands together, because the nuzzling is about to begin.*

Suddenly, the unicorn directly in front of me began to gently nudge me with his nose, head at a slight angle so the lethal horn didn't slice through my entrails. My floaty dress was thoroughly inspected, nostrils flaring, exhaled air blowing against the fabric, then his nose inquisitively nuzzled down my legs, whiskers tickling my bare calves as his upper lip wiggled over the arches of my feet and then pushed at my toes. For one terrifying moment I thought he might bite me, but no, his massive head was slowly rising up again, gentle snorts getting louder as the nostrils came in line with my shoulder, then one ear. The unicorn's upper lip tickled its way across my forehead, touching my hair, accompanied by a series of snorting grunts as he absorbed my human smell and, hopefully, lots of love vibrations, although it was fair to say that I was probably emitting, right now, more fear than a hostage being held at gunpoint.

Suddenly the creatures backed smartly away, heads tossing alarmingly. My terror was interrupted by what I can only describe as a harmonious chord filling my head, each individual note sounding and spelling out letters which my brain somehow pieced together as one word.

*Namaste.*

I remained rooted to the spot, wondering if fear was sending me mad. If not, where was the melody coming from? And what did 'namaste' mean? Wasn't it something to do with yoga?

*The music is coming from the unicorns,* said Josh, *and 'namaste' is a universal greeting. It's literal meaning is 'I bow to you', which is what the four of us have done. Trust has been established and, more importantly, love given and received.*

Music was now filling the very air around us. It was having a strange effect upon me, as if my body was being wrapped in the lightest sheath of silk, instantly soothing and calming.

*Never underestimate the power of music,* said Josh. *In biblical accounts, King Saul was reportedly soothed by the melody from David's harp. The ancient Greeks also believed music had healing effects. Many cultures are steeped in musical traditions. It can change the mood in a jiffy – from stimulant to sedative.*

I stood in the clearing next to Josh, statue-still, and watched, mesmerised, as the unicorns tucked their legs under their bellies and dropped to the ground.

*Why are they lying down?* I asked, puzzled.

*If you stop nattering and quieten your mind, you will hear them talking to you.*

*What do you mean, stop nattering? You're the one nattering. You haven't stopped nattering since we got here. Saul this and David that and—*

*Hattie?* said Josh, sounding slightly exasperated,

*Yes?*

*Be quiet and listen!*

I pursed my lips, but did as he suggested and tried to think of nothing at all which, it turned out, was extremely hard to do. You see, there was an annoying and persistent little voice in my head that wouldn't shut up. Even more irritatingly, I realised that the little voice was my own. Good heavens. It wasn't my conscience speaking so… oh! This must be the ego. *How dare Josh tell you to shut up! I do hope you're going to put him in his place?* Yes, definitely the ego chuntering away. I mentally frowned and put on my best 'I'm the boss' voice. *Oh do bloody well be quiet!* A split second of shocked silence ensued which was enough for me to focus attention on the unicorns' song. The one sitting opposite me was regarding me with eyes like liquid pools of chocolate, willing me to understand what he was saying.

*Sit yourself*

*Upon my back*

*Thread fingers through my mane*

*And hold on tight*

*As I rise right up*

*And gallop across the terrain*

*We'll jump the trees*

*The moon*

*The stars*

*We'll canter in beams of light*

*And then we'll bid a fond farewell*

*Until we meet in dreams at night*

For some reason my eyes inexplicably filled with tears as the unicorn's message translated in my brain and went on to blossom within my heart. Without any fear or trepidation, I walked towards this majestic creature and, hitching up my hemline, straddled the velvety back. I didn't care if this was a dream, whether the Halfway Lounge really existed, or whether I was having some weird out-of-body crazy experience. All that mattered was the here and the now. Ahead of me, Josh was astride his own mount and he turned to give me an enquiring look, one that asked if I was okay with this? I nodded, and he responded with a smile that lit up his face and, with it, my entire being. I was with the man I loved and sitting on a unicorn. What more could a girl want?

# Chapter Thirty-Seven

Thirty seconds later, it transpired that one thing this girl definitely wanted – nay, needed – was the riding ability of a Grand National jockey and the body of Lester Piggott. As we set off at a brisk canter, I bounced around like a sack of potatoes. I'd rather hoped the floaty dress would attractively stream out making me look like one of those elegant actresses in a commercial, cantering her steed across a barren moor. Instead the dress was bunched up around my knickers and the only thing streaming was my eyeballs. No wonder jockeys wore goggles. I clung on grimly to the mane, concentrating on Josh ahead, trying to emulate his effortless riding style.

*Come on, Hattie, you can do better than that*, he laughed.

*I'll have you know that the last steed I rode was a donkey on Margate beach.*

*And there was me thinking you could ride like Zara Phillips.*

*Funny*, I gasped, daring to release one hand from the unicorn's mane to brush some hair out of my eyes.

*What's happened to your powers of manifestation?*

Oh! How stupid of me. I'd been so caught up with this whole crazy experience that I'd completely forgotten that, right now, I wasn't a human with limitations, but instead some sort of cosmic being with super powers. Suddenly I was riding as if born in the saddle and everything was flowing beautifully… the unicorn's mane, my hair and the hemline of my skirts were all rippling perfectly. We didn't jump the trees, moon or stars, but we did canter out of the forest, sail effortlessly over a fallen tree trunk, straight onto a golden beach that I immediately recognised. Margate. There had been many a perfect family moment spent on these sands as a child. I chuckled inwardly. There were no donkeys to be seen anywhere today, of course.

I let my feet stretch down, noticing that my strappy sandals had disappeared, and my legs were bare. I'd subconsciously manifested a change of clothing and was now wearing a bikini top and shorts. Better. Much better.

'I agree,' said Josh, reverting to spoken language.

I looked across at him, and nearly swallowed my tonsils. He was trotting along beside me, wearing the same glowing white swim shorts he'd worn when we'd been at the beach. His torso looked even more tanned than previously, but just as muscular as the last time we'd stripped off at the water's edge. I found myself discreetly adding a bit more tone and definition to my own abdomen. After all, no one wants a muffin top spoiling the look of their shorts.

We bounced along companionably, letting the cool seawater play over our mounts' legs, splashing up and eventually soaking us, so much so that we didn't protest when the unicorns waded in a little deeper, then deeper still, until they were swimming with heads extended, horns pointing up like sailboat masts. Their long manes and tails flowed out on the waves like wet seaweed.

'Happy?' asked Josh, as the warm waters washed over us.

'Very,' I replied, smiling contentedly. 'This place was a firm family favourite when I was a child. I can remember coming with my mum and dad and bringing a school friend along. We had a bit of a falling out over who'd caught the biggest crab in the rock pools. Such big stuff when little, yet little stuff now I'm looking back as an adult.' I sighed. 'Funny how one's perspective changes as we move through the years of life. Now, when I think back on days like that one, it's with nothing but a warm glow. There were so many happy moments enjoying picnics on the sand, and my mother's laughter when a bold seagull once stole my dad's sandwich.'

'I'm glad you're remembering happy stuff, Hattie,' said Josh. 'You've had some heavy experiences since your arrival here. It's good to remind yourself that there has been much joy in your life, too.'

'Yes,' I nodded, my voice as soft as the gently lapping water all around us.

Neither of us spoke for a couple of minutes, just enjoying the moment, the here and now of peace and mental relaxation. Josh was the first to break the silence.

'Do you think you're ready for the next bit of reviewing?'

The past was waiting, and my shoulders drooped.

'You know,' I said carefully, aware that I was attempting to wriggle out of it, 'someone once told me that you can't get on with the next chapter of your life if you keep re-reading the last.'

'Point taken,' said Josh, 'except in your case, Hattie, you weren't getting on with the next chapter anyway. Let me quote the big man up there' – he nodded skywards – '"the best can't find you, until you put the past behind you".'

'But I *had* put the past behind me,' I said obstinately. 'It was all neatly tucked away in its various boxes, lids tightly on.'

'But you weren't reconciled with the past. And that is what needs addressing.'

I shrugged. Something told me I wasn't going to get out of this.

'A little while ago, you nosily asked whether I was in love with someone,' Josh said.

I inhaled sharply. 'Yes. I did. And you mentioned in a roundabout way that you were in love but declined telling me who she was.'

'If you go back in order to find your way forward, you'll also discover who I'm in love with.'

My heart rate bounced unpleasantly. 'Is it someone I know?' I croaked, aghast at what might be revealed on this journey of self-discovery and forgiveness. That was all I needed. Coming across Josh somewhere in my murky past, shacked up with some gorgeous creature no doubt, perhaps not so readily recognisable because, in real life, he wasn't as tall, tanned, gorgeous or hot as he was in this altered dimension.

'You haven't known me previously,' he assured me, reading my thoughts.

I flushed, hoping that he hadn't read the bit about not looking quite so hot.

'Can't you just tell me who your lady love is?' I asked.

'I'm not allowed to,' he replied.

'I won't tell anyone if you don't,' I grinned.

He laughed. 'It's something you have to work out for yourself.'

I sighed, resigning myself to another review and whatever it might throw up. As if sensing both my mood and decision, the unicorns changed direction, heading back to the mainland. On impulse, I leant forward and threw my arms around my unicorn's neck, rubbing my hands up and down the wet fur.

*Thank you for your love*, I whispered.

Almost immediately came a musical chord of reply.

*Om shanti shanti shanti.*

Somehow, I knew what the message was. Peace. I smiled and tipped my head up to the sky, closing my eyes and letting the lemon light tickle my eyelids. But when I next opened them, I was once again back in my old bedroom at Mum and Dad's, and the only sign of any unicorns were the static images on my childhood quilt. And I knew that, downstairs, Nick was waiting to speak to me.

# Chapter Thirty-Eight

As I faced Nick across the threshold of my parents' house, his face registered surprise at the vision before him – a washed-out, red-eyed woman with her hair standing on end. Last time he'd seen me I'd been glammed up, and languorously sprawled across the sheets of his bed.

'Why are you here?' I asked, my voice hoarse.

'To see you, of course,' he said, his astonished expression switching to one of concern. 'Come here.' He opened his arms, and I flew straight into them.

'You didn't need to come by,' I said, snorting unattractively and desperately hoping I didn't get snot over his immaculate suit.

'I wanted to make sure you were okay,' he whispered into my ear. 'I wasn't sure if—'

'What?'

He hesitated. 'This sounds a bit lame now… somewhat stupid… but I wasn't sure if you regretted our time together and,' he shrugged, 'perhaps stayed away from the office because… ' He trailed off, his voice suddenly sounding uncertain.

'Oh my goodness, did you think that I was avoiding you? Was embarrassed, or something, and made up some excuse to skive off?'

He held me tight and stroked my hair. 'Something like that,' he murmured. 'I can see from the state of you, however, that this wasn't the case at all.'

A little part of me danced with joy. The gorgeous Nicholas Green had diverted his way home from the office because he'd spent his working day fretting that the dalliance with his secretary might have been regretted on her part. Surely that meant he cared a lot about me? I was secretly thrilled.

'Would you have missed me if I'd never come back?' I whispered.

'Yes,' he said. 'I've never had a secretary as efficient as you.'

At the time I'd thought Nick was bantering, but it was only now, in this review, that I realised he might not have been completely joking. What was that expression? Ah, yes. *Many a true word said in jest.* But the young Hattie, standing in the hallway in her new lover's arms, chose to construe his words as those of endearment.

'I'm so sorry for your loss, Hattie.'

'Thank you,' I mumbled.

'Was it a very close family member who died?' he asked gently.

I froze. I'd never mentioned Martin in the workplace. I didn't have that closeness with the other secretaries who moaned about their husbands, kids, or their thickening waistlines, and not necessarily in that order. I'd deliberately failed to mention the lack of a significant other to Nick because, well, my relationship with Martin had been slowly dwindling anyway – and certainly from the moment I'd clapped eyes on my new boss. Now didn't seem the time to tell him the finer details of who had passed away.

'It was a long-term friend of the family,' I quickly explained, 'but it was the suddenness more than anything. It wasn't expected and came as a tremendous shock.'

He nodded. 'Heart attack?'

'Well—'

'Was it instant?'

'Apparently so.' That much was true from what we'd been told.

'In some respects it's the best way to go. Rushing around one minute, maybe on the commute to work, then a sudden cardiac arrest out of the blue so that' – he clicked his fingers – 'you're suddenly saying hello to the angels. Literally here one minute, then gone the next.'

'Y-Yes,' I stuttered, not at all comfortable with this line of conversation. I didn't want to talk about Martin, his demise, or anything that reminded me of him. This particular Monday had seen me in an altered state. There had been too many shocks in too short a space of time, and my emotions were badly out of kilter.

'Take as long as you like off work,' said Nick, his expression now one of kindness.

'I'll be back tomorrow,' I replied.

'Is that a good idea?' Nick protested. 'I don't want you weeping over your keyboard, diluting the coffee with your tears, and greeting clients looking like a road accident.'

I flinched at Nick's choice of these last two words.

'Believe me, that won't be the case,' I said firmly. 'I'll be absolutely fine. I just want to carry on as normal and get on with my life, and that means I'll be behind my desk at Shepherd, Green & Parsons bright and early in the morning.'

'Well as long as you're sure,' he said.

'Never more so.'

'Good.'

For a moment we just stared at each other, and then he put his finger under my chin and tipped my head up, before lowering his mouth gently to mine. I welcomed the kiss and melted against him, unaware of my parents watching from the shadows above.

# Chapter Thirty-Nine

How much my parents heard or saw from the landing, I wasn't sure. All I know is that the moment Nick left, they came down the stairs looking grim. Despite my mother's earlier assurance that my love life was my business, I couldn't help noticing that her mouth was puckered like a cat's bum, and my father's set in a line so straight it could have been used as a ruler. They went through to the kitchen where Mum immediately lit up a cigarette, sucking hard on the nicotine stick and adding to the fretwork of lines around her mouth. But whatever their private thoughts were on seeing their daughter kissing another man hours after her boyfriend had been killed, they tactfully didn't voice them. I was grateful for that.

I went back to work the following day, desperate to embrace a sense of normality. Outwardly I was calm. Inwardly, I was in freefall. There was a complete denial about what Martin had done prior to his shocking death. I was coping – if you could call it that – by resolving to never think about Martin. If any thoughts about him encroached, I'd immediately push them away. If Mum or Dad mentioned his name, my distancing technique was such that his name translated as someone I only vaguely knew.

The week passed in a blur, and I had zero recall about what Martin had done. I was going through the motions. Nick, knowing that I needed distracting, made sure I was kept busier than ever. On the Friday night he wished me a pleasant weekend and it was only then that I snapped out of auto-pilot. I was still seated at my desk, pounding away at my keyboard, before I realised everyone was putting their coats on.

'Is it Friday?' I asked, genuinely astonished at where the week had gone.

'Yes,' he said, looking amused at my dumbfounded expression. 'What are you up to this weekend, Hattie?' he asked gently.

'Oh,' I gulped, 'well, I'm not too sure.' Now didn't seem the moment to say that I had keenly hoped I'd be spending some of it with him. I was desperate to move on and make fresh memories. Happy memories. I'd always thought Nick was gorgeous, but his attractiveness had also increased because I now saw him as the passport to move further away from what had happened. But he wasn't making any overtures to share his time off with me. He'd kept his emotional distance throughout the week, but I'd put that down to him wanting to give me space after—

My mind immediately veered away from thinking anything else.

'A-And you?' I asked brightly, determined not to sound needy or look disappointed at my exclusion from whatever his plans were. I had a wobbly moment of wondering if Erin from Accounts had made a reappearance in his life and declared that she no longer wanted a reunion with her cuckolded husband, and that the only get-togethers she wanted were with Nicholas Green in a horizontal position.

'I'm seeing my daughters,' he said. 'My ex-wife grants me occasional access if I've been a good boy and jumped through all her hoops. This is one such weekend.'

'Ah, right.' Yes, of course, he had Lucinda and Charlotte from his marriage to the first Mrs Green.

'Of course the real reason the girls will be staying with me is because Amanda has a new boyfriend and wants some free time to invest in her budding romance. Her last relationship didn't end well. She was livid when Lucinda had a nightmare and burst in on her and Keith in the middle of the night.'

'Oh dear,' I said, cranking up a smile. 'Were they caught in a compromising position?'

'Well, not Amanda as such. Apparently it was Keith's backside in the air.' Nick gave a wicked grin. 'That was the last anyone saw of him, poor sod'– he gave a mock shudder – 'it's enough to render one instantly impotent.' I giggled, and his face softened. 'It's nice to see you laugh again, Hattie. Anyway,' he said, hurrying on, 'the girls will be staying tonight and tomorrow. No doubt they will chat long into the night, so by the time they go home on Sunday evening they'll be tired and crotchety, and I will be accused of being a lax father.'

'I'm sure you're a very good father,' I said, desperate to prolong his company on a one-to-one basis now that everybody else had gone home. I quickly saved the document I'd been working on, then logged off. 'I'll walk to the lift with you,' I said, pulling my jacket off the back of my chair and picking up my handbag.

'Sure,' he replied, momentarily looking away to greet Barbara, our office cleaner. She swung through the doors carting a Henry vacuum cleaner in one hand and a bag of dusters and wipes in the other. 'I'm taking the girls to Legoland on Sunday,' Nick said, turning his attention back to me. 'Hey, just a thought but… ah, no… you won't want—'

'What?' I asked eagerly.

'Well, I just wondered if you fancied coming along? But I can appreciate that hanging around with an eight- and ten-year-old might not be your idea of fun, so forget—'

'I'd love to,' I said breathlessly, before he could change his mind. I didn't care one bit if there would be a couple of little girls on the scene, just so long as their father was there, too.

'Okay,' he said, looking surprised. 'I'll pick you up Sunday morning.'

'Fabulous,' I said, my heart lifting for the first time all week. I couldn't wait to spend the day with him and his two darling children. I wondered what they were like. At that age they'd still be at primary school, unspoilt for sure, unlike the moment they went to secondary school and morphed into prepubescents exchanging ankle socks and sweetness for Doc Martens and Attitude with a capital A.

Needless to say, the meeting with Nick's daughters was an unmitigated disaster.

# Chapter Forty

When Nick turned up at my parents' house at nine on Sunday morning with two squabbling children in the back of his car, my mother's eyeballs were on stalks.

'Married with *children*?' she asked.

'*Separated* with children,' I crisply retorted.

'And you're about to jump in feet first and play happy families, right?'

'I'm going to Legoland,' I said through slightly gritted teeth. 'I've been invited along to have some much-needed fun.'

'Ah yes, L-e-g-o-land,' said Mum, scratching her chin in a parody of contemplation, 'the place where every grown-up goes to let off steam. Correct me if I'm wrong, Hattie, but I could have sworn that adults went to Chessington or Thorpe Park, which isn't, after all, a million miles away.'

'There are height restrictions at Chessington and Thorpe Park. You can't take two little girls to theme parks like that, can you?' I retorted.

'Indeed you can't,' said Mum, 'so I rather suspect this trip is about his daughters, not you. Instead you'll be going along as an unpaid nanny, taking his girls to the loo, assisting with pants and tights, and buckling up their shoes.'

'Lucinda and Charlotte are eight and ten, Mum. Not two and four. I don't know anything about kids, but I'm pretty sure they are past the potty-training stage and are able to use a toilet unaided.'

'Hmm,' said my mother, sceptically, 'well I hope you know what you're letting yourself in for. Oh look, the great man himself is getting out of the car. Probably to give his ears a couple of minutes' respite from the din those kids are making.'

Nick was now walking up the garden path. He did look slightly frazzled and was repeatedly raking one hand through his hair, as if already weary. Behind him, the car was now rocking as the girls thumped each other. Good heavens, and I'd thought it was only little boys who resorted to fisticuffs. I noticed that Nick's crumpet-catcher sports car had been replaced with something more sober for today's outing. This must be a spare vehicle kept for such occasions. It was an old Citroen Picasso, its roomy boot stuffed with children's paraphernalia. Two pink bicycles dangled off a metal contraption at the rear of the vehicle.

'Hi!' said Nick, as Mum opened the front door. Gordon Bennett, why was she hanging around? 'You must be Hattie's sister?'

Mum melted quicker than an ice-cube in a microwave. 'You're not the first person to think that,' she cooed.

'This is my mother,' I said to Nick.

'Nick,' he replied, shaking her hand.

'You may call me Penny,' said Mum.

'Well he's hardly going to call you *Mum*, is he?' I muttered under my breath.

'Hattie's told us so much about you,' said Mum, ignoring me and turning on the charm. 'And those must be your two dear little girls?' She nodded towards the rocking car.

'Yes,' said Nick, as the car alarm began shrieking from all the hoo-ha coming from within.

'Aren't they just *dar*ling?' said Mum, over the din, as net curtains the length of the road began to violently twitch.

'Shall we get a wiggle on, Hattie?' asked Nick, trying not to look harassed. 'Are you not taking a coat?'

'No, it's a decent enough day. I'll be fine with this hoodie.'

'Right, lovely to meet you, Penny,' said Nick, already backing away, visibly psyching himself up to return to the racket within his car.

'Have a great time!' my mother called to his retreating back. I shoved my feet into some trainers and made to go after Nick, but Mum's hand caught my wrist in a vice-like grip. 'Do you have any headache pills?' she hissed.

'No. If you need some, I think there's a packet in the bathroom cabinet.'

'Oh they're not for me,' she said, eyes wide and feigning innocence. 'I'm thinking of you. Believe me, you're going to need them before the day is out.'

I tutted crossly. 'Don't be ridiculous. They're just little children.'

'No, they're not,' said my mother, eyes narrowing at the girls still fighting within the car.

'What are they then?' I asked sarcastically. 'Monsters? The devil's offspring? Evil itself dressed in pink with pigtails?'

Mum gave a tinkle of laughter. 'No, darling. I do believe the terminology is much simpler and something a seasoned mother like myself can spot at two paces.'

'Oh?'

'Otherwise known as "spoilt brats".'

'Goodbye, Mum. I'm not sure when I'll be home.'

'See you later, Hattie,' said Mum cheerfully, 'I would say have fun, but I know you won't.'

As I marched defiantly towards Nick's car, I wished that sometimes my mother didn't have the propensity to always be right.

# Chapter Forty-One

'Girls, girls,' said Nick, as I slid into the passenger seat next to him. 'Settle down and say hi to Hattie.' He glanced across at me. 'Charlotte is on the left, and Lucinda is sitting behind you.'

'Hello there!' I said, in my best *Five Have a Wonderful Time* voice, although I had a sneaking suspicion these children had never read an Enid Blyton book in their lives. As I swivelled round to face them, I saw they both had iPads in their laps and iPhones on the seat space between them. Definitely not book readers. They stared at me with furious blue eyes, their mouths set in a mutinous line. Where had I seen those expressions before? Ah yes. Mum and Dad. Both of them had looked exactly like this after witnessing Nick kiss me in the hallway last Monday evening. Well, wasn't I just flavour of the month right now! I gave both children a winning smile which was met with scowls. They were incredibly alike, and if it hadn't been for an obvious height difference in the shoulders, could have been mistaken for twins. 'My goodness,' I chirped, 'aren't you both beautiful young ladies.' My pathetic attempt to charm was met with identical withering looks. Silently, they turned their attention to their iPads. 'Well,' I said, to no one in particular, 'I think this is going to be a splendid day.'

In no time at all we were on the M25, but half an hour later we were at a standstill.

'Are we nearly there yet?' asked Charlotte.

'No, unfortunately not,' said Nick, drumming his fingers on the steering wheel. 'What on earth has happened?' He turned on the radio, pressing buttons in search of a traffic update.

'I need a wee,' said Lucinda.

'You'll have to hold on until we get to Services.'

'What's Services?' asked Charlotte.

'It's where the toilets are,' I said helpfully.

'I wasn't talking to you,' said Charlotte rudely, 'I was talking to Daddy.'

Right. That put me in my place.

'Ah, here we are,' said Nick, listening intently to the traffic update. 'Oh no. A ten-mile tailback due to an accident.'

'I'll have an accident if I don't have a wee in a minute,' said Lucinda.

'There's a grassy bank over there,' I said pointing, 'and some trees to hide behind. Do you want me to take you over there?'

Lucinda stared at me as if I'd just suggested dancing naked in the moonlight. 'I'm not weeing in front of all these people,' she said, one arm making a sweeping gesture at the motionless traffic all around us.

'You wouldn't have to,' I said, making my voice placatory, 'the trees will shield you and I can stand in front of you. No one will see.'

'There's no toilet paper,' she said, jaw jutting out.

'I have a tissue,' I replied, burrowing up my sleeve for my one sheet of Kleenex I'd hurriedly stuffed up my arm earlier on.

'Ewww, I don't want your tissue,' said Lucinda, 'it will be full of bogies.'

'Ohhh, you just said *bogies*,' said Charlotte. 'Mummy said that's a bad word.'

'The tissue is clean,' I assured her, 'and you're very welcome to it.'

'No thanks,' said Lucinda, 'I'll just have to wet myself.'

'Oh come *on*,' said Nick in exasperation. 'Sorry, but I'm not sitting in this.' Suddenly he was manoeuvring the car, darting and squeezing the vehicle through gaps until we were driving on the hard shoulder.

'Er, Nick, I'm not sure you're allowed to—'

'There's no traffic cameras on this stretch,' said Nick, 'and if a cop car comes along I'll say it was an emergency and my daughter needed to pee.'

'Um, right,' I said, as we shot up the hard shoulder, a torrent of horns blasting in our wake.

'Police cars are allowed to do this,' said Charlotte, bouncing around with excitement. 'Let's pretend we're a police car, Luce,' she nudged her sister. Suddenly the back window was buzzed down and both girls were emitting ear-piercing wails, emulating a speeding patrol vehicle. The noise went right through my head, and I was suddenly reminded of my mother asking if I had headache tablets on me.

# Chapter Forty-Two

We arrived at Legoland two hours later than planned. Nick hadn't been in the best of tempers to find, when we had finally got off the hard shoulder, that the Services had been closed for refurbishment. Lucinda, despite threatening to wet herself every thirty seconds, held on until Nick paid for the Legoland entrance tickets which were... *how much*? Good heavens, since when did a family day out cost so much? And we hadn't even stopped for lunch yet. Both children clamoured to get on their bicycles after Charlotte haughtily informed me she never walked anywhere, and most definitely not around a theme park.

'Oh look,' I called, just as both girls were about to pedal off, 'there's a toilet. Would you like me to take you?'

Lucinda screwed up her face in rage and yelled, 'We're not babies, you know, and anyway, I don't need the toilet any more.'

'Are you sure?' I asked, bemused at how a child's bladder could one moment feel as though it was going to burst and the next, seemingly stretch to the size of a hot air balloon accommodating any number of Slush Puppies and Coca-Colas that Nick bought every thirty minutes throughout the day. No wonder they were both hyper.

'Head towards Miniland, girls,' Nick called after them, as they pedalled off.

'Shouldn't we keep up with them?' I asked nervously, as Lucinda and Charlotte disappeared out of sight.

'They're fine,' said Nick, slowing to a stroll and taking my hand in his. The sudden romantic gesture caught me off guard. In a nanosecond the tension in my shoulders melted away, and I felt myself relaxing. So what if the girls cycled off? The whole place was enclosed. If they did happen to lose their bearings, they both had mobile phones and were obviously savvy enough to use them.

I inhaled a lungful of air, releasing it with a sigh of contentment. This was more like it. For a moment I allowed myself a happy daydream, pretending that I was Nick's wife… yes, another wife… and that Charlotte and Lucinda were *our* children, and this was a family day out for the four of us. I imagined passers-by smiling indulgently at the handsome couple with their beautiful blonde children tearing around in high spirits.

'Isn't this wonderful,' I said, smiling happily.

'You're enjoying yourself?' said Nick, looking surprised.

'Of course,' I said. Didn't he understand that I'd be happy going anywhere so long as he was by my side? 'Aren't you?'

'Can't stand these places,' he replied cheerfully. 'I guess I'm just not a true family guy.'

'Of course you are,' I said loyally.

'Don't get me wrong, Hattie,' said Nick, giving a little shrug, 'I love my girls unconditionally, but I find them damned hard work.'

Charlotte and Lucinda reappeared a minute later, scattering some birds pecking at dropped chips, repeatedly ringing their shrill bicycle bells and demanding we hurry up.

'Oh look,' I gasped, as miniature versions of famous London landmarks came into view. 'Canary Wharf… City Hall… the Millennium Bridge… what amazing detail,' I enthused, bending to inspect some tiny pigeons which, according to an information placard, were the smallest models and used just five Lego bricks each.

'It's boring,' said Charlotte, looking mutinous, 'and anyway, we want to go on some rides, don't we, Daddy?' She beamed up at her father.

'We most certainly do!' he said, causing Charlotte to shoot me a triumphant look. 'Come on, Hattie,' said Nick, as the girls flung their bicycles down on the ground and skipped off, one either side of Nick and holding a hand each. I was left to pick up the bikes and adopt a half-walk, half-crouch, making me look like a hunchback. They headed off in the direction of the Dragon's Apprentice, a mini rollercoaster, which was perfect for kids but far too small for someone of my height, and with legs even longer than Nick's. As Nick hopped into a carriage behind the girls, I opted to watch from the side, still hanging onto the bikes, all the while smiling brightly.

The sun, which up until now had been little more than a pale watery blob, suddenly disappeared behind a bank of dark clouds. A gust of wind sent an abandoned drink carton rolling across the ground, and I shivered. The weather was changing. Cold air filtered through every fibre of my hoodie until it felt like it was penetrating my bones. Too late I realised I should have brought a coat. Nick and the girls were suitably dressed and, anyway, they were busy roaring around on rides, dashing between attractions, constantly on the move and staying warmer than me. My position was mostly static, holding the wretched bikes as the three of them whizzed around on the Duplo train, then beamed down at me from the Aero Nomad. Actually, it was just Nick who beamed. The girls ignored me throughout, except on one occasion when Charlotte attractively turned her head one-hundred-and-eighty-degrees and stuck her tongue out without her father seeing. I shivered on the sidelines, my nose turning pink and my lips a fetching shade of blue, until the heavens opened forcing the girls to squeal and abandon any further rides.

We made a dash for the nearest fast food place – well the others did, I was still impeded and imitating Quasimodo, but with bikes rather than bells. Nick spent another small fortune on sugary drinks and burgers oozing fat, topped with slices of plastic cheese between cardboard buns.

'You look frozen, Hattie,' he said. 'Leave the bikes outside and warm up.'

'But what if they get stolen?' I said, dithering between the call of hot chocolate or guarding the damn bicycles.

'It doesn't matter if they get stolen,' said Lucinda, 'because we're too big for them now and, anyway, Daddy said he was going to buy us some new ones. Didn't you Daddy?' she smiled at him adoringly.

'I did, angel.'

'Surely only one new bike needs to be bought,' I said, brow puckering. 'Lucinda can have Charlotte's outgrown bike.'

'But that wouldn't be fair,' said Lucinda, looking aghast. 'You wouldn't make me have Charlotte's old bike, would you Daddy? That would be so cruel.'

Nick roared with laughter at his daughter's precociousness. 'Of course it wouldn't be fair, darling heart. Daddy will buy you *both* new bikes. Oh look, there's an empty table over there. Let's grab it.'

Lucinda gave me a 'so there, ha ha!' look, before scampering over to the vacated table with her sister, while Nick joined the food queue. I stayed with him on the pretence of helping, but in fact was reluctant to sit alone with the girls. I didn't want to be on the receiving end of their obvious dislike. Finally, carrying a loaded tray apiece, we made our way over to the slightly grubby table.

'Sit down, Hattie,' Nick said, indicating a chair. 'That's it. And you, Lucinda, can sit here next to me. You, Charlotte, can sit that side of the table next to Hattie.'

Charlotte immediately looked like she'd swallowed a gobstopper.

'I'm not sitting next to *her*,' she shrieked, catching the attention of some nearby parents who gazed at me uncertainly. 'Mummy says we should never talk to strangers, and we don't even know *her*.'

'That's enough,' said Nick mildly.

Charlotte complied with her father's wishes but not before shuffling her plastic chair closer to Nick, making sure there was as much distance as possible between her body and mine. I chewed on my greasy burger, trying not to feel miserable. The children were quiet for a moment as they busied themselves poking straws through plastic lids on drinks. Lucinda sucked on her straw, sly eyes under an overlong fringe peering up at me. She smirked and turned to her father.

'Daddy, whatever happened to Caroline?'

'Who?'

'That really nice lady you went out with. Remember? She was so pretty and kind. She bought me a Barbie doll. I wanted you to marry her.'

'I preferred Janey,' said Charlotte. 'She didn't interfere' – she gave me a pointed look – 'and kept her opinions to herself.'

Nick scratched his head and looked bemused. 'Since when were either of you so interested in my girlfriends? Anyway, I like Hattie now.'

'We don't,' said Lucinda who, being the youngest, could get away with being more outspoken than her sibling.

I flushed the colour of the sticky bottle of ketchup on the table, but Nick simply hooted with laughter. He noticed my mottled complexion and leant over.

'Take no notice of them,' he whispered in my ear, then kissed me on the cheek.

Lucinda glared at me. I found myself volleying back the triumphant look she'd thrown me earlier, but almost immediately chastised myself. *For God's sake, Hattie. They're flipping kids! Act your age and not your shoe size. You're not back in the playground.* But the trouble was, Lucinda and Charlotte made me feel like I was.

The downpour eventually stopped. The children, mercifully, jumped back on their bicycles leaving us briefly alone together.

'Do they hate all your girlfriends?' I asked tentatively.

'Yes,' Nick chuckled. 'Hey, don't take it personally. They gave Caroline and Janey a hard time too. They are also vile to any new man that takes an interest in my first wife.'

'Good to know,' I said, trying to laugh it off but still feeling ridiculously hurt. I reminded myself that these were two little girls displaying emotional fallout from their parents' failed marriage. It was perfectly natural to feel possessive about their mother and father, and dislike newcomers encroaching on their splintered family.

Before leaving the park, Nick insisted both children use the loo.

'I'm not stopping at the Services,' he warned, 'so go with Hattie, please.'

I trailed after them as they crashed into a vacant toilet stall together. Inside my own cubicle, I hung my handbag on a peg and pulled down my jeans. What a day. I was cold, wet and my morale had done a complete bunk. From elsewhere came the sound of someone gustily breaking wind, which sent Lucinda and Charlotte into a fit of giggles.

'Oooh, someone just blew off,' said Lucinda in a telltale voice.

'How rude,' said Charlotte, adopting a hoity-toity tone, like that of an adult. 'Where *are* that person's manners?'

'How dare you,' screeched an indignant voice. 'I've got an upset stomach.'

Both girls tittered naughtily before launching into some energetic raspberry blowing.

'Oops, 'scuse me,' said Lucinda, 'my tummy isn't right', and let rip with another string of farty sounds.

'The minute I get my backside off this toilet, I'm going to report you kids,' came a furious squawk.

'Oooh, I say,' said Charlotte, making sounds like a deflating balloon, 'my bum seems to be on fire.'

'Girls,' I warned, hastily zipping up my flies and erupting out of my cubicle, just as a Vera Duckworth lookalike catapulted out of hers.

'Can't yer keep yer bluddy kids under control?' yelled Vera, purple with rage. 'Call yerself a mother?'

Whereupon another cubicle door flew open revealing Lucinda and Charlotte, both sporting peeled back lips and snarling faces.

'*She's* not our mummy,' shrieked Charlotte, '*she's* just another horrid woman like you.'

And with that the pair of them darted out leaving me stammering apologies to Vera.

Thankfully, the pair of them fell asleep on the return journey. I'd presumed that Nick was going to drop me off first. Instead we eventually drew up in a beautiful tree-lined road, fringed with elegant houses.

'I thought I'd get them back, so we can have a bit of us time,' he murmured.

'Oh, that's nice,' I said, perking up.

He let himself out of the vehicle and disappeared around the back, unstrapping the bicycles and then getting the girls' weekend bags out of the boot. At the sound of doors opening and closing, Lucinda and Charlotte sat up and stretched.

'We're home!' Lucinda squeaked with delight.

'Say goodbye to Hattie,' said Nick, as the children scrambled out of the car, eager to put as much distance as possible between us.

'Bye, darlings,' I quavered after them. They ignored me. They belted off, running up to the smart front door of a swish house. It looked like the type of property owned by someone who worked in the money markets – or, in this case, someone who'd had a lucrative divorce settlement. I couldn't help staring. My goodness, it was very different to the bachelor pad Nick was renting. I wondered if he missed this place. Stupid to think he didn't. The door opened, and a glamorous woman greeted her daughters. Naturally the kids were all smiles. For the first time since I'd clapped eyes on them, they looked angelic. Charlotte then spoilt it by discreetly showing me two fingers, while Lucinda flipped the bird. Good *God!* What horrible, horrible children! I immediately felt wracked with guilt for thinking such thoughts, but couldn't help it.

I watched as Nick and Amanda exchanged brief pleasantries, and couldn't help noticing how stunning she was. Her hair, professionally blow-dried, curled attractively over her shoulders, and her clothes looked expensive and chic. I felt shabby in comparison, my blonde mop tangled and damp from wind and rain, my nose still pink from the endless cold of the day.

When Nick eventually returned to the car, he tucked himself behind the wheel of the old Citroen with a sigh of pleasure.

'I don't know about you, Hattie, but I need a stiff drink and something decent to eat – and most definitely not theme park fare. There's a charming Italian bistro just around the corner. Fancy it?'

'Looking like this?' I protested, indicating my damp jeans and dishevelled hair.

'You look fabulous,' he said, winking, 'and anyway, don't worry about those clothes. It's what's under them that counts. You have the patience of a saint and the body of an angel which – I might add – I want to caress for all eternity.'

Suddenly I didn't give two hoots about his precocious children. In that last sentence, Nick Green had made it clear he was interested in me long-term, and I couldn't wait to encourage this, thus putting emotional mileage between the past and, well…

My face was wreathed in smiles as we went into the trattoria together, arms linked, looking like a proper couple with eyes only for each other.

'You're amazing, Hattie,' he said, as we glugged gratefully at our red wine.

'So are you,' I said, the wine emboldening me.

'Do you like children?' he asked, after a moment's silence.

The question caught me out. Was he testing me? Thinking, perhaps, of me in a future step-parent role?

'Well, er…' I shrugged.

'You can be honest,' he laughed. 'Have Charlotte and Lucinda put you off having kids forever and a day?'

Wow, he *was* testing me. His mind must be flitting off to the distant future, thinking about starting all over again with me, maybe another baby or two in the equation.

'I can't say I've ever really had much to do with children,' I said carefully, 'but yes, of course I like children. I'm certainly not averse to them, if that's what you mean.' Didn't want him thinking that I'd never oblige with a son and heir.

'That's good to hear,' he said, looking relieved. 'So you won't mind if Lucinda and Charlotte join us again at some point?'

Oh. He *had* been testing me, but not in the way I'd imagined.

'N-No,' I stammered, privately thinking I couldn't imagine anything worse.

And then he said something that further disconcerted me.

'I love my daughters to bits, but I don't ever, *ever* want any more children. So if you do,' he said, not unkindly, 'it's best you find yourself another boyfriend before we get in too deep.'

On the one hand I was delighted to hear Nick refer to himself as my boyfriend. But on the other, I was dismayed at his emphatic tone about never wanting to be a father again. Especially when those words came winging back four months later.

# Chapter Forty-Three

*Do you want to take a break, Hattie?*

From somewhere far away, Josh spoke quietly in my head. Suddenly I felt drained. Whether it was from the day at Legoland in the bitter cold, the effects of the red wine, Nick's warning about never wanting children again, or simply being on the receiving end of Lucinda and Charlotte's endless loathing, a wave of tiredness washed over me.

*Yes, please*, I replied.

In the blink of an eye I was back in the Halfway Lounge with Josh. I put my hands to my temples and massaged vigorously. I felt as though I'd just been pulled from a giant cosmic tumble dryer churning a muddle of mismatched garments. Right now, I was struggling to keep up with events. One moment I was shopping in Tesco, the next riding unicorns on Margate's sandy beach, and in yet another instant I was plunging back into the past with an ex-husband and two kids that couldn't bear to share their airspace with me. Hell, the likes of Trump and Putin didn't need to go to war with missiles. All they needed was an army of Charlottes and Lucindas to infiltrate their countries and both governments would be fleeing for the hills.

'And that is precisely why it's a good moment to take a pause in your review,' said Josh, with wry smile.

'Eh?' I said, frowning in confusion.

'Charlotte and Lucinda.'

'What about them?'

I was sitting down on one of the squashy sofas, still wearing the damp jeans and hoodie that I'd been wearing when having dinner with Nick in the trattoria.

'Here,' said Josh, passing me what looked like the same glass of red wine that I'd been enjoying earlier with Nick.

'Thanks,' I said, taking a greedy glug. I'd forgotten how Charlotte and Lucinda had the propensity to drive me to drink.

'Hmm, definitely needs addressing,' said Josh, more to himself than me.

I took another sip and regarded him over the rim. God, he was good-looking. And so much nicer to be with than Nick. I felt as though I could always be myself with Josh. No need for airs or graces, or worrying about my appearance or having to impress with good behaviour.

'Won't you join me?' I asked. 'I hate drinking alone.'

'Sure,' he grinned, as a glass of red liquid materialised in his hand. 'Cheers!'

'So,' I said, kicking off my trainers and tucking my legs up on the sofa, 'what exactly needs addressing?'

A comfy chair appeared out of nowhere, close to me, and Josh sat down. The light in the lounge seemed to dim to one of intimacy and ambience. Good heavens, all we needed now was a roaring log fire and this would be just blissful.

'I agree,' said Josh, as the lounge morphed into a cosy country pub, complete with log-filled hearth crackling and popping away. The place looked familiar, but I couldn't place it.

'You do realise you are completely messing with my mind,' I said, arching one eyebrow.

'Nonsense,' he grinned. 'This is all meat and beer to a woman like you.'

'Is it indeed?' I bantered back, thinking how lovely it was to be with him again, and wishing it could be forever.

'However,' he said, holding his index finger up by way of pointing something out, 'Charlotte and Lucinda have left impressions upon your soul.'

'Here we go again,' I sighed, 'but yes, I don't doubt.'

'Not good impressions either.'

'They were challenging kids.'

'Ah, but it's not the challenges that left the impressions. It's the way you felt about them that is the issue.'

I shifted uncomfortably in my chair, not liking the turn in conversation.

'What do you mean?'

'You didn't like them, did you?'

'Josh, that's an awful thing to say,' I protested, trying to dance away from the truth. 'They were just little girls.'

'But very disagreeable ones, right?'

'Well, yes, I suppose' – I blew out my cheeks – 'but they couldn't help the way they were.'

'Maybe not at that age,' Josh agreed, 'but later, when you became a family with Nick, and when they were old enough to know better.

Their dislike of you became out-and-out hatred, and that was when you found yourself struggling even more with your own feelings about the girls.'

I blanched. Put so concisely, it sounded awful hearing that two human beings detested me for no reason other than that I'd dared to once love their father, and that their hatred had darkened my feelings towards them.

'They harboured hopes that their mother and father would one day get back together,' I said, knowing that I was making excuses for them. 'They had dreams about them all being reunited and living happily ever after. A lot of kids from broken homes have the same aspirations. I'm sure many step-parents all over the country are on the receiving end of occasional vitriol.'

'Sure. But again, Hattie, I will remind you that right now this isn't about how *they* felt. It's about how *you* felt, and how your thoughts scarred *you*. You know, it's perfectly okay to dislike a couple of kids.'

'Is it?' I asked, astonished.

'Of course. They gave you a hard time and you reacted like any human being would. You distanced yourself. It's a protection mechanism. It doesn't mean you're some sort of monster.'

I considered this. Hearing Josh talk about Charlotte and Lucinda in such a matter-of-fact way made it all sound so reasonable. The truth was, for years I'd beaten myself up over never bonding with Nick's daughters. Don't get me wrong, I'd tried. From the days of pretending we were a jolly blended family, making picnics for outings, attempting to be some sort of grown-up sister to them when holidaying together, and later, when they were teenagers, suggesting we all go shopping and have a fun girly time. I'd thrown cash at

them, which they'd grabbed. But the love I'd done my damnedest to
dredge up had been chucked back. Then came a further recollection,
later still, of the two of them as the young women they became
and now were, coldly telling me that neither I nor my precious son
meant anything to them. They'd blatantly announced that they
didn't care if they never saw either of us again. It had hurt. Indeed,
there had been years of hurt. So much so that, in my darkest, most
despairing moments, I'd detested them almost as much as they'd
detested me. I'd resented the number of Christmases that had
been wrecked by two spoilt brats who had grown into two most
unpleasant young women.

It had all come to a head on our final family Christmas together.
The very last time Nick and I were together as husband and wife,
and Fin had wrongly been accused of smashing Charlotte's expensive
make-up palette. Nick had popped out to the garden shed to get
some logs for the wood burner and missed the altercation.

'Do you know how much that cost?' Charlotte had snarled, her
face contorted with rage as Fin had cowered away.

'I never touched it,' he'd bleated, 'it was you who dropped it.
I saw you.'

'How dare you lie, you nasty little piece of shi—'

'That's enough, Charlotte,' I'd interrupted, the lioness in me roaring
into life. I didn't care how either of these girls treated me, but I would
not have my darling boy on the receiving end of their nastiness.

'Don't you speak to me like that,' said Charlotte, her eyes narrowing, 'you're not my mother.'

'No, but I *am* Fin's mum, and I won't have him made a scapegoat
for your clumsiness.'

Lucinda had sidled over, joining her sister and, huddling close, given Charlotte moral support. They'd stood there, two pairs of ice-blue eyes meeting mine, full of loathing. Charlotte had inclined her head, as if considering me for the first time. When she'd next spoken, her voice had been low.

'We hate you, Hattie,' she'd hissed.

'Good to know,' I'd quipped back, 'because I hate you too.'

In that moment I'd meant it, and my expression must have confirmed it because both girls looked shocked, the hurt on their faces mirroring what they'd spent years dishing out to me without a second thought. But within seconds, I'd regretted my words. I was older than them. Supposedly wiser. Instead I'd sunk to their level. And I'd detested myself for that.

'But there's no need to beat yourself up about it, Hattie,' said Josh, gently bringing me back to the present. 'In that moment, you felt protective of your son and were indignant. Years of frustration rose to the surface and in one teeny, tiny second, you lowered yourself to their vibration. That doesn't make you a bad person.'

'Doesn't it?' I said miserably, taking another swig of wine.

'One hundred per cent,' said Josh kindly. 'You did everything you could to give those girls a second family base with emotional security. However, I need to flag up that this is an important moment in your review break.'

'God, I feel like I'm still reviewing, except doing it from this halfway pub.'

'In a way you are, but this is an easy matter to clear up, so long as you can now make peace with yourself over the retort you made to Charlotte. Do you feel able to?'

I considered Josh's question. It didn't need a lot of thinking about. 'Of course. I don't want to bear grudges. The past is over and done with. Lucinda and Charlotte are part of that past and were simply casualties of a marital fallout. If Nick had married someone else instead of me, then that lady too would have been on the receiving end of their hatred. It was the same with Nick's second wife. They didn't want anything to do with her – and the same applied to any girlfriend of Nick's the moment the relationship started to look serious. It wasn't personal, and anyway, I never really hated them. That's too strong a word.'

'So you no longer hate yourself for reaching the end of your tether?'

'No, and you're right,' I nodded, 'I'm not a bad person.'

Almost immediately I experienced the weirdest feeling. It was as if a pair of invisible hands had pushed themselves through the wall of my stomach, separating all the skin and muscles, and were busily rubbing away some inner part of me; as if I'd had a blocked intestine which, after all these years, had suddenly cleared. As though confirming such a thought, my guts gurgled alarmingly.

'Perfect,' said Josh. 'The energy is flowing again. You'll be amazed how much better you will feel when you're back in Earth time.'

'Thanks,' I grinned.

'Parenting is a hard task,' said Josh.

'Do you speak from experience?' I asked. Josh had revealed that he was in love with someone, but hadn't said anything about them having children together. For some reason my heart lurched at the thought.

'No, I don't have any children, Hattie,' Josh replied.

I found myself slowly exhaling with relief. Now why was that?

'Have you never wanted any?' I said, aware that I was probing, but trying to make it sound as if the question were as casual as asking if he liked milk in his tea before pouring or after.

He laughed knowingly. 'Hm, you're back to asking things about me. You know I'm not meant to tell you anything.'

'It's just an innocent question, Josh. Why on earth can't you answer it? It's called conversation.'

'It's also called nosiness,' he laughed, 'something you have a lot of, but I find it very endearing.'

'Really?' I asked, as a thrill of delight rippled through me. I so wanted Josh to feel something of the way I felt about him, and this was as good a start as any. There were also plenty more nosy questions I could ask if he found it charming. 'You're so knowing and wise where Charlotte and Lucinda are concerned, I'm sure you'd make a great dad.'

'I'll let you into a secret,' he said, dropping his voice as if the walls might have ears. The mischievous twinkle in his eyes wasn't lost on me. 'I'm not a father... yet!'

'Ah... so... oh! You're a father-to-be?' My spirits, which had been so uplifted only moments ago, seemed to sink right through the conjured-up pub's scuffed oak floorboards. 'Congratulations,' I said in a strangled voice.

'Thank you, said Josh, inclining his head graciously.

Well wasn't that just peachy? Not only was my lovely, gorgeous Josh in love with some other lucky lady, but plainly she was big with child too. *His* child. Josh regarded me with amusement, as if he was having a private joke at my expense.

'And when is the baby due?' I asked, trying to inject a bit of enthusiasm into my voice.

'In Earth time, not for another eighteen months.'

I frowned. 'Eighteen months? But how—'

'No more questions,' he said cutting me off.

'Right,' I sighed, resuming my contemplation of the floorboards.

'Otherwise you'll get me into trouble, and my job as your co-ordinator will be taken away. And I really don't want that to happen,' he added softly.

I looked up sharply, just in time to catch a look of extreme tenderness on his face. So much so that, if I wasn't very much mistaken – if this red wine wasn't blurring the edges and, indeed, if this whole weird experience wasn't muddling my clarity – one might be inclined to interpret it as a look of longing. But before I could reflect on that any further, he interrupted my musings.

'Are you ready to return to the past, Hattie?'

I drained my wine glass and nodded, staring into the flames of the roaring log fire. I knew what was coming next. Even though I recognised it needed reconciling, I didn't like it one little bit.

# Chapter Forty-Four

'What is it you want to tell me, Hattie?' said a man's voice.

Not Josh's. I tore my eyes away from the flames of the log fire and found Nick sitting opposite me. We weren't alone. The place was heaving. I knew immediately why the pub had seemed so familiar. It had once been Nick's local. Quaint, low-beamed and very relaxing with a stress-free ambience. He'd often brought me here in the early days of our dating, and we'd enjoyed many a charming pub supper. Its cosy atmosphere and down-to-earth clientele was one of the reasons I'd opted to tell him my news here, rather than at his flat. I'd felt it might be more prudent to have people around us, so he wouldn't go ballistic and create a scene. Well, he might do the former, but definitely not the latter. Nick wasn't one for public meltdowns.

'Er, yes,' I cleared my throat. 'Yes.'

'Yes?'

'Yes, I need to tell you something.'

'We've already established that,' Nick laughed. 'What's up with you, for goodness' sake? You're behaving like someone with an enormous secret that's grown so big it's going to burst out of you, ripping apart the very seams of your clothes.'

I couldn't have put it better if I'd tried. Whilst the seams of my clothes weren't coming undone, the zip on my jeans certainly was. In fact, I couldn't remember the last time I'd been able to do it all the way up. The stud button hadn't met for weeks.

'Do you want another drink first?' I asked.

'No, don't want to lose my licence,' Nick nodded at his pint. 'What about you? Wouldn't you rather change that soda water for a glass of wine?'

'Er, n-no,' I stammered, 'the s-soda water is fine.'

Whether it was the tremor in my voice, or that Nick suddenly registered I was declining my usual tipple, his facial expression and body language changed in a flash. His back visibly stiffened, and he sat so still I wondered if he'd suspended breathing. Suddenly there was a silence between us that became heavy and horribly protracted. In the background, noise continued. There was the merry ding of the pub's old-fashioned cash till followed by a clatter of coins. The punters continued chatting, their collective conversation sounding like bees humming, punctuated by the occasional guffaw. All around us people were having a joke and relaxing. It was just in this snug corner, by the open fire, that a hushed tension prevailed. And still we stared at each other.

'Do you or do you not have something to tell me?' said Nick, at length. His voice sounded so different. Harsh. Like that of a stranger.

'Yes, I do,' I croaked, struggling to voice aloud what needed saying.

'Go on, spit it out,' he said, his mouth disappearing into a thin line. I hated it when he did that. It made him look so mean.

Unnerved, I took a sip of soda water and promptly choked. He didn't blink as I sat there, coughing and spluttering. Eyeballs streaming, I dipped into my handbag for a tissue.

'I'm waiting,' he hissed.

I swiped at my eyes and thanked God I was telling him my news in a public place.

'I-I have a feeling you've already worked it out,' I said, desperately hoping I'd be let off the hook for actually saying it.

'I'm not second-guessing what you want to tell me, Hattie,' he said bleakly. 'I'll ask you again. What do you want to tell me?'

There was a pause while I dug deep for some much-needed courage.

'I'm pregnant,' I whispered.

'You can't be,' he immediately volleyed back.

'But I am.' My voice was barely audible. He looked so angry. This was awful.

'It can't be mine,' he said, his eyes hard as flint. 'I've never taken chances, not even if a woman has told me she's on the pill. I know too many guys who have been trapped by a woman playing the card that you're now trying to deal me.'

'I haven't been unfaithful,' I said, aghast that he could think I'd want to sleep with anyone other than him. 'Accidents happen.'

'No they don't,' he said, 'not to me.'

'Well this time, it *has*,' I insisted miserably. 'But it's okay. I'm not trying to trap you. You don't have to whisk me into the nearest Registry Office and make an honest woman out of me. Nor do I expect you to raise the child with me. I'll see to it.'

Relief flooded across his face. 'Good. I'll pay. Obviously.'

I stared at him in confusion. 'Pay?'

'For the abortion.'

'Who said I'm having an abortion?'

'You just said you'd see to it.'

'Yes, I meant, as in bringing up the child. I'll see to it.'

Nick stared at me incredulously. 'You'll *see* to it?' he repeated, his voice going up an octave. 'This isn't a bloody tin of baked beans you're talking about, Hattie. You're talking about nine months of pregnancy and a life-long commitment. How the heck are you going to "see" to having a kid when you're still living at home with your mum and dad, and sleeping in your childhood bedroom, eh? Are you under some sort of misguided impression that you'll simply shift over in bed, and make a bit of room under that childish unicorn quilt so you can tuck Baby in alongside you? Is that what you're naively thinking?'

Well, yes, something like that. Put like that, the idea sounded preposterous.

'I'm sure—'

'Sure of what? That Mummy and Daddy will be thrilled to bits they're going to have a grandchild? Delighted that their daughter will become a stay-at-home mum and they have to fund not only you, but a kid that grows at the rate of knots?'

'They won't object—'

'Well I bloody do!' he roared, causing the background hum to dip as several eyes pinged over to the couple in the corner clearly having an exchange of words. Nick slammed his pint down on the table, causing it to slop everywhere.

Oh God. I should have told him at his flat after all. He was giving me exactly the reaction I'd sought to avoid by being in a public place. Instead we were making a spectacle of ourselves. My face flushed an unfetching shade of beetroot. He shifted in his seat to stare at those bold enough to gawp in our direction. Eyes slithered away. Men studied their drinks while women whispered behind their hands.

'Get rid of it,' he said, turning back to me.

'I can't.'

'Don't give me any bollocks about it being your body and your decision. It takes two to make a baby. Therefore, it takes two to decide whether to keep it.'

'I really can't—'

'Now you listen to me, Hattie,' Nick interrupted, his face turning an unattractive shade of magenta. 'I do *not* want to be a father again. I do *not* want another child. Do you understand?'

'Yes, but—'

'I'll sort it out,' he said, picking up his dripping pint glass and draining the contents in one gulp. He set the empty glass back down with an air of finality. 'Leave it to me. I'll find a private clinic and book you in. You'll get the best care and—'

'But—'

'No buts.'

'WILL YOU LET ME SPEAK!' I shouted.

Once again there was a hush as this time the entire pub ground to a halt. It was Nick's turn to look uncomfortable.

'Aye, let the lass speak,' quipped someone as another tittered.

'Is this really the place to have this conversation?' Nick hissed.

'It's as good as any,' I retorted.

The punters once again turned back to their drinks, resuming conversation. When the volume was at a suitable level to stop anyone overhearing, I leant in closer to Nick.

Debbie Viggiano

'You're absolutely right.'

He immediately looked happier, thinking I was seeing sense from his point of view, but he was misunderstanding me, and I was quick to rectify that.

'It does indeed take two to make a baby,' I continued, 'but that baby is carried by *one* person. Me. Not you. So don't you ever, *ever* tell me what I can and can't do with *my* body. Is that clear?' My voice caught in the back of my throat and I broke off, struggling for composure.

He regarded me furiously. 'Exactly how pregnant are you?' he demanded.

'Four months.'

'Four *months*?' Nick gasped. 'Why the heck have you kept so quiet about it?'

'I didn't know,' I said.

'Didn't know?' he repeated, his expression one of disbelief. 'How the hell could you not have known, Hattie?'

Yes, indeed, how could I have not known? However, I was speaking the absolute truth. It was everything after this moment that became a lie.

# Chapter Forty-Five

*Your vibration is changing to grey, Hattie. I can tell you're distressed. Shall we resume the review in the Halfway Lounge?*

*Y-yes please*, I stammered.

The pub disappeared and, with it, Nick's angry face and the inquisitive clientele who had still been casting us the odd surreptitious glance, curious to know what was going on with the angry man and the young woman with huge scared eyes.

'Oh, Josh,' I said, my voice despairing. 'What must you think of me?' And with that I burst into tears. 'Sorry,' I bleated, as a box of tissues manifested in mid-air. Josh was clearly expecting the full waterworks. Again.

'I've told you before, Hattie,' he said gently, 'there is no judgement. You're not here to repeatedly beat yourself up. You're here to make peace with yourself and let the past go in a mindful and self-healing way.'

'It wasn't very mindful and healing for Nick though, was it?' I howled.

'I hear what you're saying, but he didn't have to stay with you. Later, he made that decision for himself.'

'Under duress.'

'Duress or not, it was ultimately his choice. But this isn't about Nick and, anyway, karma later played out its hand to you for your actions.'

'What do you mean, karma?'

'That old law of cause and effect came into play after you and Nick got together. You know what I'm talking about, don't you?'

'You mean the bit where—'

'Hang on, we're getting ahead of ourselves,' said Josh, interrupting me. 'One thing at a time. Firstly, everything happens for a reason. Nick had outstanding parenting issues to address that were left hanging when he dumped the first Mrs Green for the second Mrs Green. So rest assured that he got to deal with those issues when your son was born.'

'This karma stuff is beyond complex,' I said, trumpeting noisily into a second tissue.

'Life is full of complexities,' Josh agreed, 'and yet there is simplicity in the most complicated of things.'

'You're not convincing me,' I said, giving a watery grin.

'I don't need to convince you, because that's not what this is about. Let's start with why this situation arose in the first place.'

'You mean, why I lied to Nick.'

'If you want to put it that way, although I think the word "lie" is rather a strong one, don't you? Let's try another word. What about "deluded"? It fits the circumstances. You literally duped yourself into believing Nick was the father of your unborn child. And that's understandable.'

'Because of what happened with… ' I almost gagged saying his name aloud, '…with Martin?'

'You wince every time you say your ex-boyfriend's name. That also needs addressing. But yes. With Martin. You had a total mental block about what happened. A coping mechanism came into play and your memory acted like shutters clanging down, blocking out the fact that no contraceptives were used which, in turn, obstructed you questioning why your period was late, month after month after month, until your jeans didn't do up and your belly had the start of a swell.'

I reddened, not entirely at ease discussing my menstrual cycle with a man who, for heaven's sake, wasn't even my GP. But then again, I seemed to be talking about no end of embarrassing things with Josh. If he wasn't fazed, then presumably I shouldn't be.

'Yes, I understand what you're saying, and you're right. I was in denial. But there did eventually come a point where I realised it wasn't just my body that was about to go pear-shaped. My whole life was crumbling around me.'

'It was a stressful situation, Hattie. There's no doubt about it. Your memory block lifted enough for you to finally buy a pregnancy kit, but that was all. You'd been banned from Martin's funeral, which also kept a lot of much-needed grief at bay and unwittingly aided the denial and memory block.'

I nodded, accepting Josh's explanation, because hearing him voice it was lifting the lid on the whole sorry episode. Everything was flooding back with clarity and I found myself admitting important things that I'd never allowed myself to acknowledge before: that what had happened was not my fault. No was no, and whether he'd been drinking or not, Martin hadn't taken notice of that. Afterwards, I'd convinced myself that I was to blame. That Martin had been hurting from my ending the relationship, so it was only natural for him to want to hurt me back. That perhaps he'd genuinely thought we were sexually play-acting a 'catch me if you can' scenario. I'd told myself that perhaps I was at fault for going to his apartment to end the relationship, allowing him to misconstrue things and that, callous as it seemed, I should have done what hundreds of other women so often do – dumped him by text. Such an action would have avoided misunderstanding on his part and vulnerability on mine.

All these unleashed thoughts came rushing back to me. I'd blamed myself and, disgusted, shoved it from my mind. Whenever the memory had threatened to return and overwhelm me, I'd simply turned my back on it all, mentally distancing myself and berating myself: *It's your fault, Hattie*. I'd done something stupid. Handled it badly. End of story. Much better to move on and make a fresh start with a man I'd loved from afar for the last six months.

Despite the trauma of what had happened with Martin, I'd had no compunction about sleeping with Nick again. Firstly, a part of my brain had shut down, consequently putting distance between myself and the event. Secondly, I'd welcomed my body joining with Nick's. It had been cathartic. Cleansing. The action became the cement in the brick wall that I'd put up over Martin, and I concentrated only on having a fun time with the man I adored. So when I missed my period, I told myself it was just a hormonal blip. I was now well and truly in denial, you see. And that denial remained steadfast when the second period failed to make an appearance. And then the third. I refused to acknowledge what was going on in my body. It was only when I could no longer do up buttons on waistbands that a chink appeared in the cemented-up wall. It was only a small chink, you understand, but enough to send me scurrying off to the local pharmacy. An over-the-counter pregnancy test was purchased and, later, I trembled as the twin lines turned blue. And *still* I refused to acknowledge Martin's role in my new situation. Never. Not in a month of Sundays. This baby was Nick's. Of that I was adamant.

# Chapter Forty-Six

'So,' said Josh, bringing me back to the present again, 'you've recognised why the delusion was established about Fin's father, and reviewed with fresh eyes the reason for the denial, and you now understand the precursor to that action. Martin raped you Hattie. What happened was never your fault.'

'Yes,' I sighed. God, what a mess. Years and years of emotional chaos. 'But, Josh, deep down I *did* know. You can run from the truth, but it has a way of constantly catching up with you. Every now and again that carefully constructed wall would threaten to crumble... a brick would fall out... sometimes several... and I was like a builder on amphetamines hastily patching it all up. I was constantly checking the foundations didn't wobble and, if they did, scrabbling to find other ways of propping it up in order to maintain the illusion. Anything – and I mean *anything* – that would allow me to continue convincing myself that none of us were living a lie. As the years went by, that wall became a barricade with barbed wire along the top.' I shook my head. 'I've never admitted any of this to anyone. Nobody knows the truth, Josh,' I said sadly. And then I recoiled in horror as a thought occurred. 'Is part of my being here also to do with owning up to my son? Do I have to tell Fin?'

'No.'

'But… that doesn't seem right, somehow.' I licked my lips nervously. 'It smacks of dishonesty.'

'Okay, so let's discuss the idea of potentially telling Fin. Think carefully, Hattie, and answer me one question. What purpose does it serve?'

I shrugged. 'Well, I'm not sure, as such. Doesn't he have a moral right to know?'

'You tell me. Would it be beneficial for Fin – and Nick for that matter – to deal with this socking great bolt from the blue? Can you anticipate their reaction? Do you see them jumping for joy at such news? Can you be sure their relationship would remain unchanged? Do you think they'd happily accept this bombshell – the circumstances of Fin's conception followed by Martin's awful demise – and simply give you a hug and say, "Heyyy, no harm done!"? Or do you think such action might, in fact, open a stinking can of worms that benefits nobody other than you from an offloading perspective? The latter of which, I might point out, you're now doing anyway, so therefore it has no benefit for anyone in your family, least of all Fin and Nick.'

'Right, well, put like that, no. It's better to stay schtum.' I could feel my eyes filling up again. 'But I feel so guilty, Josh.'

'Okay, well you can drop the guilt right now, because I'm going to tell you something that will rock you.'

'What?' I asked tremulously.

'Nick is Fin's father.'

I stared at Josh, gobsmacked. 'You mean… all these years… oh my God! Are you telling me that I've been mistaken all this time?' I couldn't believe my ears, but my body was majorly reacting to Josh's words. It felt like huge invisible shackles were falling off me, leaving me beyond joyous. Elated. Dear Lord, I was flying with happiness. No more would I mentally flay myself believing I was guilty of lying! 'But… but I don't understand. There are too many physical resemblances between Martin and Fin. He has the same smile as Martin. Certain expressions…' I trailed off, suddenly uncertain, doubting what Josh had told me.

'Hattie, look at me,' he said softly. I gazed up and saw such compassion in his eyes, such immense kindness, it brought a whopping lump to my throat.

'Remember when I told you that even the most complex situations have simplicity?'

'Yes,' I said, my voice quavering slightly. I felt like I'd just stepped off a merry-go-round of madness but was in danger of being pushed back on it. I didn't want to be full of fresh doubt and find myself once again spinning endlessly, like the lie I'd been living.

'I was telling you the truth, Hattie. Out of this complex situation there is one certainty. Nick *is* Fin's father. Think about it. Who raised your son? Who helped you with broken nights? The endless colic and, later, teething? Who wiped Fin's brow when he had a fever? Who came to stand at the school gates as you waved your little boy off on that first day? Who shed a tear with you? Who always rushed from work to be by your side if there was a problem – like the time Fin had a fall and ended up in hospital with concussion? Even when you split, he remained involved with his son. He's still there for Fin. Whatever Nick lacked as a husband, he has given in spades as a parent. So ask yourself again, Hattie. Who is the real father of your child, and your heart will instantly answer.'

'Nick,' I said, without any hesitation.

'Yes, Nick. You see, it doesn't matter whose DNA went into making up the flesh and bones of your son, it's who has been *there* for him. And the answer to that question – and has always been the answer to that question – is Nick. So now you understand that Nick is indeed Fin's dad. He always has been. Always will be.'

I nodded, knowing every word Josh was saying was true. Understanding and euphoria rippled through my core. There was no need to reveal the past to Fin... Nick... anyone... because it didn't matter. It simply wasn't relevant.

'Exactly,' said Josh, reading my thoughts. 'You can't change the past, but you can make your peace with it, and move on.'

Tears were pouring down my face now, but I was smiling. Josh pushed himself up from his easy chair and opened his arms. It seemed like the most natural thing in the world to spring to my feet and walk straight into his embrace. He held me tight, and I hugged him back, hard. From a place deep within my heart, another oppressive layer shook itself free. I felt like I was standing on the threshold of a brand new future. A future where everything was shiny and bright and – at last – untainted. Nick and Fin could carry on enjoying their father and son relationship, which was, after all, what they'd always had. And always would.

# Chapter Forty-Seven

As Josh continued to hold me, for one crazy moment I was tempted to thread my fingers through his hair and pull his mouth towards mine. The jubilation of discovering Nick was truly Fin's dad was almost like a physical sensation. I could have sworn I was literally *feeling* happiness flowing through my veins. It was heightening everything – including the effect Josh's touch was having upon me.

'You need a review break,' said Josh, gently releasing me from his arms.

'I think you're right,' I said, letting my hands fall reluctantly to my sides.

'Do you still feel like you're "flying with happiness"?' he said, his eyes twinkling playfully.

'Y-e-s,' I carefully replied. 'I know that look you're giving. You're going to suggest we do something crazy.'

'You're getting to know me so well, Hattie,' he beamed.

*But not nearly as much as I'd like to*, I privately lamented, wondering how Josh would react if I told him I was not only in love with him but wanted to push him down on the squashy sofa I'd just abandoned, leap on top of him and cover his face in lots of frantic kisses. He'd probably have a coronary – if such a thing were possible in a place like this.

'What have you got in mind?' I asked, wishing that he would reply, 'You', before striding over and pulling me back into his arms and lowering his lips to mine and snogging me roughly, but gently, but firmly, but softly, but—

'Are you all right, Hattie?' he asked.

'Sorry?' I gasped. Good heavens, why did my mind have this habit of wandering off into fantasyland?

'You've gone all pink.'

'Ah, y-yes, it happens sometimes.'

'Does it?'

'Mm. Sometimes I get all hot and bothered.'

'Really?' said Josh, his eyes doing that infuriatingly attractive twinkly thing again.

'It's just a hot flush.'

*A hot flush, Hattie? At your age? And even if you were old enough to experience such a thing, it's hardly romantic to mention it. Do you honestly believe Josh would like to be included in reflecting upon the finer nuances of your hormonal system?*

'Right, well so long as you're okay, let's press on. Your thought processes have manifested an interesting excursion.'

'Really?' I said, eager to get off the subject of my red face and curious to see what Josh was hinting at.

'Come with me.'

He caught hold of my hand and led me to the Halfway Lounge's door. I'd stepped through this portal a few times, and now I wondered what lay beyond on this occasion. It reminded me of a television programme I'd watched as a child, where different shaped windows had been presented to the viewer with a guessing-game of what lay beyond. As Josh opened the door, I let out a little cry of surprise.

We had stepped into the cockpit of a hot air balloon and, even more thrilling, were already at two thousand feet drifting through the sky… a proper sky this time, with a bright sun and soft puffs of clouds. I breathed in deeply, relishing the fresh air, the swathe of Kent countryside below, and the sensation of having the world at my feet. With a jolt, I realised that I truly did have the world at my feet. It was right back home, and waiting for me.

Josh and I didn't talk for a while, allowing ourselves to just 'be'. We drifted in companionable silence, with only the occasional blast of the burners for company.

'I've done this before,' I eventually murmured.

'I know,' Josh smiled. 'Your eighteenth birthday present from your parents.'

I nodded. 'We went as a family. When the balloon took off, I was terrified but, weirdly, having Mum and Dad there too also made me feel safe. I'd never thought it possible to experience both fear *and* security at the same time, until that moment,' I chuckled at the memory. I was lucky to have such wonderful parents and, again, was reminded of the good stuff in my life. 'I've promised Fin the same birthday experience when he's eighteen.'

I broke off, suddenly feeling incredibly homesick. It didn't matter what had happened in my past. The only thing that truly mattered was the future. And oh, how I wanted to return home and have that future waiting.

'Let's press on with your life review, Hattie,' said Josh. He took my hand and gave it a gentle squeeze of reassurance.

I didn't reply. The balloon excursion had been a smooth experience. But now, something far bumpier was awaiting.

# Chapter Forty-Eight

We were back in the Halfway Lounge, me sitting on the squashy sofa, and Josh once again ensconced in the easy chair opposite me. Both of us were enjoying an après flight aperitif of some sort. I had no idea what it was, but it reminded me of brandy. Perhaps Josh had given it to me as a fortification measure for what lay ahead. Despite knowing I was shortly in for a choppy ride in 'review time', the balloon jaunt had left me feeling strangely energised.

'It's true,' said Josh, picking up on my thoughts. 'You've basically done the cosmic equivalent of charging a battery. In your case, you were the battery, and the flight was the electrical charge. Which is good, because there's a lot coming up. However, there is now light at the end of the tunnel – as everyone says on Earth. The end, Hattie, is in sight!'

'And then I can go home?'

'Yes. You will soon be returning to normality.'

'Good,' I said, adopting a chipper tone. Home. It was what I so wanted, although I was dreading saying goodbye to Josh. I had a horrible feeling that absenting myself from him would break my heart. I had visions of drooping around the cottage sighing a lot. Disappearing with Buddy for long, pensive walks. My mother regarding me beadily as she puffed away on one of her ciggies. Perhaps I would have to take myself off for a spot of counselling.

COUNSELLOR: *Broken heart, you say?*
ME: *Yes (reaching for handy box of tissues placed on functional table).*
COUNSELLOR: *It happens to the best of us. Where did you meet?*
ME: *On the astral plane.*
COUNSELLOR: *Don't think I know it. Ah, wait, Berkshire?*
ME: *No. Heavenwards. It didn't take us long to get there.*
COUNSELLOR: *Heaven… er, as in the afterlife?*
ME: *That's right (perking up). At one point, I was in a hot air balloon.*
COUNSELLOR: *(reaching for notepad and scribbling frantically) Barking mad… delusional… but not a threat to society…*

I wondered if Josh would miss me. Probably not. Twinkly eyes and the occasional bit of flirty banter did not mean he felt the same way about me. And anyway, even if he did, it wasn't possible to be together. I wondered if there was a way to unite these two worlds? I felt like there might be, but couldn't quite put my finger on it. But it was no good pondering this dilemma. Not yet anyway, because a far more pressing one was about to happen.

'Are you sure you're ready for this, Hattie? There's no pressure. We have all the time in the universe.'

'No, not at all, it's fine,' I said hastily, taking another slug of the brandy-like liquid. I drained the glass and put it on the floor by my feet. 'Tell me how to travel to the next bit of reviewing.'

'That's easy. Firstly, close your eyes and relax.'

I sat back, my lids fluttering shut.

'Good. Now, concentrate on the flavour of what you've been drinking,' said Josh, 'and acknowledge the echo of its taste on your tongue.'

I focused on the subtle nuances and discovered I could name the ingredients. Impatiens, Rock Rose, Clematis, Star of Bethlehem, Cherry Plum… good heavens, how did I know this?

'What are you doing?' said a male voice.

My eyes snapped open. Nick. I'd left him by a roaring log fire in the pub where I'd broken the news to him that he was an expectant father. But now the scene had shifted. We were back in his apartment. The bathroom, to be more precise. The wall-mounted cabinet was open. Something small and hard was in my hands. From my safe place, I once again found myself both peculiarly watching *and* reliving an old drama.

I glanced down at a bottle of Rescue Remedy caught between my fingers. The lid had been removed and, from the taste in my mouth, it was apparent I'd delivered a hefty squirt of the stuff under my tongue.

'It's a flower remedy,' I replied.

'A what?' Nick frowned. He didn't believe in anything 'alternative' and had a distinct aversion to anything that wasn't conventional. Ask him about Chinese medicine and he'd have told you that the only herbs he liked were those with his crispy duck. He peered at the bottle in my hands. 'What's it for?'

'Um, stress,' I mumbled, faintly embarrassed. I sensed, rather than saw, him rolling his eyes. I'd stashed a couple of bottles of the stuff, which were only small, behind my floral shampoo, which I knew Nick wouldn't touch and had therefore thought a good hiding place for the remedy.

'It must be working,' he quipped, 'because I've never known you so uptight.'

I screwed the lid back on and hastily shoved it in the cabinet. It was then that I caught sight of my belly. Good heavens, it was huge. My mind flew off and did some mental calculations on exactly how pregnant I was. It came to me in a flash. Around six months, and I'd been living with Nick for the last two. I shut the cabinet door. It was mirrored and reflected the view beyond the bathroom window. Outside, a round-shaped bonfire of orange was rapidly sinking beyond the horizon, turning the sky into a canvas of grey and purple feathery clouds shot through with gold. It looked beautiful. Unlike me. I was shocked at the tired young woman gazing back at me in the mirror. I turned away and regarded Nick properly.

He was dressed casually, but smartly enough for me to know that he was off out. The scent of freshly applied aftershave hung in the air between us.

'Thought I'd pop in on Tod and Jackie. They're having a bit of a drinks do.'

Tod was Nick's charming brother, married to the insufferable Jackie who was a big-breasted monumental bore and totally up her pert little backside.

'I told them to expect me about eight-ish, so I'd better get a wiggle on. See you later, Hattie.'

I leant back against the sink, momentarily rooted to the spot. It was Saturday night. He was going out. Again. Leaving me alone. Again. This pattern had started about a fortnight ago, but in the last week the pace had picked up dramatically.

'I'll come with you,' I said impulsively.

Nick swung round, his face neutral, but for a split second I'd seen his look of alarm.

'Is that a good idea?' he asked, arranging his features into an expression of caring concern. 'You said you weren't feeling well. I don't want you overdoing it, darling.'

'Don't be daft,' I tutted. 'How can chatting with your brother and sister-in-law be overdoing it?'

'It's quite a crowd they've invited over. Nobody really sits down at these types of events. They all stand about clutching warm drinks, rocking back on their heels and making inane conversation. It's pretty boring in all truth. I'm only going because Tod begged me to keep him company. Ninety per cent of the crowd are Jackie's friends, and we all know what planks they are.'

'You sound like you don't want me there.' It was said lightly enough, but Nick knew I was challenging him.

'Don't be silly,' he said, but his tone held no conviction. 'You're the one with elephant ankles at the moment, not me. If you want to aggravate them further by not keeping off them for the next few hours, that's entirely up to you. Shall I wait for you to get changed then?'

He was calling my bluff. I was about to double-bluff him and say, 'Two seconds, let me exchange this awful smock for my poshest maternity tent', but my bravado was interrupted by a wave of nausea. I'd discovered that there was no such thing as morning sickness in this pregnancy, but evenings were an entirely different matter. Unlike the cheerfully worded advice in the text books, the affliction hadn't subsided as the pregnancy progressed. I clutched the basin as my face turned the same colour as the porcelain.

'Darling, you can't possibly come with me. You look awful.'

'Thanks,' I muttered.

'I don't mean that horribly,' he assured me, 'but I can see you're not feeling fab. Come into the lounge. Get those feet up and I'll make you a ginger tea before I go.'

He was all concern now, leading me out of the bathroom, into the open-plan kitchen-living area. My eyes widened slightly at the change in the flat's appearance. What had once been a chic and minimalist bachelor pad now looked like it had been invaded by several branches of Mothercare. Mum was the culprit. She wasn't Nick's biggest fan, but once she'd known a baby was on the way, she'd decided to make the best of the situation. Her feelings might only be lukewarm for Nick, but she was determined her grandchild would be the most loved baby ever and was revving up to be a besotted grandma.

I worked my way through the obstacle course. So far, we'd amassed a cot, boxed-up playpen, a pram that converted into so many different things the manual would have to accompany me wherever we went, several large boxes of flat-pack nursery furniture and bagful after bagful of baby clothes. I had no idea how we were going to fit all this into the small second bedroom. Currently it was Nick's office, and only just about accommodated a small desk and filing cabinet.

I flopped down on the sofa, trying to ignore the nausea and not dry heave in front of my partner.

'What time will you be back?' I asked, as Nick busied himself with the kettle and rifled through an assortment of fancy teas that I never usually drank, but which I was now steadily working my way through. There were teas to help you relax, detox, wind down, or perk up, depending on one's required mood. None of them seemed to be working for me, but I suspected that was down to my mismanagement of my life, which was full of endless aggravation. I was either dealing with Nick's daughters' contempt, or my parents' anxiety, but also, and worst of all, the silent anger emanating from a man who had so obviously felt boxed into a corner. After Nick had *finally* calmed down about the pregnancy news, he'd given assurances of wanting to be with me and our child. Nonetheless I knew he was festering with resentment.

Perhaps I would have coped better if I'd *felt* better, but there seemed to be no rhyme or reason to this pregnancy nausea. My main diet consisted of ginger biscuits and tea whilst prostrate on the sofa. My reading tastes had changed too. Once I'd endlessly devoured trashy novels, but now I avidly read mother and child magazines, thumbing through glossy pics of expectant mothers looking rosy-cheeked and dewy-eyed as they bloomed away. Unlike me. I looked washed-out and knackered, and the only blooming going on was of the blooming awful variety.

'Here,' said Nick, passing me the tea.

'Thank you,' I said, and sipped gratefully.

'So,' Nick raised his eyebrows at me, 'you won't be joining me after all.'

'No, best not. You're right. I'd only be a wallflower, and there's nothing worse than a wilting wallflower at that. You go. Give Tod and Jackie my apologies and have a nice time.'

'Sure.' He bent down and pecked me on the cheek in the same manner as one might dutifully kiss an aged aunt. 'Here,' he said, passing me one of my expectant mum magazines. 'You can have a flick through whilst enjoying your tea.'

'Thanks, I've not read this one.'

'Right,' he said, gathering up his jacket hanging off the back of a chair. Even chairs were doubling up as wardrobes since I'd moved in. The apartment wasn't generous with closet space. 'Don't wait up.'

Seconds later, the flat's main door clicked shut. I was on my own. I took another sip of tea and began skimming through the magazine pausing to read, with interest, an article entitled 'Sex During Pregnancy'. Really? Did anyone honestly have sex in pregnancy? I'd imagined nobody would particularly feel like it. I certainly didn't. The last thing I wanted was a tongue landing in my mouth when I was gagging. Not that it would happen right now. There had been no invitations from Nick to participate in nookie, so absolutely nothing was going on under the duvet. In fact… I paused to remember the last time we'd done *any*thing other than snuggle, spoon or cuddle. It had all ground to a halt pretty much since moving into the flat. There had been the briefest brushes of lips on cheeks, like the one delivered earlier as he'd said goodbye. But no passionate kisses. Nick had been honest and told me it wasn't personal, but he didn't find expectant women attractive. But then again, I could see where he was coming from. Lying on the sofa impersonating a beached whale was not a pretty sight. It wasn't just my stomach that was swollen. My ankles were accessorising nicely, folding neatly over my shoes, and my face looked permanently bloated. The antenatal nurse had told me it was fluid retention and would go after the birth.

Despite all these inconveniences, I loved my bump. My hand rested upon it now, stroking it tenderly. Nothing was more pleasurable than lying in the tub and watching a tiny fist or foot shoot out, making my tummy shift like a human sand dune. I took another sip of tea and continued reading, boggling slightly at one expectant mum's under-the-cover pregnancy tale.

*Dale absolutely loves me when I'm pregnant, so much so that he jokingly says he's going to keep me in the Pudding Club until I hit the menopause, ha ha ha! He likes running his fingers through my hair, which, thanks to all those surging hormones, is always lusciously thick and shiny. More than anything though, Dale adores my boobs. Pregnancy always makes them double in size. I'm a big girl anyway, but the minute those twin lines on the pregnancy tester turn blue, my chest gets so massive it makes Katie Price's look like two thimbles on a tablecloth. Sex in pregnancy can be very comfortable if you lay back on lots of cushions and let your partner concentrate on the bit of you that is going to give you both the most pleasure. Breasts easily fit into this category. To spice things up, Dale's favourite is bringing a can of whippy cream into the bedroom. The sexiest thing in the world is having your man transform your twin peaks into cream turrets and then lick it all off. It's good to experiment too. Eton Mess works well, although the meringue's sugar makes things a bit sticky…*

I took another sip of tea and cogitated. Perhaps this was where I was going wrong. Nick wasn't a big fan of cream, but he liked berries well enough. Maybe, instead of retiring to bed in an outsized pair of pants and a nightie in extra-extra-large, perhaps I should whip everything off to reveal some strawberries impaled on my nipples.

I was just wondering if raspberries might work better, when the telephone rang.

'Hello?'

'Hey, Hattie. How are you doing?'

It was Nick's brother, Tod.

'Hi, I'm fine,' I said, and then mentally smacked myself. If Tod thought I was okay he'd wonder why I wasn't coming over this evening. 'Actually, I'm a bit under the weather. But I don't like complaining.'

'Ah, Jackie was the same when she had our boys. It will be worth it in the end, you'll see.'

I smiled at his words. 'I don't doubt it. Anyway, what can I do for you, Tod?'

'Much as I love hearing your dulcet tones, Hattie, I'm actually after Nick.'

'Nick?' I repeated, surprised. 'But he should be with you.'

'Oh?' Tod sounded confused.

'Your drinks party.'

There was a stunned silence at the other end of the line.

'Isn't it tonight?' I prompted.

'Ah, the *drinks* party,' said Tod.

Even though he wasn't in the same room as me, I could sense his brain whirring.

'Yes, how silly of me,' he continued, giving a forced laugh. 'I'd forget my head if it wasn't screwed on. Oh, hang on, someone's at the door, must be some guests arriving. Okay, no worries, Hattie. I was only calling Nick for a chat, but I'll be able to natter to him all night now. Fantastic!'

'Er, yes,' I said, doubtfully.

'Bye then!' said Tod, and with that the line abruptly disconnected.

I put the handset slowly down and stared blankly at the page I'd been reading. I was fully aware that my hormones were all over the place, but I wasn't so emotionally addled as to realise that Tod knew nothing about the drinks party he was supposedly hosting, and that Nick must have lied about where he was going this evening. I had a feeling that I was going to need a lot more than whippy cream to fix this.

# Chapter Forty-Nine

It was long after midnight when Nick crept into the flat. He stumbled around in the dark, believing me to be asleep, stubbed his toe on the end of the bed and emitted a muffled oath. I lay there, inert, as he slid under the duvet. He settled on his side, facing away from me. I turned over.

'Who is she, Nick?' I said, addressing his back.

In the gloom, I saw the mound next to me stiffen.

'What are you talking about?' came his cautious reply.

'I'm talking about your fancy woman,' I said, suddenly sounding like an actress out of *EastEnders*. *Honestly, Hattie, who says 'fancy woman' these days?*

'Eh?'

'You 'eard.' Oh God, I was even talking like her now.

Earlier, after putting down the phone to Tod, I'd rehearsed this moment over and over. In my head I'd planned to question Nick in a cool and calm manner. A bit like an icy female detective inspector questioning a suspect. My tone would be measured. Confident. But steely too. Nick would instantly crack and deliver a sobbing confession. However, in the reality of the moment, my BAFTA-nomination line of questioning had dwindled to a one-liner spat out as a harsh accusation worthy of Kat Slater.

The bedside lamp flicked on.

'What the hell are you talking about?' Nick demanded, shifting on the mattress so he could peer at me. His brown eyes were full of anger as they bored into mine, which were both screwed-up against the sudden light and attractively bloodshot from bawling.

'Where've you bin… been?' I cried.

'At Tod's,' Nick enunciated, as if talking to a rather dense person.

'Liar!' I shoved him hard in the chest.

'I can't believe you're being so ridiculous,' Nick hissed. 'You know perfectly well I went to Tod and Jackie's drinks party. You were even thinking of coming with me, remember?'

'Except Tod rang about an hour after you left asking to speak to you. He seemed very surprised to hear he was playing host to a large gathering of friends, but quickly recovered himself and covered for your lies. Why weren't you with him when he called?'

'Because,' said Nick through clenched teeth, 'I popped in on Mum first. In case you'd failed to notice, she's a widow, hasn't been very well lately, and appreciates the occasional visit.'

I opened my mouth to say something, but nothing came out. There was an element of truth in Nick's explanation. Doreen had recently had a series of chest pains that had frightened her, but other than being diagnosed with mild angina and prescribed beta blockers, she'd been given a clean bill of health.

'I asked Mum if she fancied coming along with me, but she declined, saying she wanted a quiet evening in front of *Strictly* with dear Brucie and darling Len.'

It was true that Doreen adored *Strictly Come Dancing*, enjoying the late Bruce Forsyth's banter, and had a soft spot for Len who reminded her of her dearly departed husband.

'Right,' I said, finding my voice. That still didn't explain Tod's apparent surprise that he was having a bit of a do, but then again, I hadn't physically seen Tod in person to bear witness to his astonishment. Had I simply imagined his reaction? I was no longer sure.

'What was that, Hattie?' said Nick sarcastically, theatrically cupping one hand around his ear.

I frowned. 'Sorry?'

'Apology accepted,' he said, eyes flashing.

It was a look I'd seen many a time in the workplace. A look that dared a colleague or tricky client to question him further.

'Now if you don't mind, I'd like some kip. I'm picking up Lucinda and Charlotte at nine in the morning.'

My stomach lurched. Oh no. What 'fun' day had Nick got lined up for us all?

'Don't worry,' he said, as if reading my thoughts. 'I know you're not up for cycling around Bedgebury's cycle trail or taking them swimming afterwards.'

'N-no, quite,' I said, trying not to sound relieved at being exempted. 'Quite tiring for you though,' I said sympathetically, attempting to claw my way back into his good books.

'Yes, which is why their mother is coming along too.'

'Amanda?'

'I do believe that is the name of the girls' mother,' Nick retorted.

'B-but you don't usually do things with Amanda,' I said, my heart starting to pound uncomfortably. What was going on here? Happy Families Part Two?

'Amanda is currently between boyfriends, and the girls asked if their mum could come along. Is it a problem?' he asked, tetchiness evident in his voice.

'No, of course not,' I said, determined to be relaxed about it. After all, Nick was hardly likely to be getting his leg over with Amanda in front of two young girls now, was he?

*And why would he anyway, Hattie?* sneered the little voice in my head. *You know what your problem is, don't you? You're unreasonably distrustful. Pregnant and paranoid. What a combination.*

*Oh shut up*, I mentally snapped back.

*Talking to yourself too. It's meant to be the first sign of madness.*

'Right,' I said crisply, flicking the duvet up and over my shoulders as I eased myself back against the pillows. 'Best switch that light off and get some shut-eye.'

Seconds later the bedroom was once again plunged into darkness. The mattress rocked under me as Nick walloped his pillows, plumping them up before flopping heavily against them. At length he spoke.

'There's nothing going on between Amanda and me,' he said gruffly.

'I didn't say there was,' I protested.

'No, but I know how your mind works. That ship has long sailed. Understand?'

His tone was gentler now. Conciliatory. I nodded, not that he could see.

'Of course,' I said, making my tone light, even though I felt as if an invisible hand were squeezing my larynx.

'Good. Friends again?'

'Yes,' I said, as my eyes brimmed without warning. Bugger these pregnancy hormones. Heightened sensitivity and over-reaction seemed to be the norm, but it was very draining.

'Night, sweetheart,' he said. Moments later a warm hand reached out and patted me on the bottom, a bit like a master affectionately patting a faithful old dog on the rump.

'Night,' I replied. I lay there, eyes leaking tears that slid sideways into my pillow, soaking my hair and making strands of it stick damply against my cheeks. Within minutes Nick was gently snoring. I remained awake, getting up twice in forty-five minutes to relieve my bladder, thanks to the baby lying on it. And all the while the little voice in my head taunted me with its incessant chatter.

Despite Nick's reassurances, I felt edgy and badly out of sorts.

# Chapter Fifty

On the work scene, I soldiered on until my seventh month of pregnancy. There was nothing in the Employer's Handbook to say I couldn't continue being Nick's secretary, and anyway, thanks to Amanda's divorce settlement for Charlotte and Lucinda, we needed every penny. I left the office laden with flowers, a ton of baby paraphernalia and enough teddies to fill a toy shop. I dumped everything in the flat's kitchen-lounge and looked around me in dismay.

'Perhaps you can spend the next few weeks getting the baby's nursery organised,' suggested Nick.

'Yes, I'm sure bending down and putting together flat-pack furniture will be a doddle,' I said tartly. These days my tone always seemed sour, possibly aggravated by the endless indigestion and acid reflux.

Nick got as far as busting open one cardboard carton, and spreading the contents over the last remaining bit of floor space. Five minutes later, he irritably abandoned it.

'Putting furniture together isn't really my thing,' he said, scratching his head at the unfathomable instructions. 'Can't you ask your father to come over and help you? After all, it was him and your mum that bought most of this stuff.'

'Fine,' I snapped.

In truth, I was reluctant to ask for their help. Since getting together with Nick, I'd felt a need to justify this relationship to my parents. Consequently, I'd rather overdone it, showcasing him as some sort of knight in shining armour who'd crashed into both my life and my heart, so attentive I could hardly breathe without him regularly taking my pulse and checking I wasn't having the vapours. My parents also believed I was a popular step-mother figure in a newly blended family, and that my influence with the girls had been so magical both Lucinda and Charlotte had morphed into two sweet little girls who adored me. My mother was keen to practise her granny-to-be skills and kept badgering me to set a date to meet 'Nick's little darlings', which brought me out in a cold sweat whenever the subject arose.

Antenatal appointments were running closer together at this stage of the pregnancy. I made friends with a group of other first-time expectant mums. One of them suggested we start up a coffee morning club and keep it going once the babies were born. The idea was to support each other and encourage our newborns' social skills from the off. I was both thrilled and horrified – thrilled to be invited into their homes to share our pregnancy experiences, but horrified at the thought of reciprocating the invitation. Where would they sit? I had visions of pointing to the kitchen worktops and saying, 'If you could all squeeze in somewhere between the kettle and condiment jars. Ah, perfect!'

I shoved the thought away as I now set off to my new friend Melanie's house, which was on a small development just around the corner. She greeted me like a long-lost friend. Funny how you can bond with some women so quickly. We'd done just that as I'd mindlessly scratched a tummy rash in the doctor's waiting room. Melanie had been shifting uneasily on one of the plastic chairs. Catching my eye, she'd grinned.

'I should be sitting on a rubber ring,' she'd whispered. 'The baby's weight has given me terrible piles which I'm reminded of every time I waddle past our local.'

'Why's that then?' I'd whispered back.

'Because the pub is called The Purple Grapes.'

I'd giggled at her frankness.

'Why are you scratching?' she'd asked.

'Itchy tummy.'

'Hmm. Not quite as catchy. Can't see them naming a pub after that.'

I'd giggled again. What bliss to share such intimate details with someone who understood.

She opened the door to me now, and I sailed in, pregnancy smock billowing out behind me.

'God, it's so hot,' she said, fanning herself. 'Go on through, Hattie. The others are already here.'

The others were Jenny, Karen, and finally Carol and Sue who were expecting their first child together. Carol was as round as a brewery barrel, thanks to Sue's bachelor brother providing several syringed donations. Everyone was getting increasingly nervous and excited as their due dates loomed. Carol and Sue held hands throughout. Every now and again Sue would reach across and fondly rub Carol's tummy. I felt a stab of jealousy. Nick had never done that. Oh, he was caring enough, but these days it was in a fatherly way. I didn't want a father, because I already had one of those. I wanted a tender, loving partner.

Jenny, Karen and Melanie said their husbands were all so excited about their bumps. Nobody seemed to be in my situation – a *sort of* step-mum with *sort of* step-kids. And none of them lived in a cramped flat.

I tried not to feel envious when, after coffee, Melanie took us upstairs to a pale pink nursery smelling of fresh paint with a beribboned crib awaiting its occupant. We all made dutiful murmurs of approval, and then Sue told everyone how she'd worked every evening after work for a fortnight to finish a blue and white room for their eagerly awaited little boy. This prompted Karen and Jenny to tell us how their husbands had spent the last few weekends prepping their babies' nurseries in neutral colours because both couples – like me – wanted the gender of their babies to be a surprise.

'What about you, Hattie?' asked Melanie. 'You don't know the sex of your baby. What colour have you chosen for your baby's nursery?'

'Cream,' I answered. 'Well, it will be when Nick has painted it.'

Currently the walls were still Grotty Grey.

'Isn't it ready yet?' asked Karen, looking faintly alarmed.

'No. He's been manic at work, but he's definitely going to do it this weekend,' I replied, nodding my head vigorously up and down. I wasn't sure who I was trying to convince. Karen or me.

'Yes, you must get him busy with a paintbrush as soon as possible,' she said. 'We could go into labour at any moment.'

My baby chose that precise moment to give me a hefty kick which set off a gentle flurry of Braxton Hicks contractions. Karen was right. There wasn't a second to lose. The flat's spare bedroom currently remained home to Nick's computer and desk. It really was time to out it. There was no room for a crib in our bedroom. Nick's ridiculously vast sleigh-bed took up so much space there was hardly room to manoeuvre around its leather sides. I felt an overwhelming urge to cry. And when I got home again, I did.

Exactly when was my partner going to get involved? If he wasn't at the office, he was out. Every day after work there was some reason or other to pop in on Tod and Jackie, or Doreen who had supposedly had a funny turn and wanted to see him, or else he was off to see Charlotte and Lucinda who, now the baby was so close to being born, were apparently playing up and wanting lots of reassurances that Daddy would still be *their* daddy. I didn't question Nick's movements because I didn't want to annoy him. His reasons to absent himself always sounded genuine, and risking making him angry wasn't good for either me or the baby.

Walking back into the coolness of the flat, I stepped over the clutter and howled. I was making such a racket that, at first, I didn't hear the telephone ring. I wiped my eyes and picked up the handset. It was Dad.

'Hello, love. Mum and I wondered how you are.'

'Yeah, really well,' I lied.

I could hardly tell my father that Britain's unexpected heatwave had caused me to sweat so much I had thrush between my breasts, or that I'd erupted in a chronic hives-like rash over my bump that endlessly itched, despite copious amounts of calamine lotion. The antenatal nurse had told me I was suffering from 'pruritic urticarial papules and plaques of pregnancy'. The good news was that it was harmless for both mother and baby. The bad news was that I'd likely be stuck with it until after the baby was delivered. On the upside, the pregnancy nausea had finally abated.

'Is the nursery finished?'

'Um, no,' I admitted. 'We haven't even started work on it.'

'You mean you're two weeks away from your due date and have nowhere for that little babe to rest its head?' asked Dad in disbelief.

'Nick's been sooo busy at work,' I said defensively. 'It's been hectic. He got as far as opening one of the flat-pack cartons but was interrupted by, er, urgent emails that couldn't wait.'

I could have sworn, at the other end of the phone, I heard my father harrumph.

'Anyway,' I gabbled, 'I thought I'd get on with it myself. I have a real urge to sort things out.'

I'd read about the nesting instinct, where women felt a sudden overwhelming need to scrub their house from top to bottom, plump up pillows and marvel at the shine on their newly mopped floor. However, I couldn't see the floor to mop it. What wasn't covered in paraphernalia was obliterated by my enormous bump. Bending down was impossible. I thanked God I was having a summer baby, so my toes could feel their way into flip-flops rather than struggle with socks and boots.

'Let me and your mum come over and give you a hand, love,' said Dad. 'We'll soon have the nursery shipshape for you.'

'Well...' I hesitated. If only Nick was more practical in the DIY department. But time was marching on. At this rate the baby would end up sleeping in an emptied-out drawer. 'If you're sure you don't mind, that would be lovely.'

'Course we don't mind, love,' said Dad. 'We'll come over first thing in the morning. We'll get that little room repainted in no time at all, and the new furniture sorted in a jiffy.'

Which was just as well, because two days after my parents had transformed the grotty grey study into a pretty nursery in biscuit and cream neutrals, I went into labour.

# Chapter Fifty-One

Nick had been most insistent that the baby would be late, basing this assumption purely on Amanda's pregnancies with Lucinda and Charlotte.

'Trust me, Hattie. I don't know anyone whose baby ever arrived on time. Amanda was two weeks late with both girls, and had to be induced.'

So confident was he of being right, he had no hesitation of attending a business meeting in Manchester the night before I went into labour, and went ahead with booking himself into a hotel.

'Do you have to go?' I'd asked, feeling slightly panicky.

'Yes. A client is bellyaching, and I'm the most senior person to deal with it. Stop fretting, darling. Manchester is only four hours away. It's hardly the other side of the world. If anything were to happen, I'd jump straight back in the car and be with you for the final push.'

Except he wasn't.

I climbed into bed that evening and turned off the bedside lamp, and within two minutes I became aware of an ache in my lower back that hadn't been there when I'd pulled the duvet up to my chin. The ache faded, only to return. I switched the light back on and swung my legs out of bed. Standing stock still, I waited. There it was again but… wait… now it was moving around to the lower abdomen. Gentle but most definitely there. I glanced at the bedside clock. It was a little after eleven. Nick should still be up. I reached for my mobile phone and rang his number. It went straight to voicemail. Which meant he'd switched his phone off. I felt a frisson of anger. How dare he switch the bloody thing off when I needed him?

'Nick,' I said, my voice shrill with alarm, 'I'm pretty sure the baby is on its way. Can you call me, please?'

I hung up and wondered what to do next. Should I ring my parents? I knew Mum and Dad would have retired to bed an hour ago. They weren't night owls and were always asleep by ten. I dithered, not knowing whether to disturb them or not. It would be nice to have a hand to hold but, knowing Mum, she'd probably get into a panic. I had visions of her green-faced in the delivery room, clutching the bed I was spread-eagled upon, whilst administering herself gas and air. Dad was the calm family member, but no way was I having the midwife inviting him to peer between my legs the moment the baby's head crowned. I found myself making an 'ooooh' sound as another gentle wave came along. *Think, Hattie, think.* I tapped out a message to Melanie.

*Are you awake, Mel? I think I'm in labour, and Nick's away on business xx*

The mobile exploded into life making me jump so violently I nearly dropped the damn thing. It was Melanie.

'Are you sure?' she squawked down the line.

'Well I'm ninety per cent certain. It feels different to the Braxton Hicks contractions.'

'Omigod, is it awful? Are you in agony?'

'No, it's bearable. It's like period pains. Sort of crampy. Kind of… ' I broke off and let out a low moan.

'That didn't sound like a period pain,' she squeaked, her voice sounding panicky.

'Ooh, that one was a bit more uncomfortable.'

'Hattie, have you got nobody with you at all?'

'Er, I'm on my own,' I said, as a finger of fear curled its way around my heart. I could hardly drive myself to hospital.

'Do you want me to come with you?' she asked.

I so wanted to say yes, but the last thing Melanie needed whilst huge with her first child and facing the unknown, was to witness me giving birth. What if it went wrong? What if I writhed around in agony and put the fear of God in her? What if there was blood all over the place. What if—

'Absolutely not,' I said, cutting off the horrific technicolor scenario my brain was starting to churn out. 'I've left Nick a voicemail. He's probably picking it up right now as we speak and getting in his car for the drive back.'

'I can't believe he cleared off to Manchester,' said Melanie, her tone of voice letting me know that her own husband would not have been permitted to go any further than a radius of five miles.

'It was business, Mel,' I said, leaping to defend my absent husband. I seemed to be doing a lot of that lately. 'He has a very demanding job. As one of the senior partners, he has to… ooooooh,' I gasped.

'Hattie, make sure your overnight bag is by the door and get off this phone. I'm calling an ambulance.'

'But I—'

'No buts. Just do it.' The line went dead.

I neatly re-made the bed Nick and I usually shared, then substituted my outsized nightdress for a voluminous maternity dress. Reaching into the wardrobe, I pulled a woolly cardigan from its depths. The summer days were currently warm and full of sunshine, but the nights still tended to be cool. I waddled out into the hallway where my overnight bag had been placed a couple of days earlier, awaiting this very moment. Now that it had arrived I felt nervous, and very alone.

I leant against the doorframe as another contraction made itself known. As it gently ebbed away again, my mobile pinged a text message. I pounced on it eagerly, hoping it would be Nick.

*Ambulance is on its way. I'm going to bed now, but please send me blow-by-blow details by text. I'll pick them up in the morning when your darling babe will finally be here! Good luck and lots of love, Melanie xxx*

I smiled, but then grimaced as another contraction made itself known. Where was Nick? Right now, I needed him more than ever. I tried his mobile again but found myself listening to him inviting me to leave a message. I cleared my throat before speaking.

'The ambulance is on its way,' I said, my voice cracking slightly as the enormity of what was happening caught up with me. 'I hope to see you in four or five hours, so we can welcome our baby together. Drive carefully.'

In the distance I heard the wail of a siren. The ambulance was almost here. On impulse, I opened the nursery door. The hall light spilt into the tiny room illuminating the transformation within. On the left wall, a junior wardrobe snuggled up to a chest of drawers with a baby-changing mat resting upon its surface. On the short wall behind me, a shelving system housed an assortment of baby products and soft toys. Opposite, the window was framed with curtains covered in dancing teddies waving multicoloured balloons. Finally, on the wall to the right, was a cot. Its waterproof mattress was covered in lemon sheets and a soft blanket, overlaid by a quilt that matched the curtains. It seemed to silently reach out to me, letting me know it was awaiting its occupant. I leant forward and stroked the shiny wood, just as the flat's intercom loudly buzzed.

Snapping off the nursery light, I picked up my overnight bag and went to answer the door.

# Chapter Fifty-Two

Some say the pain of contractions is different from normal pain, and that your body naturally helps you cope by releasing endorphins which change the perception of pain. Either way, alone and apprehensive, I heaved a sigh of relief when arriving at the labour ward where I was greeted by a sweet young midwife by the name of Annie. By this point I was walking like a constipated duck and my vocabulary was down to two words. 'Ooooh' and 'ahhhhhh'.

'Hello, Hattie,' Annie smiled in welcome. She had a kind face, and I immediately felt both comforted and confident that I was in good hands. 'We're in this together,' she assured me, 'and I'm going to be here all the way for you, right up to placing your baby in your arms. Are you ready to metaphorically roll up your sleeves and do some hard work?'

'Ooooh,' I nodded.

'Excellent,' she replied, helping me over to the bed. 'Are those your notes you're holding? Ah, yes, they are. Let me relieve you of them. That's it. Let's see. Okay, Baby's daddy plans to be with you for this. Excellent. Is he parking the car?'

'No, I came in by ambulance. He's away on business, you see, but he should have received my message by now. I expect he's beetling down the motorway as we speak and frantic with… ooooh,' I gasped as another contraction rolled across my abdomen. My tummy felt rock hard.

'Of *course* he's on his way,' said Annie stoutly.

I nodded gratefully but didn't enlarge on the fact that Nick was two hundred and fifty miles away. I didn't want Nick seen in a bad light, because he'd gone so far away when his pregnant partner was about to go pop. Funny, there I was, all set to leap to his defence again.

'Will I have enough energy to do this?' I asked, once I'd caught my breath. 'I was hoping to get a night's sleep before labour started.'

Annie chuckled, and looked up from the notes. 'Ah, the little darlings never take things like a few zeds into consideration. However, you'll be pleased to know that in the first stage of labour you can rest between contractions, while your body gets on with gently opening the cervix. Behind the scenes there's all sorts of hormones and endorphins revving up ready to give you an extra boost when we get to the second stage of labour, which will be where you'll need to push. But that's all a few hours away. First of all, let's get you settled and comfortable.'

She fussed around, helping me slip out of my maternity dress and into a gown. I noticed there was an easy chair, a beanbag and mat allowing the mum-to-be to move around in labour and change position. Annie took my pulse, temperature and blood pressure and then asked to check my urine. She then felt my abdomen to work out the baby's position, listened to the heartbeat and checked the progress of dilation.

'My goodness, there's no dignity here, is there?' I laughed. 'I mean, I've only known you a matter of minutes, and already you've peered at places even my partner hasn't recently seen.'

She laughed and nodded. 'Yup. I always tell my ladies to leave their pride on the doorstep and collect it on the way out. Hey, we're both girls together, and I can assure you I'm not seeing anything I haven't seen hundreds of times before.'

'I'm looking forward to being able to bend down again,' I said. 'Previously, I never appreciated the luxury of being able to zip up a pair of boots. Not that I could wear any at the moment anyway. My ankles are huge.'

'The swelling will quickly subside after the birth,' Annie assured me. She put the notes to one side and placed some sticky pads on my abdomen, which were wired up to a monitor. 'That pregnancy rash looks sore,' she commented.

'It's been very itchy. When will it go?'

'Soon after delivery, and those purple stretch marks will eventually turn silver and fade.'

'Pregnancy certainly leaves its mark on the body. Do you have children?' I asked, trying to take my mind off another contraction. They were bearable, but still strong enough to make me grimace. I wondered how it would be by the time we got to the 'hard work' stage.

'I don't have children yet, but I'd definitely like a couple at some point.'

'That's nice. I used to think I wanted two, but I'm not sure I want to go through this again.'

'Oh every woman says that,' Annie laughed. 'You'll be back, mark my words.'

'Are you not put off, after everything you see here?'

'Nope,' she smiled. 'The end result makes it all worthwhile. You'll see! Is your partner excited to be a father?'

'Oh tre*mend*ously,' I lied. 'He can't stop talking about it, and makes jokes about us having a baker's dozen. I told him that one is quite enough, and… ooooh.'

'Breathe it out, that's it, well done. Baby's heart rate is perfect,' she observed looking at the monitor, 'and it's all going splendidly.'

'Do you have a boyfriend?' I asked eventually. I knew she wasn't married because her left hand was bare.

'Yes, but I don't think he's The One,' she replied. 'I believe you know instinctively if you want to spend the rest of your life with someone, and so far I haven't had that feeling.'

'I know what you mean,' I agreed. 'As soon as I saw my partner I lost all interest in anyone else. He captured my heart from the second I met him.' I omitted telling Annie about Nick at that point still being married to Wife Number Two with a couple of daughters under his belt from Wife Number One, and immediately deflected any potential questions from her by asking one myself. 'Why are you doubting your boyfriend as a lifelong partner?'

Annie wrinkled her nose. 'Instinct. He has a job, but never seems to have any money. I mean, fair enough, some women go fifty-fifty when on a date. I appreciate it's expensive eating out in restaurants, or taking in a movie at the local cinema. But I very often end up paying for the pair of us. I'm a midwife, not a millionaire. If he can't fund his share of a date, he's not a good bet as a life partner. I don't think I could rely upon him to chip in with the bills. And what if I have children one day and give up work for a while? Who will put bread on the table? I don't wish to sound materialistic,' Annie said hastily, 'I'm just being practical.'

'Of course,' I said, completely understanding where she was coming from. Heavens, I knew only too well what it was like to penny-pinch now I'd given up work. We were never going to starve, but I couldn't see us ever getting on the property ladder either.

'What's your partner like?' Annie asked.

'Incredibly extravagant and generous,' I lied, giving an apologetic smile. Annie was lovely, with a cosy manner that probably had a lot of her patients confiding in her as she distracted them from contractions, but I wasn't about to wash all my emotional laundry in the delivery room. I didn't want to think about Charlotte and Lucinda's recent demands for a pony, or Amanda having a hissy fit because she'd not managed to meet her nail technician that week. I just wanted to concentrate on my own little baby for now. I felt a thrill of excitement knowing that in a few hours I would be a mummy too. I just wished Nick would hurry up and get here.

The minutes ticked by and turned into hours. Annie made no comment that Nick hadn't shown up. I had no idea if Nick had picked up my voicemail, but was now at the stage of labour where I didn't care. I'd moved about, paced, squatted, leant against the easy chair, slumped over the beanbag and wanted to roll up the mat and chomp down on it. Annie assured me all this was perfectly normal, and that so far this was a textbook delivery. A doctor popped in a couple of times to make sure all was well, and an anaesthetist told me that it was too late for an epidural, but thankfully the lovely Annie remained my one constant, distracting me with chatter, praising my progress and urging me on. I realised I'd not texted Melanie with the promised blow-by-blow details. But then again, what did she expect me to write?

*Don't worry about a thing, it's a stroll in the park! xx*

Hardly. If she wanted the absolute truth it was more likely to be something along the lines of:

*The midwife is doing sterling service letting me crush her hand. I'm now at the 'hard work' stage and bellowing like King Kong. My nether regions periodically feel like they're being blowtorched. My hair is stuck attractively to my face, which, from all the pushing, is a mottled shade of pink and white, and I've burst a blood vessel in my left eye. Other than that, it's a complete doddle! xx*

I clamped the gas and air mask over my face and breathed deeply. A clock on the wall showed it was coming up to seven in the morning. As I screwed my face up against another contraction, Annie gave a shout of encouragement.

'The head is crowning... I can see your baby's hair! Would you like me to get a mirror so you can see?'

'Yes, please,' I panted, as Annie obliged. 'Short back and sides?' I joked feebly.

She hooted with laughter. 'You have such a wonderful sense of humour,' she said, patting my hand. 'I'm not meant to say things like this, but you've been one of my favourite patients. We've had such a lovely chat, and it makes such a nice change not being sworn at.'

'Women swear at you?' I gasped.

'Sure,' she nodded. 'I've been punched and bitten too. But the air has always turned blue at some point.'

I didn't reply as I was in the middle of another powerful contraction. There was absolutely no control over them. My body was doing what it was programmed to do, taking on a life of its own as it delivered the life within.

'Fan-*tas*-tic, Hattie. The head is out! One superhuman push for me, and your baby will be born!'

I felt like I was coming towards the finishing line of a long race, like a marathon runner, my body urging me on, to give just a little bit more, and yet a little bit more still, with Annie standing in the wings metaphorically waving a flag as she cheered me on. I gave a final, almost animal-like bellow, my body reaching the point where pain becomes euphoria, and a tiny grey-skinned baby shot into Annie's hands.

'You did it!' she cried, as I collapsed back on the bed. 'Here,' she said, presenting me with a teeny wizened face which was rapidly turning pink. 'Congratulations, Hattie. You have a baby boy.'

'Oh thank-you-thank-you-thank-you,' I said, half laughing, half crying with joy. I cradled my tiny son as Annie gave me an injection to speed up delivery of the afterbirth.

'Do you have a name for him?' she asked.

'We decided on Fin for a boy,' I replied.

'That's lovely,' she beamed. 'Okay, Hattie, I need to take Fin back for a moment to clamp the umbilical cord and take care of a few other things, like weighing and bathing him. But I'll make sure I do everything right by the bed, so you can see him and the bonding process isn't interrupted.'

'Yes, of course, thank you,' I said, passing my precious baby back to her. 'I'm so grateful to you, Annie. I couldn't have done this without you.'

In that moment, something passed between us that was beautiful, profound and moving. Two women had connected on a very intimate and private level as, together, we'd welcomed this tiny miracle into the world. The moment was shattered by Nick crashing through the delivery room doors, just in time to see the midwife holding his son in her arms.

'Oh my God!' he said, looking both shocked and horrified.

'Don't worry, darling,' I assured him, 'in some ways I'm glad you weren't here to witness a very undignified show on my part.' I smiled wanly. 'Annie here has been an absolute star.'

It was then that I realised Nick's horrified reaction wasn't because he'd missed the birth of his son, but was directed at the midwife, who was holding our baby and staring at Nick with her own appalled expression. There was a moment where nobody spoke, and everything was freeze-framed.

'Is Hattie your partner?' Annie eventually croaked, her voice barely audible.

'I can explain everything,' Nick muttered, raking one hand through his hair.

'I don't think so,' said Annie, her tone suddenly cold.

'Wh-What...' I stuttered, aghast at the drama being played out in front of me. 'Do you two know each other?'

That was when the air in the delivery room finally turned blue.

# Chapter Fifty-Three

How do you get over discovering that the woman who helped bring your son into the world was also your partner's lover? The pain was raw. As was the humiliation. The euphoria, like a punctured milk carton, instantly leaked away, curdling the joy.

'Give me back my baby,' I hissed, staring at Annie as if she'd just sprouted two heads and four sets of fangs.

Suddenly I sensed, rather than saw, Josh nearby. Like the umbilical cord that had attached Fin to me, I felt a tugging sensation, as if something or someone was trying to pull me away from this scenario.

*Step back from this moment, Hattie*, he said, speaking directly into my head.

*No way, Josh*, I replied, resisting the pull of energy like a spider scrabbling against the suction of a vacuum nozzle.

*Hattie, you have to let go of the hatred that has entered your heart. You must return to the Halfway Lounge.*

*NOOOOO!* I mentally screamed, and it seemed as if the very ground trembled as my protest reverberated through my head and the delivery room, rattling the hospital walls and squeezing through every pore of its brickwork. Through the window, I could see the trees beyond shaking as if caught up in a vicious gale.

*Hattie, it's vital to release the years of negative energy that you've stored within your mental and emotional bodies. Why don't you want to take a break?*

Why indeed? Even though this was a life review, it was as real as the moment when I'd lived it. I needed to confront Annie. Apart from anything else, the overwhelming power of nurture and nature was pumping through my veins. I wasn't going anywhere.

*I'm not leaving my baby*, I sobbed, as Annie wordlessly passed Fin back to me. I hugged him tight, hot tears splashing onto his hair, still wet from amniotic fluid.

*So be it*, said Josh.

Suddenly the delivery room was flooded with a swirling mist of different coloured lights. I clutched Fin to me as whirling clouds of violet, pink, gold and indigo washed over and around me. I felt like I was sitting in some sort of giant washing-up bowl with this rainbow of colour acting as a detergent, rinsing its light through me, lifting and cleaning away years of hidden grot.

'I'm so sorry, Hattie,' Annie was saying. I stared up at her through my brimming eyes and saw that she too was crying. 'I had no idea, I promise you.'

And even though I knew Annie had said this to me sixteen years ago, back in that moment I'd blocked her words out. Erased them. All those years ago, it had suited me to not remember. It was so much easier to put the blame at her feet, rather than Nick's. Yet again, I was excusing him, desperately trying to exonerate him, because I didn't want to sully my perception of him at that point in my life. I wanted to believe that Annie had been a temptress, temporarily luring my boyfriend away from me in a very weak moment. Because if I didn't hang on to that thought, then I would surely go insane with grief.

*Listen to her*, Josh urged. His was the voice of reason in this moment of madness.

'Do you forgive me, Hattie?' Annie was saying, the tears flowing freely down her cheeks. This time there was no escaping what she was saying. No pretending. No blocking. Her words seemed to take form in the strange mist, taking on a light of their own as they rose up from her mouth into the strange atmosphere. Her question was now suspended over my head, wavering in the light, spacing itself out so that each single letter shimmered like a brightly coloured jewel, hovering a few moments longer before suddenly collapsing in on themselves and liquefying: now running through my hair, washing over my skin, trickling over every part of my body until the question she'd asked repeated itself like an echo so deeply within me that I felt as if it had touched the very spark that had ignited my own existence. *Do you forgive me, Hattie... forgive me, Hattie... forgive me, Hattie?*

I stared up at her pretty face, her features marred by distress, and saw the pain in her eyes. Something deep in my soul stirred and responded. Annie was innocent. She'd unwittingly got caught up in this drama, as much a victim as I was. She was just as shocked. Just as horrified. And instead of hating her, this time my heart went out to her.

'There's nothing to forgive,' I replied. And I meant it.

She squeezed my hand and gave me a watery smile.

'You're a lovely lady, Hattie,' she whispered, her voice thick with emotion and sorrow. 'I'm going off-duty now. Another nurse will take over.'

I nodded, tears once again pouring down my own cheeks as she stepped away from the bed. Without even bothering to look at Nick, she calmly walked out of the delivery suite and out of our lives. As the double doors swung shut behind her I looked through the strange light at Nick. He was openly weeping. He moved towards the bed and held out his arms to take Fin. Wordlessly I handed the baby over, watching the lights whirl over him, knowing that he was weeping with joy to hold his son, and weeping with shame at what he'd put me through.

# Chapter Fifty-Four

The weeks ahead were challenging to say the least. I was desperate to turn to someone for moral support, but there was no one. I couldn't tell my parents. I just couldn't. The thought of Mum's horrified expression before she said, 'I told you so.' Or Dad clenching his fists impotently, fighting down the desire to march round to the flat and bop Nick on the nose for sending his daughter into a depression which, so far, I'd blamed on postpartum blues. Nor could I tell my little group of new-mum friends at our cosy coffee mornings, as we discussed our problems. Melanie was struggling to breastfeed and fretting. Karen was bottle-feeding and beating herself up with guilt that she hadn't put her baby to the boob in the first place. Jenny was hollow-eyed and tearful from the endless broken nights, while Carol and Sue were frazzled from baby Ben screaming the house down every evening with colic.

'What's little Fin doing to get you down?' asked Melanie, clocking a moment where my internal angst had fleetingly registered on my face.

The urge to unburden was huge. I'd actually got as far as opening my mouth, on the threshold of letting the whole sorry saga spill out, only to snap it shut again after mentally picturing the scenario:

'Oh it's nothing to do with Fin. He's a poppet. Doesn't give me a moment's trouble. No, it's his father who's the cause of my misery. I found out Nick was playing doctors and nurses with the midwife, and now I want to join in and castrate him without anaesthetic.'

They'd be horrified, although admittedly they'd thank their lucky stars that all they had to bleat about was sore nipples or the price of Aptamil. Bizarrely, the one person I wanted to reach out to was Annie. Once I'd even telephoned the hospital, only to discover she'd transferred to another, but because of the Data Protection Act I wasn't allowed to know which one.

At home my moods fluctuated wildly.

'It was just sex,' Nick had protested, ducking out of the way as I'd hurled one of Fin's teddies at him. It had bounced off his head and landed on the laminate flooring, issuing soft growls from the sound gadget sewn within its stuffing. In that moment I'd wished the bear was real so that it could rip Nick to pieces. Instead my outbursts of anger were doing a fine job of attacking him.

'It was just a release,' Nick said on another occasion. 'You were out of service. It meant nothing!'

'Well it meant something to me,' I'd hissed back. After being a disinterested boyfriend all through my pregnancy, suddenly he'd turned into the model partner. He loved Fin to pieces and didn't mind sharing the broken nights. He was also trying to claw his way back into my heart by availing himself of anything that needed doing. Never had the flat been so thoroughly vacuumed, and never had I drunk so many cups of tea made by him. Nor did his attention end there. Suddenly Nick had abandoned fulfilling Charlotte and Lucinda's wish to have a pony, and cash was available to spoil me with bouquets of flowers, scent and jewellery, all of which were meant to prove his love and devotion. Hardly a weekend went by without Nick whisking me off for candlelit dinners, while my besotted parents babysat their little grandson.

Eight weeks after Fin's birth, Nick was keen to resume our sex life. We'd spent the last two weeks tentatively kissing each other. However, before it could lead anywhere I'd always ended up angrily pushing him away. The start of intimacy seemed to set off a mental string of pornographic images in my head of Nick with Annie. I knew that things couldn't carry on like this and, one day, got as far as picking up the phone to make an appointment with a relationship counsellor. When the flat's intercom buzzed I'd jumped guiltily, hastily putting down the handset as I'd wondered who was outside. Nick had been at work and not due home for another hour. Answering the internal phone, I'd been surprised to hear Tod's voice.

'Hey, Hattie. I was just passing and thought I'd pop in and see my handsome nephew.'

'Sure,' I said, genuinely pleased. I liked Nick's brother enormously, although my feelings remained unchanged towards Tod's wife, Jackie. She was still, to put it bluntly, a two-faced bitch.

'Hey,' said Tod, sweeping into the flat's narrow hallway a minute later. He gave me a bear hug. 'Great to see you.' He thrust some flowers at me.

'Lovely,' I said, wondering if I had any vases left to accommodate yet more flowers. 'Have you got the day off work?'

'Yeah, something like that,' said Tod, raking one hand through his hair just like Nick often did.

I mentally raised an eyebrow at Tod's subdued tone, but made no comment. If he wanted to tell me what was wrong, it would come out at some point.

'Fin's in his cot, napping. But you can tiptoe quietly into the nursery and have a peek at him. I'll put the kettle on.'

I walked through to the kitchen-lounge and rifled through the cupboards. Damn. No spare vase. I put the flowers in the sink and filled it with cold water. I'd have to trim them right down and make them fit into a large mug. I busied myself with the tea. I had just set the cups on the occasional table when Tod returned.

'Your son is gorgeous,' he said, removing a basket of laundered baby-grows from the sofa. He flopped down with a heavy sigh. 'Seeing the little chap makes me quite broody.'

I smiled as I sat down at the other end of the sofa. 'Are you thinking of adding to your family?' I teased. 'I'm sure Jackie might be swayed.'

Actually I was pretty sure Jackie would most definitely *not* be persuaded. She'd made Tod pay for a breast enlargement and tummy tuck last year, and was far too self-obsessed to return to the delights of regurgitated milk all over her designer clothes. Tod gave a hollow laugh, as if reading my thoughts.

'No, Hattie, there won't be any more babies,' he said sadly, picking up his tea. 'In fact, there may not even be a marriage for much longer.' He sipped thoughtfully.

'What?' I gasped, shocked.

Tod fiddled with the handle on his cup. 'I went to see a solicitor today, to make tentative enquiries and find out how much it would cost to pay Jackie off and start afresh.'

'But why?' I asked.

'Because she's having an affair with her personal trainer.'

'No!'

'Yes. She thinks I don't know.'

'Tod, are you sure? That's a heck of an assumption, and surely you should talk to her before you file for divorce.'

'Oh I recognise the signs, Hattie. Let's just say this isn't the first time my wife has played away. But it might well be the last. I'm done with all this gut-wrenching misery. The boys are at university and in digs. They're old enough to stand on their own two feet. I quite fancy a bachelor pad.' He glanced around the kitchen-lounge. 'A place like this would suit me down to the ground. There would be no Jackie, supposedly going off to the gym every evening reeking of scent and dolled up to the nines, then coming home hours later with her lipstick kissed off and her hair mussed up, making out she went on to the salad bar with her girlfriends for a gossip while she crunched on carrots all evening. Yeah, right.'

I carefully set down my mug of tea.

'I know what you're going through,' I said quietly.

Tod looked wary. 'You do?'

'Yes. I found out, quite by chance, that Nick was seeing someone while I was pregnant with Fin.'

Tod looked at me, his face a picture of guilt, and then his eyes slithered away. I felt a frisson of shock.

'You *knew*?' I gasped.

Tod set down his own tea and rubbed his eyes with the heels of his hands.

'Oh God,' he said, his voice muffled.

'Why didn't you tell me?' I whispered.

His hands dropped down into his lap with a light slapping noise.

'Don't put that on me, Hattie,' he said, shaking his head slowly. 'What sort of person tells their brother's partner – a heavily pregnant one at that – that her guy is shagging around?'

'How did you find out?' I asked, my voice barely audible.

'Nick is like Jackie. They're two of a kind. There are always signs. Nick would drop in on the pretext of seeing me over something quite irrelevant, and then, having legitimately secured his alibi by saying he'd spent some time with me, he'd beetle off. His aftershave often clashed with Jackie's perfume. At one point I even suspected they were seeing *each other*.'

I paled, and Tod realised he'd overstepped the mark.

'Sorry, sorry, I shouldn't have said that,' he said, running the palm of his hand in agitation over his cheek and chin. 'And no, before you even ask the question, they were not seeing each other, and never have. I don't think either of them are quite crass enough to poo on their own doorstep. But I did take Nick to task when he dropped me right in it over that damn drinks party I was meant to be hosting.'

I nodded, as my mind flipped back through pages of memory... Tod ringing the flat to speak to his brother... his bemusement that Nick was on his way over to attend their apparent soirée. He'd swiftly recovered and gone on to cover Nick's lies.

'If it makes you feel any better,' he added, 'I never met the woman.'

'I did,' I said quietly.

Now it was Tod's turn to pale.

'How the hell did that happen? Did you walk in on them?'

'No. She was a nurse. Or, to be more precise, a midwife. She delivered our baby.'

'Good *God*, Hattie,' said Tod, looking appalled. 'So… so what's going on between the two of you? Have you kissed and made up?'

'He's apologised, insisting it meant nothing. Suddenly he can't do enough for me. But I'm still very angry, Tod. I'm struggling to move on.'

'It takes time, Hattie.'

'How much time?' I asked miserably.

'A lot,' he replied, his expression sad. 'Look, Nick's my brother, and I love him to bits, but I've got to tell you this. He's always been a bit of a player. He's broken a lot of women's hearts and smashed up two marriages chasing after skirt. You're a lovely girl, Hattie. I'd hate to see you as another of his casualties.'

'But I already am,' I said, my eyes brimming.

'Don't cry,' said Tod, shuffling along the sofa so he was sitting next to me. He draped an arm around my shoulders, hugging me tightly to him.

'S-sorry,' I cried, 'I don't mean to weep all over you. It's just that I've not been able to tell anyone about this. I never would have guessed you've been going through the same thing, too. It's such a relief to talk about it. Not to have it bottled up any more.'

'So what on earth happened in the delivery room?' Tod gently asked. 'Did you punch her lights out?'

'No,' I shook my head, 'I had no idea who she was until Nick bowled into the delivery room a couple of minutes after Fin was born.'

Tod tutted. 'He'd miss his own funeral, that guy.'

'He was away on business, but drove like a demon once he knew Fin was on the way. He arrived to find the midwife holding our son. The two of them just stared at each other. The expression on their faces was just—'

I broke off as my voice caught.

'Don't,' said Tod, squeezing me. 'Just try and forget about it.'

'But you don't understand, Tod. She was lovely. So sweet. And she didn't have a clue that he was with someone else – or that he was about to become a father. She looked so hurt. I really felt for her.'

'Dear oh dear, Hattie. What are the two of us like, eh?'

We pulled apart and, despite our respective misery, grinned weakly at each other. But in that moment, we found ourselves suddenly staring into each other's eyes. The smiles slipped from our faces as we gazed on and on. And then, subtly, Tod shifted his position. Slowly, very slowly, uncertain whether to do this or not, he lowered his face to mine. I didn't flinch away, but nor did I fling my arms around him. In that moment, we were simply two casualties from our respective relationships tentatively reaching out to each other. I wondered if sparks would fly when our lips met. As his mouth came down on mine, I was thankful for the fact that there was zero chemistry, and I knew it had been the same for him too. When we pulled apart, the relief was evident on both our faces. Too late we spotted the shadow in the doorway.

'Well, well, well,' Nick drawled. 'What have I interrupted here?'

# Chapter Fifty-Five

Tod and I sprang apart like deflecting magnets, our knees bashing against the occasional table, upsetting our tea cups so dark liquid puddled across the surface.

Tod jumped to his feet, hands out in a calming gesture.

'This isn't what you think, Nick.'

'With the greatest respect, Tod, I think I've been in enough similar situations to recognise a full-blown snog when I see one.'

I scrambled to my feet and scuttled over to Tod.

'Your brother was simply consoling me,' I gabbled.

'Yes, I saw.'

'Look, Nick,' said Tod. 'It was my fault, not Hattie's.'

'Ah, my brother the gentleman.'

'She's had a shitty time.'

'And that makes it okay, does it? Shall I go around to your house, Tod, and push your wife down on the sofa?'

'Tod didn't do that,' I protested.

'No, he didn't need to,' said Nick, rounding on me, 'because you were willing to prostrate yourself quite unaided, weren't you, Hattie?'

'Prostrate herself?' Tod spluttered. 'Don't be ridiculous. We were having a cup of tea together.'

'Since when did a cup of tea nearly become a fuck?' Nick spat. 'Get out, Tod.'

'I'm going,' said Tod, putting his hands up in the air. 'But it's not what you think.' He moved towards the door, and then turned back to me. 'Any problems, Hattie, just call me, right?'

'My girlfriend will *not* be calling you,' Nick said, his teeth clenched, 'because the only problem in this flat right now, is you. So the moment you leave, the problem will be gone. Have I made myself understood?'

'Loud and clear,' Tod nodded, turning on his heel. Seconds later, the flat door clicked shut behind him.

Fin chose that moment to stir, making soft mewing noises. I made to go to the nursery.

'Leave him for a moment,' said Nick, catching hold of my arm.

'He'll start crying,' I said, shaking him off.

'He's not crying at the moment,' said Nick, his tone daring me to argue. 'Sit down.'

I took a deep breath to calm myself, then perched on the edge of the sofa.

'How long have you and Tod been having it off?'

'We haven't!' I gasped.

Nick said nothing, instead scrutinising my face.

'So what was he doing here?'

'He popped in to see Fin—'

'Yeah, right,' Nick sneered.

'It's true!' I protested. 'He was feeling crappy—'

'And you thought you'd cheer him up?'

'Will you stop interrupting me, and give me a chance to tell you what happened?'

'Will it take long?' Nick said, his tone sarcastic. 'I'm just wondering whether to open a bag of popcorn and crack open a can of cola, while your lies entertain me.'

'There are no lies,' I said emphatically. 'Tod ended up having a cup of tea and telling me about his awful day. He went to see a matrimonial solicitor. Jackie's having an affair, and he's had enough.'

'So he thought he'd come around here and start an affair with *my* partner instead?'

'Just shut up and listen for a minute, eh?' I snapped, exasperation getting the better of me. 'We've both had a tough time and inexplicably found ourselves reaching out to each other. It wasn't planned. It wasn't premeditated. It just happened.'

'And what if I hadn't intercepted the pair of you?' Nick hissed. 'What else would have happened, eh?'

'Nothing. I'm not attracted to him.'

'Don't bloody give me that, Hattie,' Nick snorted.

'It was just a hug and a kiss. Are you going to insist on using this as an emotional stick to beat me with? It meant nothing!' I cried.

'Ah, touché,' said Nick softly.

I immediately realised that, in the last few weeks, he'd said those last three words to me a million times over. And I'd repeatedly flung them back at him.

'Looks like we're even, Hattie.'

'Don't be ridiculous,' I protested. 'There's a world of difference between you having a full-blown affair with Annie, and your brother and me comforting each other which led – in a moment of madness – to an unplanned kiss.'

'But who's to say that kiss wouldn't have led to anything else?'

'It wouldn't!'

'So you say, but I don't know that. No, Hattie. As far as I'm concerned, we're now the same... both as bad as each other.'

Fin's soft noises were turning into grizzles.

'I must go to him,' I said, standing up and making to move past Nick again.

Once again he caught my arm, spinning me round to face him.

'Marry me, Hattie.'

I stared at him, not quite believing what he'd said. It dawned on me that, like most people who put themselves about, Nick was jealous and possessive when it came to suspecting his own partner might have been on the threshold of betraying him. I knew he was angry with his brother, but more than anything I suspected Nick's ego was dented.

'What do you say?' he asked.

'I don't know, it's—'

'Listen to me,' he urged. 'I'll forgive you, if you forgive me. Let's put the past behind us once and for all. Start afresh. I love you, Hattie. We have a child together. Let's make it official. I want you to be my wife.'

And six months later, I was.

# Chapter Fifty-Six

Nick and I settled down to married life together, and family life with Fin. Lucinda and Charlotte weren't keen to play Happy Blended Families. They'd boycotted our wedding, which Nick was disappointed about. He'd tried to tempt them both with the promise of silk dresses and pearl tiaras, but it wasn't to be. I made noises of sympathy, but was secretly relieved. What bride, on her wedding day, wants two angry bridesmaids stomping along beside her? I certainly didn't.

The girls made it quite plain they only wanted to see their father, so I saw little of them unless their mother dictated otherwise. Sometimes Amanda wanted a weekend away, and insisted the girls do her bidding. On these occasions, they would arrive at the flat, sullen-faced and moody, complaining bitterly about having to sleep together on the sofa bed in the kitchen-lounge.

'The mattress is too hard, Daddy!' Charlotte wailed.

'And the bed is too small,' Lucinda added.

Nick, anxious for a quiet life and always ready to indulge them, instead insisted we sleep on the sofa pull-out and the girls have our bed. Despite the extra laundry this created, I went along with it because I was still hoping to ingratiate myself into their good books, if not their affections. Throughout their time with us I would wear a fixed smile, trying to jolly them up and rah-rah along as we ventured out to ice rinks and pizza places, or made picnics in warmer weather and sat on blankets at the beautiful Trosley Country Park. Lucinda would look down her nose and announce that only common people ate cheese and pickle sandwiches. I'd once cooked chicken nuggets and chips for tea, believing it to be a kids' favourite, but Charlotte had coldly informed me that they didn't eat processed chicken. Not for the first time I'd wondered how on earth these two would cope in the real world when they one day left their posh private schools. I always sighed with relief when Nick took them both back to their mother's.

We had a winter wedding. The sun shone bravely, although it was bitterly cold. Tod was Nick's best man, the two of them having made up their differences. At the mention of divorce, Jackie had instantly dumped her personal trainer and crowbarred her way back into Tod's affections. She was now pulling out all the stops to be the perfect wife, just as Nick had concentrated on being the perfect husband.

The first year of marriage was happy. Probably *the* happiest. Fin was a delight for both of us. He was a placid, easy-going child with a sunny nature. Nick doted on him. By this point we were metaphorically bursting out of the flat, and Nick suggested he might be able to afford a little house for us all. When Fin was napping, I'd sit with the local property paper, nursing a coffee, and circling photographs of houses with a biro. They were all extremely modest. Our budget was tight because Nick was still paying fortunes in maintenance for Lucinda and Charlotte. But then Doreen, my mother-in-law, had a sudden heart attack and passed away. Whilst her death was terribly sad, financially it gave us the break we needed. The sale of her large family home was split between Tod and Nick, enabling us to find a lovely place in leafy Sevenoaks.

The second year of marriage kept me busy making the house our own. I repainted all the kitchen cupboards to give them a cheap facelift, and ripped out tatty built-in wardrobes from the bedrooms, replacing them with charity-shop finds which I upcycled along with bedside cabinets and drawers. The finished result caused quite a stir with my coffee-morning mums. I found myself doing projects for them, transforming ugly old sideboards and scruffy out-of-fashion pine tables. Buoyed up with confidence, I put a business card on the cork-board at the local Spar and advertised on a local Facebook page. I'd never be a millionaire, but it brought in some much-needed extra cash, allowing me to work from home with a toddler.

It was in the third year of marriage that my female intuition hit me like a sledgehammer. Something wasn't right. I'd been so busy with Fin, the house, and my little upcycling business, I'd failed to spot the moment Nick had started coming in later from work. But somewhere along the way it had definitely crept in; the need to stay out late to schmooze clients, or the necessity of remaining at the office long after hours to focus on a tricky account without the distraction of ringing telephones. But the biggest and most obvious clue was when Nick failed to come home at all.

I'd sat in my pyjamas, curled into the sofa in front of the television, a late-night movie playing on low volume. Somewhere along the way I'd fallen asleep, waking up hours later, stiff and cold, just as fingers of early morning grey light filtered into the lounge. And it came to me in a flash that old patterns were repeating themselves. Nick had left the first Mrs Green for the second who, in turn, dumped him because he was having an affair with a work colleague. Nick had sought out female company again when I was pregnant with Fin, but what was his excuse this time? And was this the first occasion in our marriage? Or had I been too busy with my child and homemaking to recognise other occasions that just hadn't flagged themselves up until now?

My brain felt like it was spinning, trying to find the answers to all the questions. One by one the cogs fell into place and I was presented with two certainties. Firstly, my husband was a serial philanderer. Secondly, if he frequently felt the need to hook up with a lover when committed to someone else, then something had been created. A vacancy.

# Chapter Fifty-Seven

Why do people stay together in marriages that become layered with affairs, littered with tears and lashed with angry words of recrimination?

It was a question I'd asked myself many times, and frequently cogitated upon. I'd determined that whilst splitting up meant you kept your own earnings, no longer had to entertain step-kids who detested you, and could have just a sandwich for supper if the mood so took you, there were other things that simply didn't fit into that category. How do you quantify the reaction when you and your husband see your child take his first step? That is worth something, because only you and he together can truly appreciate how special it is. And there are countless other things like that which are involved when children are in the equation. The first day at school. The first wet painting. The first visit by the tooth fairy. The first football match. That first goal.

And if you divorce? Instantly there is the loss of so many traditions. What are we supposed to do at Easter? Christmas? Birthdays? Those glorious summer holidays? And I'd decided that those traditions were necessary in my life. I needed for us to be doing them together – starting with marriage itself, which still held those pledges of help and support, if not fidelity. So I listened to Nick's excuses. Whether it was supposedly crashing out from tiredness at his desk as he adjusted paperwork and contracts to appease a difficult client, or apparently having to go away for the weekend on a corporate event that excluded wives, as the years passed I swallowed the lies down like a bitter pill.

Ironically, it was Nick's brother who, over a decade later, looked at me in the same way as he had when visiting the flat on the pretext of seeing baby Fin. This time the scene had changed. We were all at a big family barbecue hosted by Tod and Jackie. Everyone was laughing, nursing their chilled wines and beers. The kids – teenagers now – were hanging out together, nursing filched ciders and well away from the Embarrassing Parent Brigade.

Sensing that I was being watched, I'd turned to see Tod's eyes upon me. He was standing by the barbecue, cooking a mountain of fodder. He'd jerked his head imperceptibly indicating I go and talk to him. Excusing myself from one of Jackie's neighbours who'd come around to complain about the smell of charcoal and promptly inveigled an invitation to stay, I'd taken myself over to Tod.

'How are you, Hattie?' he'd asked quietly.

'Fine,' I'd smiled.

'No you're not. What's with the weight loss? The strained smile? Those dark circles under the eyes?'

'Ah,' I'd shrugged, taking a swig of wine so I didn't have to say anything else.

'Those are telltale signs,' he'd murmured.

'Yup, I guess so.'

It hadn't taken Tod's prompting for me to admit that something was wrong in my marriage again… that Nick had started something. I just hadn't yet discovered it was with my good friend Pippa.

'Do you want me to have a word with him?' Tod had quietly said, flipping blackening beef burgers over the smoking griddle.

'No,' I'd replied, twisting my wine flute between my fingers. 'Give it three months and the affair will have burnt itself out.'

'It looks like it's burning *you* out,' Tod had replied. 'You know what, Hattie?'

'What?'

Tod had shaken his head slowly. 'I can't help thinking that Nick might have forgiven *me* for kissing you way back when, but I don't believe he's ever quite absolved you.'

'I suspect you're right,' I'd responded.

It was true that Nick always dragged the matter up if I dared to make a comment about suspecting him of having an affair.

'Oh, hark at Miss Virtuous,' Nick would always sneer, when Fin was out of earshot.

'I do sometimes wonder,' I said to Tod, 'if Nick has repeatedly wanted to punish me throughout our marriage for that one indiscretion.'

'Can it even be called that, Hattie?' Tod asked. 'God, one fleeting brush of the lips. Hardly a snog. It wasn't even a fumble.'

I smiled wanly. 'I guess the trouble is, Tod, I've been made to feel so guilty about it, a part of me believes it was something bigger than it actually was. When Nick walked into the flat and saw us in a lip-lock, he later told me we were even. That anything he'd done was cancelled out, because now we were both as bad as each other. Certainly, Nick would like me to believe that. That said, he'll also have me believe that he is Mr Innocent with a wife who simply has an overactive imagination.'

'That's poppycock,' said Tod quietly.

And indeed there had been nothing imaginary about spotting Nick's car outside my bestie's house and seeing, with my own eyes, their frantic coupling. In that moment, something in me had finally died. All the glue that I'd so carefully placed in the fragile bricks of our marriage had cracked like crazy paving, allowing those blocks to tumble down and batter me under the rubble. In that moment I'd metaphorically stuck two fingers up to tradition, marriage, and men. I was tired of it all.

# Chapter Fifty-Eight

*You are indeed tired of it all*, said a dear and familiar voice directly into my head. *Fin is no longer a baby, so I'm bringing you back. No protests or resistance this time.*

Like a tablecloth trick, the scenery was snatched away leaving me blinking owlishly in the Halfway Lounge. I was sitting on the squashy sofa, Josh seated opposite in the easy chair, exactly as we'd been sitting before I began such a lengthy piece of life reviewing.

'Welcome back,' he said, giving me that wonderful blowtorch smile that had the ability to melt every part of my being. 'I had to intervene, Hattie, because your aura's colour indicated you were wilting fast.'

'I was,' I nodded.

'That was the longest period of reflecting on your part since you came to the Halfway Lounge.'

I put out a hand on the edge of the sofa to steady myself. I felt disorientated and befuddled. For a while there, I'd almost believed I was reliving the past all over again in Earth time. It was good to be back to reality – ha! – whatever that was.

'I feel like I've been away for years,' I said.

Josh looked at me kindly. 'In some respects, you have. You have an iron will, Hattie. When you put your mind to something, there's no budging you, is there! Your resistance to my summons to return earlier, when Fin was a baby, was quite something.'

'Sorry, Josh, but I just couldn't bear to be parted from him. He was so tiny, so defenceless, and even though there was the drama with Nick in the delivery room, it was indescribably blissful to hold him once again as a babe in arms.'

'I understand. You have worked through some tough stuff, and cast off a whole lot of emotional chains, almost making peace with yourself and your past.'

'Almost?' I said, shivering slightly. I still felt weird. Definitely out of sorts.

'One thing remains, but we'll talk about that in a moment. First of all, you need a strong pick-me-up.'

A tall glass appeared out of nowhere, suspended in the air between us. It appeared to be full of white swirling mist, some of which was spilling over the rim, the white vapour curling like a witch's potion before evaporating into nothingness.

'What's this?' I asked, taking hold of the glass.

'An energy drink in the true sense of the word. You won't sprout wings, because you'll possibly fly without them,' he chuckled. 'Its content is harnessed from the mountain range beyond the veranda.' Josh nodded at the snow-capped peaks in the distance. 'The ingredients are excellent for eliminating any traces of leftover residual emotional toxicity, and holistically stabilising the body after trauma.'

'I see.' I didn't. Was he still talking English?

I sniffed the substance cautiously before putting it to my lips. My senses were instantly tickled with indefinable aromas, one moment cherry and vanilla, the next strawberry and mint, then pineapple and mango. It was a constantly shifting kaleidoscope of smells. The texture of the drink was bizarre, and almost impossible to describe. The nearest comparison would be like swallowing warm deliciously flavoured clouds. But instead of feeling better with every sip, I began to feel more and more upset. By the time I'd downed the last of the glass's contents, I felt like my lungs had taken on a life of their own, inhaling and exhaling air in great chuggy breaths. My expression must have alarmed Josh, because he leapt to his feet in concern.

'Hey, are you all right?'

'Ooooooh, n-n-n-noooooo,' I gasped. I was reminded of Fin, as a two-year-old, wanting his own way about something and, if he failed to get it, taking a huge breath which he'd hold until he turned purple, before releasing it as the mother of all tantrums. What was my body doing? Was it about to have a hissy fit?

Josh folded my hands into his. 'Breathe out,' he ordered.

'I'm tr-tr-trying,' I stuttered, wondering if I might be on the verge of fainting, especially as Josh's hand-holding was started some sort of internal nuclear meltdown. Suddenly he released one of his hands from mine and began to gently stroke my throat. I thought I might pass out from desire.

'Try exhaling again,' he urged, fingers still caressing my neck. It was the most erotic thing any man had ever done to me. Embarrassingly, my body was starting to judder. After two years without sex, I wondered if I might just judder right off this sofa. Instead my lips parted, and I let forth an involuntary bellow before promptly bursting into tears.

'Perfect,' said Josh, his voice matter-of-fact. 'You had some trapped emotion in your oesophagus, but it's gone now.' He produced a tissue out of nowhere and gently dabbed my eyes.

I let out an involuntary whimper as I stared at him, dazed.

'How do you feel now?' he asked.

*Like I want to be kissed*, I silently replied, knowing he wouldn't be able to read that, but a bit of me wishing he could and, if so, what his reaction might be. Would he join in, reciprocating enthusiastically, his fingers caressing not just my throat, but two very erogenous zones that, even now, felt like they were straining at the straps of my balcony bra, bursting forward like roses unfurling on a camera's fast-frame, begging to be touched, demanding to be—

'There's just one very tiny bit to verbally review, Hattie,' said Josh, cutting across my thoughts, which had taken an indecently erotic turn.

'Yes?' I whispered. I'd verbally do anything with this man, especially if it meant using tongues.

'When you were talking to Tod at the family barbecue —'

'Yes,' I said cautiously, not sure where this line of conversation was going.

'You were both discussing how Nick so easily forgave Tod for kissing you.'

I flushed pink with embarrassment. Even though Josh had assured me previously that he never judged – that it wasn't his role to do that, nor did he have any opinions about it anyway – it was nonetheless pretty monumental having a complete stranger put so many years of your life under some sort of giant microscope and endlessly mop your tears throughout.

'And you were also talking,' he continued, 'about the fact that Nick never completely forgave you for something which – as Tod so succinctly put it – *wasn't even a snog.*'

I went from pink to puce as I also recalled Tod adding on a few more words… that it hadn't even been a fumble. Thankfully Josh was alive to my discomfiture and didn't vocalise the rest of Tod's sentence.

'Also,' he added, 'you told Tod how Nick considered both you and he being as bad as each other. Indeed, how you let him talk you into believing that.'

'That's true,' I nodded, as my mind went back to the scenario in my best friend's bedroom, when I'd discovered her entwined with my husband.

*You know why I do this, don't you, Hattie?* Nick had mocked.

*Because you're a tart?* I'd answered back.

Nick had been livid at my response.

*Don't you talk to me about being a tart,* he'd hissed. *Try taking the plank out of your own eye before you start complaining about the splinters in other people's.*

'Nick was manipulating you, Hattie. Do you see that?'

'I do now.'

'You need to understand that this was Nick's escape clause to justify his extra-marital affairs. And that's his business. Something he will one day have to review himself. But for you, Hattie, in *your* review, it's time to grant yourself the ultimate kindness and forgive yourself for thinking that you drove him to behave the way he did. That was never so. A cheater is a cheater. No excuses.'

'Should I not have married Nick?' I frowned.

'You made that decision in the best interests of your son. There is no right or wrong about that particular path. You have reviewed and subsequently understood *why* you took that path, but you never quite binned blaming yourself for Nick's behaviour. Exonerate yourself, Hattie. There was no excuse for his conduct. Ultimately, and equally important, be at peace with your decision to finally walk away from the marriage. You have carried misplaced guilt about putting yourself first in this instance, after years of thinking about everyone else. You forgot that *you* are important too. You retired to your dear little cottage with your charming beagle and teenage son, pulling the whole thing around you like a giant duvet which, although comforting, has stopped you moving on with the next phase of your life.'

'Which is?' I asked, mesmerised by his fabulous blue eyes which hadn't left my face while he'd been talking.

'It's time for you to fall in love,' said Josh softly.

'I don't know how to,' I whispered, electrified by the moment, and far too shy to reveal to Josh my true feelings for him.

'Yes you do. It's as natural as breathing.' He was still holding one of my hands, the other hand now tenderly touching my cheek.

'How?' I whispered. There was now nothing natural about my breathing. I was struggling not to hyperventilate.

'You just let it happen.'

I gulped. Was it happening now? Certainly, something was. I felt woozy, but pleasantly so. Josh pulled me to my feet and it seemed as though I floated into his arms, which, gloriously, were wrapping around me.

'You've already fallen in love,' he murmured. 'I might not be able to read your private thoughts, Hattie, but I can read your aura. And your aura is the colour of love.'

'Is it?' I mumbled, my heart crashing around under my ribs like a trapped bird.

'And I want you to know that I love you, too.'

My legs nearly gave way upon hearing those words.

'You *love* me?' I gasped.

'Yes. I love you for the woman you are, the life you've lived, and the way it has shaped and defined you. I've waited such a long time to be with you, Hattie.'

'But... but... how can you be with me, Josh? You're here, and I'm... I'm... God I'm all over the place, one moment shopping in Tesco, then in this halfway place, then catapulting back to the past, pinging back to here again. How mad is that? God, I've even ridden a unicorn... on Margate beach,' I cried.

'And now you're going back to Earth,' he said, his eyes full of tenderness, his mouth inches from mine.

'No,' I protested, 'I don't want to leave you.' But as soon as I said those words, I knew that I couldn't stay here. This wasn't my home.

I was feeling a gentle tugging sensation, like when Josh had previously tried to pull me back to the Halfway Lounge and I'd resisted.

'What's happening?' I asked, clinging on to him tightly.

'Your time here is done, and my job as co-ordinator is now over.'

My hands curled around his neck, hanging on grimly as the pulling sensation increased.

'I can't leave you like this!' I cried.

'I'll see you again.'

'When?'

'When the time is right.'

'What? Are you talking about when I die? And then we'll be reunited? I don't want that, Josh! I want it now. I want—'

But before I could say anything further, the moment I'd been craving for so long finally happened. Josh looked deep into my eyes and lowered his mouth to mine. I surrendered to the moment, greeting his lips joyfully, allowing the tip of his tongue to meet mine, feeling the passion scorch between us and, as my body responded, it seemed as if the entire universe was shifting beneath the floor of the Halfway Lounge. The kiss went on and on, unfolding moment after perfect moment as I closed my eyes, melting against his body, my fingers touching his silky hair, feeling the warmth from his skin under that glowing white shirt, and my whole being sang with happiness. This was love. *True* love. I'd found it. And I never wanted to let it go—

'Yer all right, love,' said a loud voice in my ear. 'Just breathe deeply. Everything is going to be fine.'

*What?* Who was so rudely interrupting my long-awaited kiss? I wanted more. I puckered my lips up, touched something and stuck my tongue out.

'Stop licking the oxygen mask, love,' said a voice laced with amusement, 'and just concentrate on taking those nice big breaths for me.'

I flung my arms out to reach for Josh, but encountered a pair of rough uniformed shoulders. My eyes pinged open in shock.

'Welcome back,' said the voice. It belonged to a paramedic, who was bent over me. I was lying on the floor of Tesco, surrounded by tins of baked beans, feeling sick to my stomach that my dream man had been exactly that. A dream.

# Chapter Fifty-Nine

I must have drifted off again, because a moment later I was coming to inside an ambulance. Nor was I alone. On the stretcher next to me was a body. Oh my God. A *body*!

'ARGH!' I screamed, attempting to push the mask from my face.

'It's all right, love,' said the same paramedic, 'yer knocked yerself out. If yer don't need that no more, I'll take it off. Yer off to 'ospital to get thoroughly checked out. Yer can't be too careful with 'ead injuries.'

A second later the mask was removed. I regarded the paramedic with huge eyes.

'Is that person dead?' I asked hoarsely, jabbing a finger at the inert mound next to me.

The paramedic straightened up and shook his head. 'Nah, don't fret,' he grinned. 'Like you, knocked out.'

'What happened?' I croaked.

The paramedic scratched his head. 'Well, from what the store manager told us, it was somethin' to do with tripping over tin cans and—'

'I remember now,' I interrupted. 'Aisle three. The overhead sign fell down.'

'That's not what the store manager said.'

I shook my head, and instantly felt a bit sick from the movement of doing so. My thoughts were muzzy, but something was nudging at the corners of my mind. *A halfway place. A man. The former somewhere between Tesco and Heaven. The latter… a Bradley Cooper lookalike called… what was his name?* Josh! His arms had been around me. I wanted to feel their reassurance again, and hear his voice telling me all was well… that I'd see him again. *Concentrate, Hattie, concentrate.* And then everything flooded back, including Josh's words… what he'd first said when I'd found myself in such a strange and surreal place. 'You might have *thought* that aisle three's sign fell from the ceiling, but it didn't. It was an illusion created to interrupt your life.'

'I'm confused,' I said to the paramedic. My mouth was dry, and my voice felt rusty. 'So what *did* the store manager tell you?'

'He said that some'ow some shelves of baked beans 'ad collapsed causin' two people ter trip over the rollin' tins an' fall flat on their faces. Or 'eads, in this case. The pair of yer were knocked out cold. This one 'ere ain't opened their eyes yet,' said the paramedic, jerking his head at the stretcher-bed next to mine. 'But don't worry, they ain't dead,' he reassured me, seeing the horrified look on my face.

'Will they be all right?' I asked, trying to get a better look at the motionless lump.

'Ah'm sure, don't stress yerself, love. Nah, don't sit up. Yer concussed – so that's not a good idea.'

But I wasn't listening. The paramedic had shifted slightly out of the way, enough for me to get a better look at the mound beside me. It was a man. And I'd seen him before… when I'd trundled past Tesco's display of Valentine cards. My exit from the hateful aisle had been blocked by a lone figure trolleying towards me. My brain instantly replayed the scene of our brief encounter:

*'Excuse me,' I said politely, trying to wheel my way around him. For a moment we trolley danced, going in the same direction and therefore unable to pass. We both laughed at the same time. The man took this as his cue to speak.*

*'Trying to escape the Valentine aisle, eh?' he grinned and tutted, and I saw his eyes quickly check out my ringless left hand.*

*'Yes,' I smiled, adopting a rueful expression. 'As far as I'm concerned, this section of the supermarket is akin to hell on Earth.'*

*'Ah, a woman who has been burned.'*

*'Maybe,' I replied. I was still smiling, but the smile had gone brittle around the edges.*

*'Er, look,' said the man hesitantly, a sudden shyness entering his tone. 'I know I don't know you or anything… and you might think I'm being outrageously forward, but… do you fancy having a coffee?' He nodded his head at Tesco's Costa corner, which, admittedly, was emitting delicious smells of ground coffee beans.*

*I stared at him in surprise. He was handsome. Very handsome. If my mother had been with me, she'd have physically dragged the pair of us over to the Costa corner and then whipped out her diary and asked when we both had a mutually convenient date to pop into Sidcup Registry office on the way home. But the last thing I needed was a gorgeous-looking stranger issuing an invitation for coffee. It might not lead to Sidcup Registry Office, but it could potentially lead to my heart being broken. And that was a no-no. I took a deep breath.*

*'Thanks, but no thanks. I just—' I shrugged helplessly. Hopelessly. 'I can't.'*

*And before the man could say another word, I'd put my head down, tucked my elbows in, and pushed my way out of the hateful aisle full of red roses and romance.*

And now, here he was again. In this ambulance with me. But this time… this time we'd had the coffee together… and lots of other beverages too. Oh my *God*. It was *him*! My mind was clearing at the speed of light remembering rainbow drinks and tall glasses wafting steamy vapour that tasted of clouds. The incident in Tesco had been the universe's final attempt to get my path to cross with true love. But I'd rejected it, and subsequently been whisked off to the Halfway Lounge. Ignoring my pounding head, I was instead responding to the pounding of my heart.

'I don't believe it!' I cried.

'Wha'?' said the paramedic, looking alarmed at my shocked expression.

'It's Josh!'

'Josh? Do yer know 'im?'

'No.'

'But yer just said 'is name.'

'I recognise him.'

'From where?'

'The Halfway Lounge.'

'Whass that then? A pub?'

'No, it's somewhere between here and Heaven.'

'Heaven? Is that the new bar in Bexley'eath?'

But I wasn't listening. The man was stirring.

'My head,' he groaned.

'Yer okay, matey. Don't move.'

'What's happened?'

'Yer bin in a bit of an accident, but nothin' ter fret about.'

A pair of very familiar hands were pulling an oxygen mask from his face. I gasped aloud as two piercing blue eyes met mine. Josh stared back at me, taking in my slack-jawed astonishment. I definitely hadn't been dreaming. The Halfway Lounge was as real as this ambulance we were both riding in.

'Do I know you?' he asked, looking puzzled. 'You seem awfully familiar.'

'It's Hattie,' I whispered.

'Hattie,' he murmured, 'what a lovely name.'

I gazed at him, trying to work out what was going on here. He didn't recognise me, but had said I seemed familiar and questioned whether he knew me. My brain was whirring, trying to recall exactly what Josh had said in the Halfway Lounge.

*'I'll see you again.'*

*'When?'*

*'When the time is right.'*

I'd presumed Josh had meant we'd be reunited in death.

Suddenly the inside of the ambulance was filled with dazzling light. I screwed up my eyes for a moment and, as the brightness slightly subsided, saw the Josh I knew from the Halfway Lounge. He was standing there, drop-dead gorgeous in his familiar glowing jeans and shirt. My heart flipped with joy. He gave me his familiar blowtorch smile and blew a kiss, before moving over to stand behind the concussed physical extension of himself. A second later, and in a shimmer of light, he'd blended into the man beside me. I shook my head slightly, stunned by the strange series of events.

'What's up?' Josh asked. 'You look like you just saw a ghost!'

'No,' I said with a smile, silently adding, *Just the rest of my life…*

# A Letter from Debbie

I want to say a huge thank you for reading *The Man You Meet in Heaven*. If you enjoyed it, and want to keep up to date with all my latest releases, just sign up at the following link. Your email address will never be shared, and you can unsubscribe at any time.

*www.bookouture.com/debbie-viggiano*

I find everything to do with the afterlife fascinating and have devoured many a book on the subject – from the good old Bible, ordinary folk claiming to have near-death experiences, the possibilities of reincarnation, to scientists talking about quantum physics and doctors giving medical explanations as to why some people find themselves purchasing a ticket for a return journey through the Tunnel of Light.

I have dedicated this book to my beloved Nanna, long since gone from this world, but who was a major light in my own life. She used to tell me fascinating tales of how she went 'flying' at night. My father used to roll his eyes and joke she'd had one gin too many. But whether her astral tales were true or not, I couldn't get enough of them!

'Where do you go at night, Nanna?' I would ask, eyes round with wonder.

'To see Mum,' she'd reply, her tone matter-of-fact.

'My great-grandmother?'

'Yes,' she'd nod. 'It's always good to catch up with her.'

'Debs,' my father would mutter under his breath, 'take no notice.'

'It's beautiful over there,' my Nanna would say, ignoring my father. 'There are such incredible sights. Take the flowers, for example. Far more detailed and beautiful than those that grow here, with colours so vibrant I couldn't even begin to describe them.'

I always took my Nanna's stories with a pinch of salt. Until, as a young woman living with my first husband who was... how shall I put this?... a bit of a Lothario... my Nanna rang me up one Sunday morning.

'Why were you on your own last night and crying?' she'd asked.

For a moment I'd been too stunned to speak. I hadn't told my family anything.

'I don't know what you're talking about,' I'd blustered.

'Yes you do, Debs,' she'd insisted. 'I visited you on the astral because I had a nagging worry that all wasn't well. And I was right. You were in your bedroom, alone, sobbing your eyes out.'

At the time I'd been living in London digs which my Nanna had never visited. I asked her to describe my bedroom. Which she did. In perfect detail. Right down to the faded patchwork print on my Woolworths' duvet cover. Coincidence? Who knows, but my Nanna was a very canny lady.

I don't doubt that those memories of my Nanna's tall tales have spent years whirling in my subconscious. The idea for *The Man You*

*Meet in Heaven* came to me whilst in a deep sleep. The concept was enough to wake me up and have my arm making a cartoon-stretch in the dark as my fingers tiptoed towards my iPhone. With eyes screwed up against screen glare, I tapped out the story outline before emailing it off to myself to revisit in the morning. Writing a supernatural romance had seemed like such a good idea when the moon was hanging in the sky. In broad daylight, it didn't present as quite so straightforward. It's not easy to explain the unexplainable. In the end I didn't try. This is a romance about two people who meet in a 'somewhere place' and ultimately get together. So whatever your beliefs, whether deeply religious, or completely agnostic, everything within these pages is pure fiction and not based on private beliefs, or any religion or any scientific theories. It's purely the author's imagination at work to weave a tale that suits the characters' individual dramas.

*The Man You Meet in Heaven* is set in a Kent village – my own stomping ground – and features real places, including Vigo Village where the fog really does hang like a thick blanket throughout the winter months. Hattie's dog, Buddy, is a male version of my own rescue pooch and has the same endearing charm and halitosis.

I hope you loved *The Man You Meet in Heaven* and, if so, would be very grateful if you would write a review. I'd be thrilled to hear what you think, and it makes such a difference helping new readers discover one of my books for the first time.

I always like hearing from my readers, so do look me up on Facebook, Twitter, Goodreads or my blog or website.

With love,
Debbie

# Acknowledgements

This is my tenth novel, and the second with the incredible Bookouture. I am deeply grateful to the whole team, but particularly the lovely Kathryn Taussig, Associate Publisher at Bookouture, for her endless support, encouragement and reassurance, not to mention hand-holding me through the edits ('You want me to chop the entirety of that scene? Really? Argh!'). I do the writing, but Kathryn is the one who does the polishing to make every word shine. Likewise, I would like to thank Noelle Holten, Alexandra Holmes, Lauren Finger, Maisie Lawrence, and all the Bookouture authors for their assistance, friendship and amazing humour. We come together most days in a virtual place to laugh – and sometimes weep – but above all, support. A big thank you must also go to Yeti Lambregts for the wonderfully fun cover design, and Kim Nash, Bookouture's Publicity and Social Media Manager, who somehow gets eight days into a week and surely must never sleep. Finally, I want to thank *you*, my reader. Without you, there is no book. I very much hope you enjoy this one.

Debbie xx

Printed in Great Britain
by Amazon